being friends with boys

Also by Terra Elan McVoy

Pure

After the Kiss

The Summer of Firsts and Lasts

being friends with boys

Terra Elan McVoy

Simon Pulse

NEW YORK LONDON TORONTO SYDNEY NEW DELHI

SIMON PULSE

An imprint of Simon & Schuster Children's Publishing Division
1230 Avenue of the Americas, New York, NY 10020
First Simon Pulse hardcover edition May 2012
Copyright © 2012 by Terra Elan McVoy
All rights reserved, including the right of reproduction in whole or in part in any form.
SIMON PULSE and colophon are registered trademarks of Simon & Schuster, Inc.
For information about special discounts for bulk purchases, please contact
Simon & Schuster Special Sales at 1-866-506-1949 or business@simonandschuster.com.
The Simon & Schuster Speakers Bureau can bring authors to your live event. For more
information or to book an event, contact the Simon & Schuster Speakers Bureau
at 1-866-248-3049 or visit our website at www.simonspeakers.com.
Designed by Karina Granda
The text of this book was set in Adobe Garamond Pro
Manufactured in the United States of America
2 4 6 8 10 9 7 5 3 1
Library of Congress Cataloging-in-Publication Data
McVoy, Terra Elan. Being friends with boys / by Terra Elan McVoy. p. cm.
Summary: Living with stepsisters and having a bad history with female friends, Charlotte
enjoys the easy relationships that come with managing an all-male band but things get
complicated when dating becomes an issue, and she is urged to sing in public.
[1. Interpersonal relations—Fiction 2. Dating (Social customs) —Fiction. 3. Bands
(Music) —Fiction. 4. Stepsisters—Fiction. 5. Self-confidence—Fiction.] I. Title.
PZ7.M478843Bei 2012   [Fic]—dc23   2011040176
ISBN 978-1-4424-2159-2 ISBN 978-1-4424-2161-5 (eBook)

This book is in part dedicated to
Aubry, Baby Astor, and Anger Lad.
But really it is for Amy Mc.

Chapter One

I'm on my way up the stairs to my locker Monday morning when Abe comes down the other direction. He sees me and goes, "Trip's out of the band," over his shoulder, halfway past me on the staircase already.

"*What?*" is all I say back. Really, I'm thinking three things at once:

1. Oliver is such an asshole for not discussing this with me first.

2. I knew I should've gone to practice on Saturday. And,

3. Why didn't Trip *call* me?

Abe sees my face and points down the stairs. "I know. But I gotta head."

"Later," I holler. Only his leather satchel, flapping behind him, hears me.

I get to my locker and spin the combination. *What the hell? What. The. Absolute. Hell?* Has Oliver forgotten he never could have started a band without Trip? Or that I don't have anyone else to— Which is when Lish walks by. She doesn't stop, and she's wearing the same noncommittal, straight-lipped smile she's been offering me since that lame phone call of hers last weekend. But I can't think about her right now. *Trip, Trip, Trip,* is the main thing. I've got to find out what happened between him and Oliver over the weekend, and how he feels about it. Unfortunately, though, I've also got to get to homeroom and then class, while simultaneously finishing last night's reading assignment.

"I know, I know," Trip says when I round the corner after first period. His hands are automatically up at the sight of me, like I'm going to arrest him. "But it's no big deal, I swear," he assures. "Creative differences is all. It was mutual."

He's so smooth, it's like he's selling cars. Or, more, like he practiced telling me this. Which makes me feel even more left out of the decision.

"What *happened*?"

He shrugs. "We were getting stale together."

Which isn't true. Sure, they've been low-energy since school started. Even I told them so Thursday. But that doesn't mean the band has to break up.

"But what are you going to do? What are *we* going to do?" I squeak.

It's impossible to imagine Trip and Oliver not being together during 100 percent of their free time, and me with them 80 percent of that. Now Trip will need to find new ways to avoid his father too. But, more importantly, there's the Halloween dance we're playing at. Coming up. In not much over a month.

"I've got my own stuff," he tosses back, pretending to adjust his glasses.

I know he doesn't. Not, at least, from what he's been telling me in the notebook. He has the band. And his music obsession. And talking to me on the phone or online. And sometimes a dense Russian novel.

"Yeah, but what about Sad Jackal?" I can't keep my voice from rising even higher.

"Everybody in the band will manage. *Manager*." He tries to make me smile, but I just can't right now.

"But we—" My thoughts are racing.

"Hey." A hand on my shoulder. "I'll reassure you all about it while I'm in French, I swear."

I reach in my satchel, give him the five-subject spiral notebook we've been filling with notes to each other since August. This morning in English all I wrote, in really big letters, was *WTF? Are you okay?* And *Why didn't you tell me?* Standing here with him in the hall, my alarm feels both exaggerated and appropriate.

"Okay, but—" I start again.

"Okay, *Mom*." He pats me on the head. "Get yourself to inferior algebra." He raises his eyebrows toward my class door. "And here." He holds out a CD for me. "A little more old-school electronica, since you liked a few on that last mix."

It's amazing how easily this makes me unmad at him. "Thanks, I—"

"Eh." He shrugs. "It's all part of my self-serving plan, convincing you you can't do without me."

"I already know I can't do without you. Because without these"—I lift the CD—"I'm stuck listening to my stepsisters' crap all the time."

He points to the ceiling and winks, right as the late bell rings over our heads. I watch him stroll off, unconcerned, in his dopey splayed-foot walk.

All I can think, before opening the door to face my fellow math torture companions, is *I am going to kill Oliver.*

• • •

After a month of school, most of my teachers have already figured out my deal: I am the definition of an average student. I am who they need to keep the grading curve in check. This is my second round of Algebra II, though, because apparently, being too comfortable with "average" can lead to failing if you're not careful.

Still, I can't focus, even more than my usual amount of not being able to focus. I'm steaming about Oliver making this decision without talking to me about it first. I mean, if you're going to cut out the guy who creates the tunes, shouldn't you tell the girl who writes all the words? Not to mention who coordinates practice, handles PR, schleps equipment, and makes sure there are enough energy drinks around? Couldn't I have had a *hint*? And seriously, why is Trip out? He's a great guitarist. There's no way we'll find someone as good as him in time for the dance, even if we have auditions every day.

I honestly can't imagine how Trip and Oliver have gone from "We have to spend every weekend together and even dress alike" to "Yeah, well, we're not doing the band anymore." I mean, bad couple of rehearsals or no, they can't have both forgotten the awesomeness of Our Golden Summer. All we did was hang out at Oliver's house. They'd play and I'd help them play better. It was so perfect, I didn't care that Lish was gone half the time in California. I didn't care that my sister was busy with college dorm shopping, texting her new roommate, and having farewell experiences with her high school friends. The guys stopped caring about their stupid nights in the cemetery and neighborhood pranks. They almost stopped caring about *girls*. After that last gig at Nimby's went so well, Trip was so ramped up about the future that you could practically see the sparks coming out of his ears. It was all happening, and we all felt it.

And now this. Now Trip is out. And if Trip won't tell me what really happened, I'll make Oliver do it.

Unfortunately, today I only see Oliver at the end of the day, in the hardest class I have. There won't be any good conversation until later, because our teacher is merciless. Sometimes she asks for our notes without any warning, so if we're just writing bullshit or drawing pictures or whatever, trying to make it look like we're concentrating when we aren't, we're totally screwed. She's tricky and scheming like that. But, as a result, I think I'm doing better in her class than anyone else's so far.

Still, I can't resist sneaking glances at the notebook again while Ms. Neff starts class with a short film. Trip's new entry is long: a lot of it a goofy list of Things Charlotte Can Do When Not Taking Care of Sad Jackal (including a pottery class, which could be cool), but also he insists I don't need to worry, and nothing will change between me and him. Which would be reassuring if I halfway understood what changed between him and Oliver, and how I didn't see it coming.

When Ms. Neff turns the lights back on, it's time to fake my interest in those class-participation points that she says will count so much. In between people raising their hands (me included), I scrawl a note to Oliver: *What were you thinking?* I pitch it expertly to his desk, which is one over and one behind mine. When it comes back it says: *I just want more options, man. We need to have auditions. This weekend. You do a flyer?*

And you didn't tell me, why????????? I shoot back as soon as Ms. Neff's not looking.

It takes him a long time to answer, and when he does, I'm at first angered and then embarrassed by what it says: *Because I knew you would freak.*

As calmly and clearly—and *not freaking*—as I can after class, I explain to Oliver all the ways in which this is a terrible decision. I tell him he's crazy and we need to ask Trip back.

"It wasn't like I fired him or anything," Oliver says when I'm done. "And is it so wrong if I don't want to sound like everybody else?" He bangs the back of one shoe against the toe of the other.

"But Trip is just so good at coming up with the melodies and—"

Oliver's face twists for just a second. "Maybe it's because

you always show him the words first."

I cut him with my eyes. This is so not about that. It's not my fault that Trip *asks me questions about what I'm doing* more than Oliver ever has.

"Or maybe," I huff, "it's because he's been playing guitar for longer than you have, I don't know."

He presses his stick-up bangs back from his forehead and yanks his fingers through them. "Don't you trust me? Trust Trip if you don't. He's the one who left."

Because if you gave any *indication that you didn't want him anymore, he'd sense it and take off,* I want to say. I've learned at least that much about Trip in the last eight months. But then I see Oliver's let-down face, how disappointed he is that I'm not automatically taking his side. How, since summer, I've been doing more of that lately. Siding with Trip. And I *do* need to give Oliver more credit. I wouldn't be involved in this at all if he hadn't liked those poems I did in English last year, and then asked me to help coordinate. Plus, he is great on rhythm guitar, and without him there's no singer. I mean, Abe's wicked on drums, but he can't sing to save his life. And Oliver is . . . well . . . Oliver is the face, too.

"You're not out, are you, Charlotte?" For a second he looks actually worried that I might be.

I snort. "Of course not."

"Good. Because just me and Abe, decisions will never get made."

CALGARY
PUBLIC
LIBRARY

Village Square Library
Self Checkout
August 17 2019 12:43

39065157224989	2019-09-07
The game can't love you back	
39065154845023	2019-09-07
The secret history of us	
39065141317055	2019-09-07
Paper butterflies	
39065119817342	2019-09-07
Being friends with boys	

Total   **4 item(s)**

You have 0 item(s) ready for pickup

Village Square Library
Self Checkout
August,17,2019 12:43

39065157224989   2019-09-07
The game can't love you back
39065152485023   2019-09-07
The secret history of us
39065141317055   2019-09-07
Paper butterflies
39065119817342   2019-09-07
Being friends with boys

Total   **4 item(s)**

You have 0 item(s) ready for pickup

To check your card and renew items

go to www.calgarylibrary.ca

or call 403-262-2928

We both laugh. Kind of at ourselves, kind of at each other.

"I still don't like it." My arms are crossed in front of my chest, like some housewife with a rolling pin. I drop them to my sides.

He hooks his arm around my neck and steers me down the empty hall. "I'm telling you, it will be okay. This is the right thing to do. Even Trip said so, right?"

I think about the calm, even tone of Trip's stuff in the notebook today. Of his hand on my shoulder, squeezing lightly. "Well, he just said that—"

"I *know* what he said, because I talked to him. It's not like we're not friends anymore. So it's all cool, okay? Now let's get out of here. There are lists to be made! People to call!"

He pulls me out into the blinding sunshine, down the walkway to the parking lot. I'm grateful to be squinting, so he can't see in my face that I both love and hate how he was right about me freaking, and also right about how maybe things aren't going to be as bad as I think they will. How we both know this but aren't saying anything about it. More than that, I love and hate that I've already got ideas for this audition flyer.

By the time my stepsisters and I get home from school, though, some of my enthusiasm has gone out the window. Darby and Gretchen tried to outcomplain each other in the car, and then halfway home Gretchen got in another fight with her wrestler boyfriend, and we almost drove off the road when Darby reached over to turn off Gretchen's phone. Home still feels strange, anyway, even though Jilly's been off at college almost a month. I make myself a bowl of chips and onion dip and go upstairs, pretend I might do my homework, but our room—*my* room—isn't any good, because I'm not used to Jilly not being in here. Not used to her bed being made and *empty* instead of crowded with her, splayed out, talking on the phone or, more likely, studying. I'm not used to my sister sharing a room with someone new off at college: someone cooler and crisper and who won't fight about whose turn it is to do laundry.

The sun slants in through my blinds and I stretch my hands out into it, making my arms into zebras. If I'm honest, Lish is missing from this afternoon too. I don't know if there's volleyball practice right now. I just know that if I try to call my former best friend, all I'll get is a couple of rings and her voice mail.

To fill the room with something, I put in the new CD from Trip. How *did* I spend my afternoons, before? Before Lish came back from her summer with that slanty bob, and then school started and she was suddenly talking about her volleyball friends D'Shelle and Kiaya all the time and plans she never involved me in.

It wasn't that much of a surprise when Lish ditched me for real, actually. She'd been quiet on the drive to school for days, and had bailed on sleepover plans two weekends straight. When my phone trilled my ringtone for her that weekend, it was only so she could tell me her mom was uncomfortable with her driving so many people around, since she'd just had her license a few months. Lish didn't even pretend not to still be driving Bronwyn to school, and I felt a small pang inside that I didn't want to feel. The three of us had been talking about Lish getting her license (and her mom's old convertible) since last October. We planned stops at the QT to get creamy cappuccinos, and blaring the music with the top down, even in winter. While she was talking, all I could think was how we'd yet to do anything like that.

It's not like she was mean. She was just—not the old Lish. I could've tried to argue with her or beg, but I know—better than anyone—that once someone's made up her mind to leave you, there's nothing you can do to make her stay.

Not having any classes with Lish this year makes her even more invisible. But this whole semester has turned out weird, anyway. I don't have classes with Abe or Trip, and just the one with Oliver, plus lunch. I don't understand, exactly, how everyone's kind of evaporated—not just Jilly, off at college. I mean, even if I do catch sight of Lish in the halls, it's like she's a different person. She's got her equestrian boots and her skinny skinny jeans, her shiny hair. And then there's me: twice as big as her, in my thrift-store pants; my untucked, unironed button-downs; my long, tangly hair. Sometimes she truly doesn't even see me. It's like a giant wall has been lowered down between us. We're not, apparently, going to talk about it. There's no crowbar to pry it up. I'm glad I have Trip, and the notebook, and band practice with Oliver, but now even that's messed up.

Before I can truly sink into despair about it, though, my phone chimes from the depths of my bag.

I drop down on my bed to answer. "Usually, by this time of day, we've hung up the phone and moved to the computer."

"Yeah, I know," Trip says. "But when I got home, Dad was all like, 'Son, I feel like we haven't spent enough time together lately. Here's these flies I tied and these new rods, and what do you say we do some fishing?'"

"Yeah, right. So then you reminded him you're a vegetarian?"

He tries to hide his chuckle from me. "Are you suggesting the love of my own father wouldn't be enough to convert me to carnivore?"

"Well, my love of chicken wings and cheeseburgers hasn't seemed to convince you yet, so yeah, maybe."

He clears his throat. "Just giving you enough time to talk to Oliver."

"Oh. Well, that was thoughtful."

"So, did you?"

"Yeah."

"Okay, then, so?"

I am not sure what he's asking me. "So, what?"

"So, you going to abandon ship and form a band with me instead?"

I laugh. "What, a band of one guy on guitar and a silent girl with a tambourine?"

"Well, or a cowbell. And you sing, don't you?"

"No way. Not like that, anyway." I shift down to the floor, put my back against the bed frame. "You're going to be on your own, I'm afraid. At least while I'm busy trying to keep Sad Jackal afloat."

"Ah. Well, maybe I'll take up needlepoint to pass the time. Let's ponder that together, while I play you something."

This is my favorite part of our phone calls. Talking to Trip is great, but when we stop talking, stop thinking, and just *listen*, I feel really . . . connected. To him. And maybe even the rest of the world. Usually he picks the songs, but sometimes I'll find something too. We turn up the stereo, put the phone on speaker, and then just sit there (or, often, in my case, lie there), not saying anything during the music. Thanks to Trip, I've discovered all kinds of cool bands and have a giant playlist full of all the stuff he's given me.

"Okay, ready," I tell him when I've muted my own stereo and stretched out.

"This one's a good one."

I lie quiet, waiting. Soon the phone fills with simple drums, and then a strumming guitar and a bass line—repetitive, basic, sweet. The singer comes in, British and a little emo. But good. Full of a lot to feel. I focus on the words, and it sticks in me how sad it all sounds. Lost. And resigned, in a way. I'm listening to the way the drums are light but carrying everything, how the guitar provides the rhythm. I picture Oliver playing it—his eyes closed, his head slightly back. There's a lull, and then things crescendo, driving you to the end, and the singer's just repeating *"It's all mixed up"* over and over until the song disappears.

When it's finished, I feel the way I often do after Trip plays something for me: inspired, open-eyed, and sad in a way I can't quite explain. I say, quiet, "Oliver wants auditions this weekend."

There is barely a pause. But still there is one. "Well then, you'll have to take notes. Tell me all the nasty details."

"You better not hog the notebook all weekend like you usually do, then."

"I could give it to you on Friday night. *If* you come help me spend some Scoutmob Dad got for a Mexican place in Little Five."

I smile. "Nachos sound like a fair exchange for spying on your former band."

"You're so *easy*. You didn't even let me get to the part about Zesto after."

"Damn!" I pound my fist on my thigh. "I knew I should've held out for more!"

"Yeah, well. Lesson learned. I'd better go, though. Shipshape around here before dinner and all that."

"Yeah, go shine those shoes of yours," I tease. "I couldn't see my face in them this morning. I would've said, but—"

"So kind to me, as usual. But—" His voice switches to serious. "Lemme know if you ever want to play sometime, really. We could be good, you and me."

No way he honestly thinks this is a good idea. "I think my invisible-songwriter act suits me better."

"Going to have to work on my bribery skills a little more, I guess."

"More than a Zesto cone, that's for sure."

We laugh and click off.

I stare at the clock. Hannah won't be home for another hour and a half, Dad maybe not until seven. Because of Dad's massage therapy schedule, Hannah says we have *no* excuse for not getting a good handle on most of our homework before dinner. Sometimes I regret telling her, when she and Dad got the house, that it was kind of nice, having a stepmom with some rules.

I turn the volume back up on Trip's CD. I wonder if Jilly's doing homework now, what she's listening to, what kind of books she has to read. I postpone homework a little longer to give her a call, but her voice mail right away means her phone is off. She could be in class or studying in the library, maybe. Possibly she's already at dinner or coffee with her suitemates, or in chorus rehearsal. When Dad and I visited campus with her last spring, I was amazed how big everything was, how much there was to do. Jilly could be anywhere right now. It's unsettling not being able to picture her, not having her in my face all the time. I put home-work in my face instead.

When Dad gets home from his last client, he and I go grocery shopping. Hannah's making Italian tonight, which means she needs—on top of other things—one of the baguettes they bake fresh at Your Dekalb Farmers Market. It also means Dad and I buy another one for us to eat in the car on the way home.

Chewing the soft bread, Dad asks, "You girls have fun this afternoon?"

I snort. "What? Listening to Darby's whining and Gretchen fighting with the Wrestler? Not really."

"No, I meant Lish. Bronwyn. Joyriding around town, wav-ing to boys and all those other things I don't want to know about."

His attempt at Hey I'm a Cool Dad is irritating. "Why'd you ask, then?"

"Um. Because I want all my insecurities reassured that even

if you're doing things I don't want you to be doing, you'll tell me instead of making me find out about it in a police blotter?"

He's kidding. Sort of.

"Lish has practice," is all I say about that.

"The band is good, yeah?" He tries again. "Oliver seems to be doing a great job of promoting it."

Dad is one of Oliver's friends on Facebook, which is how he knows anything about the band.

I rip a big piece off the baguette, to keep him from eating all of it.

"It's pretty good, I guess. I think we're going to get some new members."

"You still writing lyrics?"

I forgot I told him about that. "Yeah."

He nods, swallowing. "Good for you. And them."

When we arrive home, we just sit in the driveway with the engine off.

We finish the baguette, staring at the house. Looking at it, I picture some of the loud (in a good way), tangled-up-energy moments that have gone on inside with Hannah and Gretchen and Darby lately. Underneath those are dreamier, farther-away memories from our old place—with Mom.

"What are you thinking about?" He is looking at me now.

"I was thinking how nice our house looks from the outside.

How it seems like, I don't know, a place with a real family."

His face is soft. "I'm glad you think that now."

There are a lot of things I could say. I don't.

He pats my knee, then wads up the plastic bread bag and shoves it under the driver's seat. "All righty, then. Thanks for coming with me."

I shrug, pleased. "The grocery store is our thing."

I miss Jilly again. But it's not like I can leave a second message, especially not a lame one that goes: *Dad and I went shopping and it made me wish you were home.*

Dad is clearly also debating whether or not to say the embarrassingly mushy thing that just occurred to him, so I reach for the door handle, push my way out.

"I'll get the bags, you get the door," I tell him, starting to unload without waiting for his answer.

Chapter Two

Wednesday morning, I take the finished copies of the Sad Jackal audition flyer with me to school. I'm armed with my roll of masking tape, to aim for the most prominent bulletin boards on campus, once Oliver gives the final okay.

Even though he sees me coming in the parking lot—and he knows what's in my satchel—I still have to wait for Oliver to unwind himself from Whitney's arms and tell Abe and the other guys surrounding him to hang on a minute, before he moves in my direction. Some new girl I think Abe's into is looking at me with this *What are* you *doing here?* face, so I just stand in the way I'm used to standing around the guys: letting their dimwit girlfriend-hopefuls know that I belong here more than they do.

Finally Oliver's there, hand extended. "Lemme see."

I try to hold the flyers so no one else can look. The picture is a vintage-looking piglet band standing on two legs and playing their instruments, with Oliver's and Abe's faces pasted over two of the pigs and big question marks over the others. It looks decent, even though it was tough to Photoshop everything to keep the ears showing. Oliver and I both thought the whole thing should be almost a little uncool, because if it was *too* cool then we'd have people who thought they were way too cool trying out. At the bottom it says, *Experienced bassist. Synth.* There are hang-down tags with the band's generic email address (which mostly I check) and the date of auditions—two and a half days from now—for people to tear off and take with.

Trying to read Oliver's face, I see Trip heading over from Chris Monroe's car.

"Are these them?" Trip asks us both, sounding excited. Too excited. That he was hanging out with Chris, instead of here with Oliver, is bizarre, but I don't mention it. Oliver flicks a slightly annoyed glance at me, and I return it before I realize I don't know why Trip's presence should be annoying at all.

But Trip doesn't notice. He takes one of the flyers, reviews it without saying anything. His eyes glimmer with disappointment and some kind of weird vindictive pride at the same time.

"What?" I don't want to be defensive, but I do want him to like it.

"Nothing." He shrugs, but he still has that look on his face.

"We wanted it to be weird," I rush, hearing a "we" coming from my mouth that means "me and Oliver" instead of "me and you."

"Well, congrats," Trip says after a beat. "It's . . . cute." To Oliver he says, "You see Simon's post last night?"

Oliver nods and wraps his arm around Whitney, who has sidled up to him from nowhere—not liking it, I suppose, that he was away from her for a full two minutes.

"Cool." Trip looks at them, then me.

Why is this awkward all of a sudden? Oliver should be joking and talking and tied up in Trip's opinion just like before. I shouldn't be feeling like a wonky but necessary third wheel, the one keeping the tricycle from propelling itself into oncoming traffic.

"I'm going to put these up." I lift the envelope, show my roll of tape.

"Good work, Spider," Oliver says after me. As I turn to say thanks, I catch Trip watching, and he doesn't look pleased. I almost ask does he want to come help me, but asking him to participate in his own replacement would just be weird.

I get four flyers hung up—the crucial one near the band hall, and three others in strategic places by the cafeteria and the library—before the bell rings. I'll do the rest later. And check back on these to see if anyone's pulled off a tab.

Walking with Trip between first and second periods is a little more normal than the parking lot scenario. Apparently two seconds after I left, Whitney was all "What's up with *that*?" about the flyers, because Oliver hadn't told her about the auditions at all.

"Five-minute tirade about his lack of communication and respect." Trip's giddy, describing it. "Finger in his face and everything."

I groan. "Could he please go ahead and dump her?"

Oliver and Whitney have been going out since the party Sad Jackal played in July, and Trip and I really hoped the start of school would break them up. As an outlet for our Whitney disdain, we have written out several little scenarios in the notebook, all of them involving Oliver dumping Whitney in dastardly and creative ways. My favorite depicts Oliver rowing Whitney out to an island, abandoning her there, and tossing out bottles with messages that say *NOT EVEN IF WE WERE STRANDED ON A DESERT ISLAND* into the boat's wake.

"She does have a great rack, though," Trip says. "You can't argue."

I swat him on the arm. "Annoying much?"

He shrugs. "I'm just saying."

"Okay, well." We are at my math class. I hold up the notebook he just handed me. "I'll return it before lunch?"

"Duh."

I watch him walk away. He must know that I do this now, because today he turns and gives me a wave before he disappears around the corner.

When I'm able to read the notebook, though, I discover that as soon as his dad heard Trip wasn't doing Sad Jackal anymore, he started pushing Trip extra hard about joining a sports team again, or else the martial arts stuff his dad's obsessed with. And it sounds like Trip's actually considering it: *The thing is, after dinner I was laying there listening to music (too late to call you, sorry), and I remembered hearing that when your body's engaged in one mindless activity, it leaves the creative part free to create.*

I'm still working on my response to him in 20th Cen. As soon as Dr. Campbell turns out the lights for the overhead projector and his eighteen-year-old notes (which he expects us to copy and memorize whether he actually lectures on them or not), the guy in front of me, Benji, turns around and whispers, "That's not history, is it?"

"None of your business," I hiss at him, indicating he should turn around and focus, which I should be doing too. We had our first test last Friday, a take-home. But Campbell managed to make it hard as hell, and I know I'll be lucky if I get a C+.

Still, I want to finish my response to Trip in time for our switch-off.

Learning ninja skills is possibly cool, I write, but then I hesitate. I want to be encouraging. I do. But Trip's dad is militant about Trip conforming to his hard-core ideals. He wants a machine, not a musician. That Trip is even considering his dad's suggestions now, especially after all the fighting they did over the summer about the band, well—it's a little disconcerting.

I just want to protect that musical genius I admire so much, I write.

I'm debating telling him I'm worried that our busy schedules might make it harder for us to hang out, when Benji, in his oh-so-not-subtleness, reaches over his shoulder and drops a messily folded note on my desk. *We should team up for these tests. You up for it?*

I look down at my two notebooks: one a distracted hodge-podge of history, one a distracted, still not fully articulated mess about—whatever. I picture my report card, probably coming up before I know it.

Sure. I write back. *When. Where?*

After class, Benji bolts from his desk, but then waits for me outside the portable building and takes my arm like we're at the opera.

"You mean it?" he says.

"Sure, Benj."

"Okay, well. I can't truly hang until four or something this afternoon. Detention."

"You have detention already?" I unhook my arm from his. It feels weird being that close to him.

He shrugs.

"Okay, so, fine," I say. "But are you really taking notes in class or not? You're not getting me to do all the work."

He slow-smiles at me, shaking his head. From under those long bangs, his eyes are serious, and he holds out his hands as if in surrender. "I will be useful."

We're getting close to the main building, the busy double doors.

"That remains to be seen," I tell him over my shoulder. "I'll meet you this afternoon."

I don't know why I think this as I walk off, but I hope to god he is not, in any way, looking at my ass.

Waiting for Trip, to hand off the notebook before he has AP Physics and I have lunch period, I try to wrap things up by telling him about Benji and how I'm incredibly curious about this "study session."

"Ah-ah-ah," I hear Trip call across the courtyard. "Editing is cheating. Raw, unbridled honesty is the whole point." He gets to where I'm sitting and stands over me.

"Oh yeah, like all the honesty in those mysteriously missing pages?"

His hand goes to his chest. "Are you accusing me of censoring myself?"

"No. I'm accusing you of not doing a better job of editing yourself. If you're going to tear things out, you should really make sure they flow—" I start flipping, to show him, though he already knows the gap from August is totally there.

"You were in a difficult place." His face is fake sympathetic. "Jilly was getting ready to leave, and school was coming up, and I just didn't think you needed to hear about me reuniting with my long-lost twin brother, who was also king of Persia and wanted me to be in that action movie with him and our equally long-lost uncle, the famous movie star."

"I don't think Persia is a country anymore." My eyebrows are frowning but my mouth is smiling.

"I think you need to work on your geography."

"That's not the point."

"You are completely right." He takes the notebook from my hands. "The point is that I'm going to be late, and we're getting nachos in only two nights."

"You're right—that *is* the point." I pat my stomach.

He moves off, back toward the stairs, and we holler, "See you—if I don't see you first!" at the same time. The late bell rings over us, leaving me to spend the rest of lunch taping more Sad Jackal flyers in the open halls.

When the notebook comes back to me before psych at the end of the day, Trip has ignored basically everything I'd said in it. There aren't any How Oliver Should Break Up With Whitney cartoons, or any comeback in Jessica Stine's defense (seeing as she is the third hottest girl in school) regarding my snark that I'm not sure whether what she had on this morning was a dress or just a T-shirt. Instead he's written, in big block letters, *DO NOT HANG OUT WITH BENJI MCLAUGHLIN*. I'm all ready to write a snappy response when Oliver leans across the aisle to bump my fist.

"Good work, Spider. The flyers look great. And did you see that six tabs are already missing off that one?"

My shoulders flush with a proud orange feeling. Why this makes me ask, "Hey, what do you know about Benji McLaughlin?" I'm not really sure.

Oliver shrugs. "Skate punk. Pothead. Basically decent. Why?"

"He sits in front of me in history." I try to say it with nonchalance. "Just wanted to make sure I wasn't going to contract some horrible disease."

• • •

After school, I wait at the empty soccer fields for Benji to get done with his detention. I'm pretending to do my film studies reading, but after about two minutes, I have to call Trip.

"What the hell 'Don't hang out with Benji'? In all caps? Like you're my mom?" I say as soon as he picks up.

"And a lovely good afternoon to you, too."

"What do you have against Benji?" I keep going. "He's a total idiot."

"Why are you studying with him, then?"

"Whatever."

"Benji is not at all interested in your Twentieth Cen. grade. Or his."

"You think I can't handle Benji McLaughlin? I handle *you* every day."

He ignores my insult. "I think you can handle him. You just might not want to. Or maybe you will." His voice is a little mean. "And he tears through girls, believe me."

Everything switches around in me then. It never would have occurred to me to think of Benji in any romantic way, but suddenly I am picturing us making out under the bleachers. I am picturing his hand in my pants.

"So what if I did? Want to?" I stumble over the words. "And besides, when did you ever spend enough time with him to know how he treats his girlfriends?"

I am glaring at the empty soccer field as though I am trying to stare Trip down. We are in dangerous, embarrassing territory this minute, him even hinting about my being with a boy. My last boyfriend, Clay, broke up with me weeks before Trip enrolled last semester, and I haven't had a date or even a crush since. Though Trip dated someone for a while at the end of the year last year, it wasn't that big a thing to either of them, and it was over before we started doing so much band stuff this summer. For most of our friendship, we've both been unattached. He hasn't been interested in anyone, and I'm not the kind of girl that boys like, anyway.

But as my long friendship with Oliver —and even Abe— has proven, when you're friends with a boy and then suddenly you have to talk about dating, it can get strange. Sure, boys want to tell you all about their hookups, until they remember—by some slip in the conversation—that you're a *girl*, and then they get weird and uncomfortable. It's important to stay expressionless when it happens, even though you also have to keep doling out girl-sided advice. Because that's why they're telling you. They *want* to know what it's like from a girl's side. But if you ever attempt doing the reverse—talking about your own hookups or crushes—and especially if you even slightly mention any kind of physical whatever, everything shuts down and gets awkward. It's safer to be completely neutral on the matter. It's safer if they don't think you have a vagina at all.

"Look." I change tactics. "It's not like I don't think Benji is a little . . . off."

"So then—?"

I can just *see* him twirling his hand in that arrogant way.

"So if *you* were in my history class, it might be different. But I have to make do with what I've got. So cut me some slack."

He's quiet a second. I'm not sure what he's going to say.

"Like maybe you should cut me some slack about not hanging with Sad Jackal anymore."

My pulse accelerates and my face warms. "When have I ever given you any crap about that at all? I think that maybe you should care less who I care whether you hang out with or not."

Yikes. That was mean-sounding. And probably not English.

"I'm just exploring alternatives," he says finally.

"Well, maybe so am I."

It feels like a fight. And yet it also just feels like a regular conversation. I'm not sure if I like either option. I'm not sure why.

"Good luck with your studying," he says. There's acid in that last word.

"Thank you." I choose not to engage.

We hang up.

"Well, that was a disaster," I say out loud.

But I only have to look at my reading for about forty-five more seconds before I hear Benji crunching through the leaves and pine needles behind me.

"'Sup," he says when I turn around. Like he's doing me a favor by actually showing up.

I stick my film studies into my satchel, pull out the notes from 20th Cen.

"I figure we should compare notes" is all I say to him.

He clomps up onto the bleachers next to me. It is gray and overcast: looking like it should be cold, making it even more uncomfortable that it's lightly humid and really too warm for a jacket, though he has one on. The minute he sits down, he rummages around in it (multipocketed, army-green canvas) and takes out a crumpled joint.

"You can't smoke that here." My whole body is on alert, looking around for anyone who might see us. Coaches, stray teachers, Principal Hammersley.

"You're right," he says, putting the joint to his lips and withdrawing a lighter from somewhere.

"I'm serious." I put my hand over his, stopping the lighter in its path. "I am not doing this if you are going to be high." I've heard enough of Abe, Oliver, and Trip's stupid pot-hazed

31

conversations to turn me off the stuff forever, if I was interested in smoking anything, anyway. "It's not part of the contract."

Benji's brown eyes level at me. "Contract?" The joint bounces on his, I notice, very plump red lips.

"I just—" I take my hand off of his. Part of me wants to wipe it on my pants. "I mean, I'm not *drunk*, so—"

"You could be."

I don't know if that means he thinks I might be, or if he's giving me permission.

"You can smoke when we're done, whatever. I don't care. But while we're working, I need your actual brain."

"You need my actual brain." His eyes are still on mine, unmoving. I stare him down. My hands are uncomfortably sweaty.

Eventually he shrugs, finally taking the joint out of his mouth and burying it back in the depths of his jacket. There's a tiny white speck of rolling paper left on his lip, but I'm certainly not going to tell him.

Instead we sit there, side by side, our notebooks splayed across our laps. I'm amazed, looking at Benji's tidy handwriting. He's got everything from Dr. Campbell's notes, plus little sidebars in the margins, tying in things our teacher mentions in his lectures. The ones that might be useful.

"You don't need me," I tell him after a minute. "Your notes

are perfect." Meanwhile I'm copying the parts I apparently missed in class.

"So, okay?" He is already reaching into his jacket, arching his eyebrows at me.

I could be a prude, or I could have him think I'm at least a *little* cool. "Whatever, I don't care."

I keep copying his notes, waving away the drifts of Benji's smoke as they head in my direction. At one point he offers the joint to me. I glare at him.

"Just being polite," he mutters.

That's all we say. When I finish I hand Benji back his notebook, tell him thanks. I feel weird that he didn't look at my own notes for more than a second or two.

"My pleasure," he says. His eyes are loose. He leans back on the seat behind us, and I see his gaze pause in the general area of my chest. "So, what now? You want to—make out a little or something?"

"You have got to be kidding." I'm glaring at him, but I also want to giggle.

He shrugs again, leans down to put the joint out on the heel of his shoe. The stubby, stinky butt gets put inside the folds of his jacket.

"Just sayin'," he goes, aloof. "We're out here, there's time to kill, I'm gonna save your Twentieth Cen. grade. . . ."

I arch my eyebrow at him, trying to joke back. "You still have to prove that part."

He can't really think that I am going to make out with him in exchange for his notes? I feel blood thumping in my neck, the backs of my knees.

"Okay, then." He stretches, climbs forward, starts heading down the bleachers. Like nothing just happened. "You need a lift home?" he offers.

"I'll walk," I say, firm, though I've never done it before.

"Suit yourself."

His indifference is a little startling. I push my hair back from my face, try to shake some sense into my head. *DO NOT HANG OUT WITH BENJI MCLAUGHLIN* is behind my eyes. I follow Benji off the bleachers, and for a second I consider accepting a ride from him, but there's nowhere for me to hurry to. Plus, I could probably afford to burn a few calories.

"Well, thanks, Benj," I say, to say something, when we get to the upper lot.

He veers off toward his car and holds up his hand in a wave without saying anything else. I'm not sure if I'm glad he hasn't insisted on driving me or if it's rude. I decide to blame it on the pot, and take out my phone, text Dad to let him know what I'm doing. I'm half a block away from school when Benji passes by me in his old brown Volvo. He beeps and waves, but he doesn't slow down.

• • •

The streets between school and home are surprisingly trashed: Chic-fil-A bags, empty plastic bottles, and, gross, a discarded diaper. At first I'm indignant about the neglect, but before long I'm imagining Sad Jackal doing some kind of neighborhood cleanup, maybe with a performance at the school at the end? I'm taking my phone out to text Oliver the idea when it rings. I'm surprised but thrilled to see it's Jilly.

"Did you ever walk home from school?" I ask her, without saying hey.

"I don't think so, why?"

"The whole way is covered with trash. It's alarming."

"You're walking? From school? What time is it?" I can hear her looking at her watch.

"It's fine. I'm almost home," I lie.

"Okay, well" is all she says. She can't do anything about it anyway, even if she wanted to. We both feel it in the air between our voices.

"So what's up?" I ask.

"I just wanted you to know that I'm not coming home for fall break," she says, voice switching to her serious-and-practical tone.

"You have fall break?" *How many breaks do you get in college?*

She charges through, fast, like she's trying to convince herself:

"Adele and some other girls are going to Savannah that weekend, and it just seems like fun, so . . ."

She needs me to tell her it's fine.

I step over some broken-up sidewalk, a plastic bag filled with what is either mud or— "Well, I didn't even know you might come home, so it's not like it's a disappointment."

"I'll be home for Thanksgiving," she offers as an apology, not even hearing what I just said.

"It's fine, Jill. Really. Hey, Hannah's letting us choose our own cereal again. No more Kashi, ha!"

"No faaaaair," she whines. But I can tell she wanted to have to soothe me a little more than that.

"Yeah, well, me and Darby managed to wear her down. Only took a little over a week, actually."

I hear her say something to someone else with her. It makes me feel insignificant. And also like she's not listening to me at all.

When she comes back she says, "Well, we have Cap'n Crunch here too, so. But, I mean, are you okay? With the break thing? I don't want you to feel like I'm . . ."

What she doesn't say is *abandoning you.*

"You aren't," I insist, too fast, though somehow, with her bringing it up like that, it's suddenly like she *is.*

"Don't worry" is all I say.

"Well—" She sounds unsure. Ever since Mom left six years

ago, it feels like I've always had to assure Jilly that there's no *way* she'd ever turn into her. It's annoying and a little unfair.

"Send me a postcard or something, okay?" I try to say lightly. But immediately it's the wrong thing to say, because it brings up all the postcards Mom sent, at the beginning. How we read them over and over, trying to decipher what more she might be trying to tell us in between those few lines.

"I mean," I go on, trying fiercely to repair everything, "just have a blast and Thanksgiving is practically around the corner, so." Although, it's still September. Halloween—our favorite holiday together—lies between now and when I'll see Jilly next. The only way I'll see her costume is if she posts pictures. The only way she'll know about Sad Jackal's performance at the dance is if I do the same. Instead of just being a part of each other's lives, we have to make time to report on them. Which makes me not want to be on the phone anymore. Why did she bother telling me? I didn't even know she was getting a fall break. I should've just let it go to voice mail.

"Okay," she says.

"Okay, then." My voice has started cramping up in the top of my throat. I am such a stupid baby.

"I'll call this weekend. Give Dad a kiss."

"Love you," I mumble. I've turned onto our street and I can see our house now. The streetlights have all come on around me, even though it's just starting to be dusk.

"Love you, too. So much," she tells me.

And then she is gone.

When I get to our driveway I just stand there, by the mailbox. Actual tears start to fall, hot and embarrassing. I don't know why I'm crying. Jilly's not coming home, but it's no big deal. She's in college. I didn't know she even *might* come home. And this is what she's supposed to do. I'm fine, really. I'm really absolutely fine. She can't be involved in every tiny aspect of my life anymore. I knew that. I know it. It doesn't mean she's turning into Mom.

Which makes me, immediately, want to talk to her. Mom.

I check the time. She'll be in her studio in the warehouse she rents with a bunch of other artists just outside of Taos. In exchange for answering the phone there, plus paperwork and maintenance things for everybody, Mom sleeps in a tiny loft upstairs. When she told me and Jilly about it, we made up all these stories about sophisticated artist parties and dark-of-night incidents with coyotes that we imagined Mom must be having. When we finally went to visit two years ago, though, Jilly said not even college students lived that way anymore.

Wiping tears off my cheeks and clearing my throat, I dial the studio phone. Mom has a cell, but it's never on. That, or she forgets and leaves it in her beat-up Jeep.

"Hello?" she says, after eighteen or something rings.

"Mom." My throat is still twitching a little, from talking to Jilly.

"Hi, sweetie. How are things?" She is breathy, loose. Like it hasn't been almost a month since we talked.

"They're okay. Classes aren't wretched yet."

"That's good. I forget—you in them with anyone?"

I tell her (again) about psych with Oliver, and then jump over school (so she won't ask about Lish) to the band, the upcoming auditions.

"I'm glad it's going well," she says. "Though I'm sorry Trip and Oliver have had a falling-out."

"They haven't had a falling-out." Irritating. "It's just that—"

"Well, I'm sure everything will work out the way it's supposed to."

She says this. Always. I know she's trying to be reassuring, but sometimes, like now, it feels more like she's just bored with my problems.

"How's your dad? And your sister?" she asks.

"They're fine. Jilly likes her roommate, and her classes. Dad has a lot of clients."

"I'm glad to know that."

It was a mistake to call, and I don't want to be talking to her anymore, but I don't want her to think I'm ending things because she asked about Dad and Jilly, either. Dad and Jilly aren't exactly fans of my mom. Mom tried at first to be Dad's friend after she left, sending postcards and calling every week and things like that, but now Dad only talks to Mom when he absolutely has to, and he's still kind of curt when he does. Jilly's a little better with her—I think she and Mom talk every few months now—but after Mom's shouting and weeping on the phone on Jilly's seventeenth birthday, things between Jilly and her have been pretty broken. This means I'm the one who has to tell Mom what's going on with them, and I don't like being in that position.

"How about you?" I ask, just to say something else.

"Oh." She sighs. "Really busy, actually. I've been doing a lot of painting, still, and some pottery, too. I've got a show coming up."

"Really?" This is supposed to be more exciting than she sounds about it. Apparently shows are harder to come by than she thought they'd be when she left us to become a real artist.

"We'll see how it turns out." Still so breathy. "It's a lot of work right now, and the gallery owner isn't exactly what you'd call cooperative, but it's a show."

"It's what you went out there for. It's great."

"It is a really good, well-established gallery," she goes on. "Downtown and everything. It's promising. And the other artists are all very good."

"Not your own show?"

"Well, no."

This explains her lack of enthusiasm. Mom's done group shows before, and they haven't gone quite the way she hoped. But maybe that's because they haven't been in good galleries, like this one sounds.

"Well, I'm proud of you."

"Thanks, honey. That means a lot."

There's a small pause between us. She isn't, I notice, asking me to fly out for it.

"I should let you get back to work, then," I say.

"Okay, hon. Well, good luck with the songs. I'm proud of you, too."

It's stupid but it does feel good, hearing her say that. Just good enough to get past my earlier funk, but I'll take it.

Chapter Three

Four guys respond to the audition flyer. Three of them are bassists. Only one does synth stuff. During lunch period Friday, Oliver and I talk over our possible backup plans. Redoing the poster, putting yet another call out on Facebook, and waiting for another week (Oliver's ideas) are all out. Trying to get Trip back, and seeing if our school's band director has any suggestions (mine) are out, too. Eventually we settle on finding out how good these four guys are, and then looking for alternatives if we have to. I'm not excited about this plan, but by the end of the day Oliver's no-worries attitude has, as it usually does, bled onto me and I feel decent.

I've been home for hours and it's almost time for Trip to pick me up for our Mexican feast when Oliver texts with the second part of the conversation—the stuff he "forgot" to ask me earlier.

Can u send everybody directions to my house?

You haven't responded to them yet? Stupidly, I haven't checked the band email in the last couple of days. I thought Oliver wanted to be the one "in charge" this time.

I'm taking 3 APs man.

Yeah ur a genius. But you couldn't do it earlier?

Whitney and shit.

Come on.

It feels like it takes ten minutes before he responds: *My Dads got this thing I have to be in a tie for in 5 mins.*

I hope you choke on that tie.

I know.

Another wait.

It's cooler if the manager does it. Makes us more professional.

I have to pause a bit before answering. Because it does. Look better. And Oliver still doesn't know the names of half the streets in our neighborhood. It's amazing he gets anywhere.

So, will u? comes in.

U aren't the only one w/ plans 2night.

Their #s are in the email box. U can just txt.

"Ergh," I growl, checking the kitchen clock. Ten minutes before Trip shows up.

Fine, I type back.

Righteous.

What time shd I come over tmrw? I am still huffy. I wish he could see that clearly in a text.

2:30?

I'll see you at 2.

Cool.

Though I can't hear it, I know he is grateful, and I know he needs me to do this.

Cool.

I hit Send right as Gretchen and Darby thunder down the stairs.

"Remind Mom I'm at Melissa's. Darb's getting a ride home from the movies," Gretchen tells me.

"*You* tell her—" I shout behind them, though the slamming door cuts me off.

How everyone—Gretchen, Darby, Oliver—just *assumes* I'll take care of everything is really annoying. But since there's no one else to do it, I check the computer and gather the numbers from Oliver's exchanges with the band guys. After that I write a note to Dad and Hannah, explaining where their children are. Then, on the couch, I compose a decent-sounding text with

Oliver's address and the audition time, debating how exactly to sign it. Manager? Charlotte? Charlotte, the Manager of Sad Jackal? As I do this, I wonder what Lish would say about me texting four different guys I've never met before. I can almost feel her gripping my arm, can hear her elated squeal. I debate calling her. I mean, it's not like we can't still *talk*. But just then the doorbell rings (Trip) and my phone chimes with another text from Oliver. Apparently, I've got plenty else going on already tonight.

It's much calmer in Trip's car. Drifty, soft-voiced singing is coming through the stereo, and being in this incubator with him, and this music, chills me out, regardless of everything else. I ask who's playing.

"You've heard them before. Come on."

I twist my face. "No fair." But then I try to listen. "Lavender Concrete?"

"They sound similar," he says, nodding. "But they're more acousticky than this guy. Which is, I have to say, a *really* big hint."

But I am truly horrible at this game.

"Um, Three Barn House?" It's a random one I remember.

"You're being silly." He punches the volume up a bit from the steering wheel. "I went to see him play? When he came to town?"

"You go to see *every*one play." The music floats around us. It's really pretty. "Come on, I want to know. I'll remember, I promise. They'll be our nacho dinner band."

"Hey, baby," he jokes. "That's nacho dinner. It's mine."

"Exactly, see?"

"Lorrie's Castle," he says.

I punch my own thigh. "Oh god, I *knew* that. I really did. But now I will remember them as *Nacho* Castle."

He rolls his eyes, but in a fake *you're annoying* way.

After eons of trying to find a parking space, both of us are really hungry, and as soon as we get seated we dive into the menus, which are taller than our heads. Nachos, obviously, we agree right away. A mountain of them with everything possible. While we're trying to decide what else, a server walks by with sizzling plates of fajitas, and we make immediate *We need that too* eyes at each other.

The nachos come fast, and we dig in. From watching both Lish and Gretchen in front of their various boyfriends, I know girls are often uncomfortable eating in front of guys. The two of them always pick at their food, because they don't want their guys thinking that they're pigs or something. But I am not like them. Partly because I don't know *how* to eat like a bird—food is just too good to take only two bites and leave it at that. But I've also seen how guys eat: both the sheer volume and the fingers-into-face-as-fast-as-possible method. There is no way, if there's food in front of him, that a guy—not a high school guy, anyway—is going to pay a lick of attention to how much or how little you're eating, except maybe to eyeball your barely nibbled-at plate and say, greedily, "You gonna eat that?"

So I don't worry about it, either with how many nachos I'm eating (I have to move fast, anyway, to keep Trip from getting all the jalapeños) or what I pile on my plate when the veggie fajitas come, about ten minutes later.

By the end of dinner, we're both greasy-smiled and utterly stuffed.

"Fried ice cream?" Trip asks, eyebrows jerking up and down.

"Not even *I* can accomplish fried ice cream right now," I groan. "And besides, you promised me Zesto later."

"Did I really promise?"

"Maybe not promised. Indicated. Hinted. Teased."

He holds his hands open. "What baby wants, baby gets."

"Not right now, though, god. Let's go on a walk or something first."

We settle the bill (nicely cheap for each of us, thanks to that Scoutmob Mr. Brewer gave to Trip) and decide to stroll down to Criminal Records, to do some browsing. Which means, for a while, I'll lose him to the vinyl section. But that gives me a minute to stand in an inconspicuous corner and reply to the texts from the audition guys. It's not like I'm trying to hide it from

Trip, exactly, but I also don't want to superfocus on the whole *Hey, we're going to replace you* element of tomorrow. All four have confirmed they'll be there, though one guy asks what color the house is and what to look for in the yard, which for some reason strikes me as really cute.

God. New guys in the band. And what if they *are* cute? It hadn't occurred to me that one of the new players might actually be interesting. The idea gives me a hot feeling around my neck, makes my jaw pop around in a circle on its hinge. So to stop thinking about it, I flip through the giant bins of used CDs, letting the stream of names fill my head, laughing at myself for only recognizing the cheesy, embarrassing ones.

When I get to the end of the bin, Trip's head-bent over the "New Releases" racks, so I entertain myself by leafing through some of the magazines I wish I had a subscription to. I'm lost in an interview in *Bust* when Trip slides up next to me, so many CDs and records picked out that he had to get a basket.

I arch my eyebrow. "You think you got enough?"

"Utter goldmine," he practically gasps. "I don't know why I don't come over here more; it's not that far."

"Because then you'd have to get a *job*."

He mock shudders, eyes rolling back.

"You good?" He is clearly not impressed with my two-disc selection.

I blink up at him sweetly. "Why should I buy music when I've got you?"

"Sheesh." But he is smiling.

After shopping we walk the rest of the way down Euclid, laughing together over the ridiculous outfits in the windows of all the specialty boutiques. Trip says he'd be embarrassed to go out with a girl who thinks leggings are pants, and I think—to myself—that on my short-waisted body, most of those wide belts would serve better as push-up bras. When we get down to the apartments of Bass Lofts, though, we gaze covetously at the lit-up windows and the cool people milling around inside, and fantasize about having our own places.

"I'm not sure I'd want to live in an old high school, though," he says. "I mean, the one I'm in is bad enough, right?"

"Well, let's try to find something better for you, then."

So we walk farther, down by the park, looking at the houses lining it. We take the next side street, to keep wandering, and then another turn, and another after that. We move deeper into a neighborhood of huge, beautiful houses: gables and deep porches and painted brick. Houses perched on tiny fenced yards, some covered in ivy, others dotted with ornamental bushes and crossed with rock-lined paths. Everything is honey-lit, everyone inside unconcerned about what's happening outside.

"Can you imagine living in a place like that?" I nod toward

the biggest one: a literal mansion hulking across the entire corner of one intersection. It's the perfect setting for women in hoop-skirted dresses and wide-brimmed hats. Men with gardenias tucked into their buttonholes.

"Maybe with a bunch of friends it would be cool," he says. "But with my dad? Probably we'd keep half the rooms closed off, to save money on heat."

I picture him and his dad in the two-bedroom house they live in. Secondhand furniture. Not much on the walls. Trip's room, crowded with his music equipment. All the weekends Trip spends at Oliver's house— its open, stylish-but-comfortable rooms, Mrs. Drake and her perpetual hostessing.

Trip interrupts my thoughts. "Do you know where we actually are?"

I peer into the shadows between the pools of street lamp light. "Um, no."

He heads for the next intersection. "Let's see what's up here."

We squint at the names of the streets, then each other. We don't recognize anything. We bust up laughing.

I slowly turn, straining to hear signs of any kind of traffic, any indication of which way we should go.

"How about—this way?" I point at the road that heads gently downhill. "Didn't we walk up a hill to get here?"

"Atlanta is full of hills. Hills on top of hills. With more hills in between."

"Well then, genius, you pick."

"I say . . ." He puts his hands over his eyes, spins around and around in a circle. When he stops, he points. "Come on. This is it."

He grabs my sleeve and pulls me down the very hill I pointed at.

"Oh, you needed your little dreidel trick to figure out what I already told you?"

"Second opinion is all," he teases.

But at the bottom of the hill the road ends, teeing off either left or right. We have no idea, so we choose right. And then when another street comes up, left. Then right again. Still, only houses and houses. No sign of Little Five Points anywhere. No brightening lights.

"You know, we could just be walking deeper into nothing," I say, starting to feel unsure.

"We could be halfway to Cabbagetown."

Which doesn't help. "Wouldn't we see the MARTA, then? Or at least hear it?" The thought of being near the MARTA, though, makes me—it's not fair, but I can't help myself—worry we could get mugged.

He can see that I'm uneasy. "Come on." He offers his elbow for me to take. "It's this way."

He leads me off to the right again, chattering about how he

used to ride his bike all up and down these streets when he was a kid. Even if he doesn't remember exactly, he insists, it's a muscle memory for him. We'll be there in no time. I decide to let him go on with his joke, and not point out that he grew up in Tampa.

But after a couple more turns, we find ourselves walking up the back side of the same gigantic mansion on the corner.

"Um," he says.

We both just stand there. I take my phone out, check the time. It's 10:42.

"You'll make your curfew, don't worry."

"But we don't know where we *are*." I'm starting to feel a little panicked now.

"Well, obviously, we need to head back down that way." He points down the street in front of us. "Because we came *up* this way, right?"

I gaze down the street. "Yes."

"And then we'll just look for more houses we recognize. They'll be our Hansel and Gretel crumbs."

"That's a good name for a song," I say, automatic.

He peers down at me with this look on his face that makes me feel . . . I don't know. Valued. Or more like . . . treasured. Or something. But then he turns and faces the street, squares his shoulders, and starts us down again, arm in arm.

"Tell me how it would go, this song," he says.

"I wasn't being serious. I just—"

"Stepmom didn't want us; Daddy was too weak!" he explodes, loud and drawly and low, like some country singer in a bar. Or someone at bad karaoke.

I giggle.

"Come on, songwritin' girl. What comes next?"

"She kicked us out of Dodge," I try. *"She threw us to the streets."*

He nods. We are bouncing now, to the rhythm of this crazy made-up song.

"And outside there were wolves, my friend," he booms. *"Witches and goblins to run from . . ."*

Immediately, I know what comes next: *"But tucked safe in our pockets . . ."*

Together we holler, both our tunes going off in different directions, *"were our Hansel and Gretel crumbs!"*

We're laughing at ourselves, but also because right then we see a house we recognize and a street we know to turn left down. This gives us immense confidence, both in ourselves and in the song. So Trip hollers out the rest of the chorus and the next verse, with me butting in every now and then to adjust a line. We actually get the chorus pretty good—*"I'm winding a trail through the woods while you sleep"*—and sing it over and over, like some kind of talisman. I catch myself being a little curious if the people in these houses think we're *together*: me and him skipping and singing in the middle of the road, but just then we pass a house surrounded by tons of security lights. Behind it we can see the edge of the park we passed to get in this neighborhood.

"Look at that," he says, panting a little.

"Wow," I gasp. "It really worked."

He crazy-grins at me. "Come on." Grabbing my hand, he runs through the unfenced yard. Another motion-detecting light springs on, but we quickly break into the safety of the park—neutral territory—both of us breathing hard.

"We did it."

"Of course we did." He winks.

It's ten after eleven—only twenty minutes until my curfew, which Dad still refuses to extend to midnight. Trip and I move fast and don't talk.

"We'll make it," he tells me, finally getting to the car.

"I know." But I don't, exactly. I won't get in *that* much trouble, but I would like to be allowed to do this again.

The music from Trip's stereo fills the quiet, until at 11:31 we slide up to the curb in front of my house.

"What did I tell you?" He is obnoxiously—and endearingly—victorious.

"I wasn't worried in the slightest," I scoff.

"You were."

"Was not. I knew right where we were. All part of my evil

plan to get you to help me with my songs, even though you're not in the ba—" I clamp my lips shut.

"Ah, yes. Well." He clears his throat and looks away from me, toward the house. "Next time you can just ask."

I put my hand on his arm. "I only meant—"

"It's cool." He opens his door, gets out. I climb out too, to meet him at the front of his car and give him a *thanks and I'm sorry* hug.

"This really was fun," I say into his chest.

His arms tighten around me. "It was."

The Hansel and Gretel song floats back into my head. Around me his hug stays and stays. Warm and strong and safe and happy. Comfortable, and right, with a glimmer of . . . what? I don't know, but it doesn't matter. Mainly I'm glad, in spite of the changes, that Trip isn't evaporating like Lish did. It makes me want to hold on to this even more—the importance of tonight.

Finally he breaks the hug, backing up a little. "Good luck tomorrow."

"Yeah. Could be a disaster. We'll see."

"It'll be great. Just make sure to tell me all about how bad they are. Deal?" His fingers point into a gun.

I point mine back. "Deal. And, hey, thanks for tonight. It was really terrific."

"It was, wasn't it?" His face is full of—something. But then it's not. "Well, good night, Charlotte."

"Good night, Trip."

And though it's chilly, and I need to go in, for some reason I don't want tonight to be over. So I stand there in the yard, watching as he gets into the car, then pulls slowly from the curb and away down my street. I keep standing there another minute, until the warm-strong feeling of his hug dissipates from my shoulders. And only then do I go inside, humming, *tucked safe in my pockets were my Hansel and Gretel crumbs.*

In the morning, the good feeling of my evening with Trip is replaced by overwhelming anxiety about auditions. Oliver's nervousness when I finally get to his house isn't reassuring, either.

"Do you think we should have snacks or something?" he says as soon as he opens the door.

"Don't we usually?" I say, pushing past. "At least chips or something? Some cheese?" I drop my bag on the chaise by the front door and move into the kitchen, to his refrigerator, start pulling out half-empty containers of prepared foods that his mom gets from Alon's and Whole Foods. There's almost a whole platter of some kind of artichoke-covered toasts that will do fine, I think, and a thing of macaroni salad. In the freezer are some Trader Joe's samosas I can heat up. But I also know, from experience, that we could just have a jar of peanut butter with a spoon in it.

"They all respond?" Oliver wants to know. He's pushing his hair back over and over. Am I supposed to notice his outfit or not? Because he does look cool in that sweater-vest and holey T-shirt, but maybe he doesn't want to seem like he's trying.

"Every one." I take out plates and serving spoons.

"Cool."

I move him out of the way to get the paper cups from an upper cabinet.

"It'll be fine," I say, though my hands are sweaty. "Gimme that bottle of Slice."

Just as he opens the refrigerator again, there are footsteps outside and we both look up. It's like someone's caught us at something.

"You greet them," I tell him, after he doesn't move.

"Right."

Watching him go, the feeling of *new* people washes through me. Getting up and going over to Oliver's on a weekend is so automatic, I didn't consider my outfit much today. And now I wish I had. At least a little. Because this isn't going to be the normal gang. This is us trying to convince other people to be with us, and it's stupid I didn't think about it before. Now all I can do is smooth down my hair, tug the tails of my rumply button-down into some variation of straightness.

But it's just Abe coming in.

"'Sup," he says to me, taking one of the samosas before they go into the oven.

I can relax, a little. "What's up?"

He shrugs. "Whatever, man. Last night a DJ saved my life."

"Okay." I half laugh, half roll my eyes. You never know when Abe is serious or joking, or even what he really means. Except for when he is seriously serious, and then he's so intense it's almost frightening. But that doesn't happen very often.

Oliver rakes his hands up and down on his skinny, dark-jeaned thighs, looking things over in the kitchen.

"Where were you and Whitney last night, man?" Abe asks him, reaching for another samosa and shoving it in his mouth.

Oliver shrugs, awkward. "Had to cancel for some thing with my dad."

"Gotcha."

Abe and I swap glances. You can tell what Oliver's not saying is that, because he forgot his dad's event, Whitney had a huge fit and so tonight he's going to have to make it up to her by doing it in some park somewhere, probably seeing a chick film after that. But rather than acknowledge any of this, I slide the tray of samosas into the oven, reach behind Oliver for a bowl for the macaroni salad. Abe coughs and pours himself a soda.

"I think we're good with the food," I say.

"Awesome." But Oliver's hardly registering. He gestures

toward the staircase and Abe and I follow him into his teenage-boy lair: the rec room downstairs.

They turn on the PS3 and get into the war game they've been working on for a while. Abe lives two doors down from Oliver, and because of this—and because he doesn't have his own practice room—he leaves his drums set up at Oliver's and basically has an open-door policy here at the Drake house. If this were Tekken I'd be able to jump in and take the loser's place, but when Abe gets shot down I know to keep my mouth shut: this is a serious game, and they can be driven almost to tears over it. I watch, and remind them where bonus packs and hidden snipers are, but my anxiousness about the new guys makes me keep getting up to see if there's anyone at the door. Good thing I'm checking, because it's only during a small pause while the game loads between levels that I even hear the doorbell.

"Got it," I tell them, though they haven't budged.

At the door are three guys, apparently all having arrived in the same old Saturn that's parked crookedly in front of Oliver's house.

"Howdy," the mohawked redhead says, lifting a black bass case covered with band and bumper stickers.

"Uh—hi. I'm Charlotte." I open the door wider. They're down the stairs before I can call Oliver and Abe up.

In the rec room, the boys all shake hands, like their dads would. The mohawk redhead kid is Eli. The other two are Sam and Sam, which is convenient, but also weirdly annoying. Immediately upon dropping their own cases, the two Sams sink into the futon to watch the game, which Abe starts up again. Eli plugs in his bass. None of them really talk. I want to ask questions, but since Oliver's focused on the game too, I'm not going to say anything. I wish we'd set up the food down here, though. Maybe I could bring it down without looking too June Cleaver about it.

"There's food," Oliver finally says, once Eli is set up and tuned.

Eli nods, but then waits politely for Oliver to take the lead back up the stairs. Neither of the Sams moves from the couch.

I follow Eli and Oliver to the main floor. I'm trying to pay attention to everything I see and feel, to tell Trip about it in the notebook later, but mostly I just wish he were here to see it himself. He would have a thing or two to say about this Eli guy, at least. I pour myself a glass of Slice just to have something to do.

The doorbell rings again, and it's this giant relief. Eli is peering deep into Oliver's refrigerator, looking for more than what I've already set out. I go to the door without saying anything.

"Am I at the right place?" the boy at the door wants to know, holding up a small slip of paper covered with tiny, antlike handwriting. He is the absolute perfect kind of cute: meaning, cute in a secret way—the way only odd girls like me notice. Glasses. Hooked nose. Close-cut black hair. Sunny hazel eyes. Bonyish wrists. Against my will, my nervous habit kicks in—my jaw going around its hinges in a circle a few times before I clamp my teeth together to stop it.

"I'm sorry." He straightens his glasses, looks at me. The slip of paper trembles just slightly between his fingers. "I'm Fabian. There's an audition? For a synth?"

He shifts a heavy-looking backpack into my view, and there's a portable amp in his hand. Behind him I see his car—small, white, hybrid-looking.

"I'm, um, Charlotte." I open the door wider. "Oliver's inside." *I'm not his girlfriend, if you were wondering*, I stop myself from adding.

"Nice to meet you, Charlotte," Fabian says, coming in. But just past the threshold, he pauses. "Is this a shoes-on or shoes-off house?"

He is so incredibly sincere. My jaw stretches itself to pop: once, twice. I force myself to quit it.

"Um. Either?" Mrs. Drake has never said anything about a rule. "Whatever makes you the most comfortable, I guess."

He looks up through his mod spectacles. "On, then," he says.

Fortunately my face is hidden as I shut the door behind him. He's stopped in the foyer, waiting for me to show him the way in, but now I'm kind of stuck behind him. We shuffle left, then right, both laugh a little. Which is when Eli comes around the corner, a plate heaped with five different new things, and goes, "Hey, man, you here too? Haven't seen you in a while."

"I am, and no we haven't," Fabian says. He is shy and friendly in a way that is just *perfect*.

I stretch a hand toward the kitchen. "We have food, if you want."

"Thanks." He nods, not budging.

"Or you can just go down." I motion to the rec room.

Fabian finally moves. I follow him down the stairs, shaking my head and reminding myself that I'm supposed to be *running* things today.

"All right, man!" one of the Sams says, seeing Fabian coming down the thickly carpeted stairs. "I didn't know *you* were gonna be here."

Fabian lifts the amp in a kind of greeting to both the Sams.

"So, we're just going to"—Oliver rubs his hands together, looks at me—"try some things out, I guess."

I think, again, how much I wish Trip were here. If for no other reason than to wink at me or something. Stick out his tongue and remind me to loosen up.

"How should we do this?" Eli says, already wiping his plate clean with his finger.

"Well, we just wanted—" I start.

At the same time, one Sam asks, "Together or individual?"

I'm not sure what he's getting at, and I'm not sure my face doesn't show it.

Abe butts in, absolutely out of character. "It'd be decent to do a song or two with each of you on bass. So we can, you know, get a sense. Fabian, you should just play the whole time for consistency." He clears his throat and nods at Oliver, who, after a second, nods back. Oliver doesn't know what to think of Abe speaking up, either.

The Sams glance at Eli and Fabian, and they all nod together. Quickly they decide on some song I don't recognize the name of—not one of ours, anyway. I don't think Oliver knows it that well either, because he has to ask Eli what key it'll be in.

I sit in the ivory leather recliner to watch, knees tucked up under my chin. Oliver hasn't told them my part in this at all, which is annoying but maybe also makes me that much more interesting. Here I am, the lone girl who is obviously important but who also is clearly not some ho-bag attached to Oliver's hip. I'm like a mystery. I hope.

The curly-haired Sam plays with them first. He and Oliver start together ably, simply. Fabian barely looks at anyone while he plays, staring down at his keyboard instead. Out of his synthesizer come some piano chords I feel like I should know. Next to them, Oliver's own chord changes are a little stumbly, but it's nothing too awkward and his voice sounds good. They stop and it's fine. Abe nods; Oliver nods back. So much nodding. The next Sam steps up. It's mostly the same thing, though Fabian's added a windlike layer of sound. At the end of it, Fabian smiles a little at the straight-haired Sam, who shrugs. He doesn't seem to care, but I like that Fabian is acknowledging him.

Eli steps up. "One two three, hit me," he counts off like James Brown. Within the first few measures, it's like all of us have straightened up a little, even Abe. Eli's playing is fierce, but so is his entire demeanor. He's biting his lip almost hard enough to draw blood, and his ferocious jerking arms and elbows are wiry and sharp.

Fabian responds to Eli's energy too: adding new things, looking happily over at Eli with eyebrows up. It's like Eli somehow brings out both what Abe is doing on the drums and what Oliver's doing on guitar. On top of that he gives Fabian a foundation to pile all that pretty, complicated synth stuff onto.

They drag it out in this crazy jam for at least two minutes past the end of the song.

"All right, then," Oliver says when they finish. The two Sams pick up the video game controls without saying anything.

We switch to one of Oliver's racing games for a while. When Abe destroys me in our final lap and it's my turn out, I run upstairs to bring the rest of the food down. As soon as I do, Eli grabs a plastic fork and finishes off the macaroni salad, straight from the bowl. It's like he already knows he's going to be able to make himself comfortable here.

It's nearly five thirty when they all finally leave. Abe, Oliver, and I wave good-bye to them from the front door and then head back in to discuss how things went. It's pretty clear who the new members are going to be, but we do have to make it official. I'm glad Fabian was so good, for a couple of reasons. And whether I like to admit it or not, it's actually really interesting how the sound is going to change with these new guys. Though Trip killed on guitar, its absence feels okay. I think even Trip would think so, and I wonder if there's a way for me to invite him to a rehearsal.

"You think they can do it?" Oliver asks. We are back in the kitchen. Abe's sitting on the counter while Oliver and I load the dishwasher together.

"In time, you mean?" Abe asks.

Oliver nods. "In time."

I picture the way Fabian just *went* with Eli, improvising all this remarkable stuff over Abe's rhythm and Oliver's chords.

"They've obviously played together before," I say.

"Right?" Oliver is excited.

"Eli is *boss*." Abe.

"So let's tell them they're in," I say, putting the last plate into the rack. We grin at each other, huge.

"I think we should practice every day next week, if they can," Oliver says. Abe nods from the counter. "Spider?"

I picture Lish and Bronwyn and their new lives, Trip taking karate classes, Jilly in her college seminars. I don't care who I used to be. Right now, meeting eyes with Oliver, glancing at Abe, all three of us are electric with the possibility of the new sound that just came out of that rec room.

"I'm yours. As much as you need."

Sunday afternoon Oliver texts.

1st practice tmrw @ 4:30. They can only do 3 days but it's ok. I sent the MP3s.

I picture Fabian, Eli listening to "Disappear," to "For Your Face." To everything else I've written, have given up to Oliver's voice. I picture their hands—okay, Fabian's hand—against his earbud, holding the sound in tight.

You sent them r songs? Already?

How else will they know what to play?

I chew on the ragged end of my thumbnail before I type: *Right.*

U have new stuff? he sends next.

New stuff?

For the dance. I thought?????

Of course. I'm lying. Maybe.

Cool.

How many? I write.

Abe thinks we need 5 at least.

I sit up straight. *Tell Abe to write them then.*

:P Urs are better.

I feel a weird tingle in the back of my throat. Praise from Oliver always feels like this—like some kind of victory. Even though it's dumb.

Whitney still off limits as material? I can't help teasing him.

Shut up.

See u in the morning.

When I drop my phone to the floor, the numbers of my bedside clock are all I see. It's 3:50. There's homework to do, reading to catch up on, notes to memorize—none of which I did yesterday because I was at auditions the whole afternoon, and then I had to write in the notebook to Trip, since he wasn't answering his phone. Now there are, at least, three songs to write (Oliver won't expect all five tomorrow), on top of that. Though I'm not sure I have anything very poetic to say beyond "Apparently it's going to be okay" and "New guy, you are so cute"—for Oliver, for the new band, and for (eeek) Fabian, I need to get over my writer's block. I open up my photo albums, grab a pen. Ready or not, there's work to be done.

Chapter Four

In the morning, I shove the sheets of legal notebook paper into Oliver's hand as he rounds the corner from the parking lot to the main building. We are in a stream of students, moving toward class.

Oliver doesn't even look down. "Cool," he says. Whitney is there, in the hook of his arm. She's making sure I see it, which doesn't even make sense anymore.

"No, I mean—" I start. But then I realize Eli is there, right behind Oliver, between Abe and a couple of other guys. From Oliver's face, I know this is not the time to discuss any of it. I picture my trash can at home, overflowing with all the lines that were no way good enough. I wish I could tell him how hard it was, since I had to do them so fast. But obviously he can't hear it right now. I think the songs are all right. I think they are, but it would be better if Oliver could just even look at them for a second, nod or something in approval. It'd be better if I'd shown Trip first.

The first one's about this ideal girl who turns out to be way more empty and cruel than you think. A girl who deceives you. Like most of the songs I've done, I had no idea I even had thoughts like that until they were written. Always, for my ideas, I can't come up with things on my own; I have to look at pictures. But looking, I can somehow hear how the photo feels, and then start writing. This one was from a photo of Lish. The second song is about animals and the things they think about the people watching them. That one came from a blurry photo of a panda I took when Jilly and I went to the zoo over spring break one time.

"There's only two in there" is all I say, half apologetic, half a warning, as we head toward Oliver's locker, which is the wrong way from mine.

He nods, neck tight, and it occurs to me that the new guys don't know who actually writes the lyrics. He wants me to stop talking about it in front of Eli. I feel a flare of annoyance, followed by one of silent pride—my songs are so good he wants Eli to think he wrote them.

"See what you think," I say last, stopping because going all the way down the hall with Oliver would totally make me late.

As I head back up the stream of other people needing to get where they're going, I do catch Oliver looking back, giving me a small, grateful wave. Which is when I also see Trip slipping by us both, over on the far side of the hallway. I want to stop him, tell him about the new songs, about the photos that inspired me. I want to at least give him the notebook, since he still doesn't know anything about the auditions. But he doesn't even look up. If I weren't going to be late, I'd totally call out to him. But I guess I'll see him during our notebook handoff after first period, which'll have to be enough.

Between first and second, though, Trip doesn't show up. Waiting for him, I feel anxious and exposed. In case he's just talking to a teacher, I wait, but it's awkward. Other kids pass by, their eyes sliding away from mine. I try to keep my face aloof, pray to god that Lish doesn't turn the corner, see me standing there without anyone. After twenty more unbearable seconds, I hurry off.

After lunch he's at my locker, apologizing. "Had to ask a question about this new project," he explains, which is what I figured, I guess. I know how he has to make good grades to keep his father off his back. But I still feel slighted somehow.

"There's a lot in here," I tell him, pulling the notebook out. "But I think you'll like it."

"Cool." He slides it into his bag. "May take me a while to get through it all."

I nod. "So where were you all weekend? I thought I'd get to thank you for Friday night at least." I try to make it sound jokey, but I feel—"hurt" is too strong a word, but I don't know what else—that he's acting like he doesn't even care.

He shrugs, shouldering through people in the hall. "Friend of Dad's came into town. I had to play Dutiful Son. And he's cracking down on Internet time."

It's weird he said *nothing* about this on Friday. "I didn't know your dad had anyone coming to visit."

"We didn't either. Army friend. Stopping over on his way to somewhere else. We went to Bambinelli's. They had a lot of beers."

I try to picture Trip sitting there, listening to his dad's friend's stories, smiling while being clapped on the back a hundred times.

"Sounds wretched."

He shrugs again as we round the corner and the thick crush of students opens up. "It actually wasn't that bad."

I stare at the back of his jacket. Normally he'd be cussing and groaning, making a show for me. And, I mean, he could've at least responded to my texts.

"Are you *okay*?" I slit my eyes at him as we get to his next class. Mine is four doors down.

"I'm fine." He looks at me like I'm Whitney-needy to even ask. "Just, fuller weekend than I thought, you know."

There's something stiff about him, something defensive, but I'm obviously not going to find out what's wrong in the next fifteen seconds.

"Okay, well, I'll see you." My eyes are half-slit, still watching.

He points a finger at me like a gun, pulls the invisible hammer with his thumb.

After school I ride with Oliver to practice, and look at my lyrics again. There's some stuff I want to add, cross out, change, though I can't tell if he's had time to read them or not.

We park in Whitney's driveway. They go inside, Whitney needing to *talk* to him. The way she said it, I wanted to lean over the shoulder of the passenger's seat and tell her to quit giving girls such a bad name. Instead I pretended I wasn't there.

Finally, Oliver trudges from around the back of Whitney's house.

"She doesn't let you out the front door anymore?" I snark as he gets in the car.

He just sits there, staring at the steering wheel. "Goddamn," he finally says, looking at me. "That girl. You know?"

I'm tempted to tell him to dump her right then. To say how she drags on him all the time and that no one else likes her. But I learned early from his thing with Carmen Finney in eighth grade that he doesn't really want my opinion on his girlfriends. So I just nod, stare back out the windshield, and wait for him to start up the car.

At Oliver's house, his mom hovers in the kitchen, offering us snacks and juice the minute we walk in. I'm plenty at home here, but it's still nice how Mrs. Drake always treats me like a favored guest. Eli arrives right after Oliver and I do, which is a good distraction from my excited nervousness about seeing Fabian again. Eli asks Oliver's mom if it's going to be okay if they're practicing down there, what with the noise and all. It is funny how polite he is, in spite of the mohawk. Abe comes in, without knocking, as usual. Mrs. Drake says hello to him and he waves, then the guys beeline downstairs. I hover in the kitchen to be helpful, and hear Eli start up the bass line for "For Your Face." I'm amazed he's learned it so fast.

"And how are your sisters doing?" Mrs. Drake asks me, wiping her hands on a towel. I tell her about Jilly, how she likes her roommate and seems to be doing well. I say that Gretchen and Darby are fine. I'm wondering if it's weird that I'm up here chatting with Oliver's mom, or if I should go downstairs.

"And you're all still getting along okay?" Mrs. Drake wants to know.

"Oh yeah." I nod emphatically. Everyone worried how me and Jilly would deal with two new sisters in the house at first. Still do, I guess, now that it's just me and them.

Watching Oliver's mom move around the kitchen in her print skirt and her cashmere sweater, I realize I'm not going downstairs because I'm waiting for Fabian to get here. That I'm jittery-dying to see him. It makes me wish I could tell Lish about him. Some girlfriend, anyway. The way I felt Saturday—the way I feel this minute—is so different than when I first met Clay, the last guy I was even semi-into. With him I was tolerant, I guess. Or maybe obedient. Everyone said he liked me and so I just liked him back. It was like it was already done for me. And it was nice. When we broke up, it sucked, but then I got over it and since then— nobody's stood out, really. Until now. *But he's just a nice guy in the band*, I tell myself, pressing my hands against my knees. *That's all.* That's what I would tell Lish anyway, if we were talking. She'd be able to tell, though, how I think his niceness stretches out of his face—down his arms and his chest—and how badly I want him to think I'm nice too. It'd be a bad idea, I guess, to like someone in the band, though. Not "I guess"; definitely "off limits." That's what I'd end up saying to Lish. What I end up saying to myself now.

Oliver bolts up the stairs then, slides into the kitchen in his socks. "Spider," he says, a little breathless. "Come down here."

I tell Mrs. Drake to let me know if there's anything she needs help with, but she waves me off happily.

Down in the rec room, Eli's moved on to another of our old songs, "Every Kind of Kindness." He stops, starts over and slows down—trying it a different way. The new pace is jarring, but good. Abe joins in, fleshing out Eli's rhythm with drum flourishes of his own. They nod at each other. It's a good fit.

Oliver sits down on the couch in front of the TV, his guitar across his lap.

"I wanted to hear what you thought," he says. And then he strums lightly, leaning close, humming in my ear so I can hear this new thing. Though it's hard to hear much outside of Abe and Eli behind us, I recognize the first lines of that "Too Close to See" song that I wrote about Lish. I feel my face brighten.

"Yeah. I mean, I think that's right."

Oliver smiles. That slow, full-lipped, wide-mouth one he has that takes up half his face, not showing any teeth. The one that crawls into his deep blue eyes from the bottom.

"I've had a couple of tunes in my head," he goes on, "but that one seemed—" Above us, the doorbell rings. We both look at the ceiling, but neither of us moves. Eli and Abe finish and fist-bump each other. To me, Abe says, "Good, right?"

"Yeah, it's good," I tell him.

"All right, then."

We hear Mrs. Drake greeting Fabian upstairs. His voice comes down through the open door: calm, quiet. Sweet.

I have to smooth my hands on the tops of my jeans to keep them from sweating. I don't look at any of the guys because I don't want them seeing my sudden anxiety. *I* don't want to be seeing my sudden anxiety. *He's just nice*, I insist to myself. He arrives at the bottom of the stairs, and—is it me? Or as his eyes go around the room, does he seem surprised, in a glad way, that I'm here?

We all say what's up, and as Fabian unpacks, the boys discuss where to start. I sit, knees up by my chin and arms hugging around my ankles. It's like watching fish swim around each other in the ocean or something, the way they bob and waver.

"I was wondering," Fabian says, "if we couldn't start with 'Disappear,' maybe." He shoves his glasses up his nose. "It might be rough, because I haven't had as much time to lay anything down, but it's such a strong song." He's apologetic, but not in a ground-scraping way.

Oliver simply nods and goes over to the mic. "Ready?" he asks everyone.

"Let's do it," Eli says. I can tell he already knows all the songs and is the type who needs little practice. Or sleep. Only food.

Abe counts off, and immediately I remember him, Oliver, and

Trip starting the set at Nimby's pool party with this song, Trip vibrating with excitement as I watched from the edge of the deck.

Now it's incredible and it's weird at the same time, hearing Oliver's voice and Abe's steady drumming mixed with these two new people, who know when to change chords and how it should all go. It's like a real band. Even more than before. A real band with real songs that I helped write. It's wonderful. And utterly surreal.

Listening, I realize maybe part of why this song always sounds so good is that Oliver doesn't play guitar. Not that Oliver isn't talented. It's just that focusing both on guitar and vocals can be a little complicated for him. But this song is all about his voice: his arresting ability to make you really *feel* what he's singing. I mouth the words with him: *"Would you help me disappear? Transparent. Invisible. Nothing. Clear."* Because of the new guys he's nervous at first, not knowing where to look, shifting back and forth. You can really see—I can, anyway—how jittery and awkward Oliver can be. I mean, I've known him since before either of us went through puberty. Most people think of Oliver as this mysterious, cool guy—a boy who has lots of friends but talks to very few; whom teachers like but are also suspicious of, because he's mischievous, skips class, and possibly cheats. To everyone else he is charming and a little dangerous. A boy with something up his sleeve. Someone everyone wants to know. And when I look at him, I see all that, too, but because I remember him from before, he's also just this too-skinny, too-hyper, too-preppy-for-his-own-good kid.

But when he's singing—the way he is now, letting go a little, getting into it—this quiet, calm, strong version of Oliver comes out. The one who makes you feel like he's really seeing you, and understands and likes what he sees.

Maybe it's this energy that makes him such a good lead singer, that makes him the boy Whitney and all the other girls wish they could grab hold of and keep close. He's someone you want to have nearby, even if he never really acknowledges your existence, because he just always makes things feel extraordinary.

Sometimes I see Oliver so much, I have to close my eyes.

Which is when I realize I've stopped mouthing words and am actually singing a little with him. I'm not the real singer in my family—Jilly is—but in helping her practice, I guess I got used to the feeling of my voice melting with someone else's. I didn't think it would feel that way harmonizing with anyone but my sister, but it's like I can hear my own voice somehow made richer, being carried by Oliver's. And his is highlighted by mine. Even singing quiet, the experience makes my whole body vibrate, like a harp long after you've plucked the last string. It's like the shell of me disappears and this other part—this raw, feeling part—rises up and takes over.

The end of the song is coming now. When I open my eyes again, I notice that Fabian's lips are parted, tongue slightly out in concentration. And the way he's so focused is totally hot. I watch his eyebrows duck down in a tiny frown, concentrating. I wonder what changes his face makes when concentrating on, um, other things. The idea of this fills me with magenta. And I understand that, as beautiful as Trip's guitaring was, something else has taken its place now—something richer. Listening, I'm out of my body, out of the room. It's like we're jellyfish, floating in the sound. We have no bones inside us, are held up only by the music.

When they finish, it takes a moment before I remember to clap. I prepare myself to go into Nit-Pick Mode, because Oliver likes it better if I'm not too gushy right away in my feedback, but mostly I think they were amazing. When Oliver looks up at me, I can see he thinks so, too.

"Well?" Abe says to me, knowing Oliver wants my opinion first.

"Overall it was good," I say carefully. "Abe and Eli, you should listen a little more to Fabian, and drop back when he comes forward, but overall you're working together well. I mean, I like it."

"I'm sorry," Eli says, rubbing his wiry red mohawk into a further state of disturbance. "But can I just—" He gestures over at me, not wanting to be rude, but clearly confused. "Can I ask who she *is*?"

"That's Charlotte," Abe says fast. Though of course they already know that.

"She's important," Oliver says, going for his guitar. And I can't help it—the smile it gives me. "She organizes things for us, writes lyrics." I think he's going to explain that part more, but he barely pauses before saying, "So, what next?"

Walking home, I can't help it. I call Trip.

"Everything's going to be okay," I say to his voice mail. "I think it's going to be really, really good." I pause a second. "But it was weird, you not being there. I just wanted you to know both those things."

Later, after dinner, I'm falling asleep in the remains of my English reading when my phone rings. Trip.

"Hey."

"That's so good," he says, his voice loose. "That practice was good, I mean."

"Are you okay?" Something is weird with him. Weirder than today at school.

"Yeah. I'm fine. I'm just—really glad."

I wait to see if he'll say more. When he doesn't, I go: "Okay, well, good."

"Yeah, it is good. It is. Reading how you describe it, you know, this weekend, it's all really good. I'm really glad."

"You said that."

"Well, it's just because I am, you know."

We're both quiet a minute. I can hear him breathing.

"Okay," I finally say.

"Okay, well," he echoes. "I guess that's all I wanted to say."

"Got a song for me tonight?"

He makes a thick swallowing sound. "Too sleepy."

I'm disappointed. And also still not sure something isn't really whack with him. "Okay, well. Good night?"

"Yeah. G'night."

My phone blinks that the conversation has ended. I think, for a second, of calling him back again. He sounded drunk. And sad around the edges. But I'm not sure how far we'd get with any kind of conversation, the way he's just repeating everything I say.

The rest of the week marches forward as normal. Trip catches up with me in the notebook, and when I get it back I spend all of lunch reading about how his classes are difficult but he feels like he might be up for the challenge. He's glad, he says, that he isn't going to be weighed down by the band this semester. When I write back, I tell him about practice (Mondays, Thursdays, and Saturdays is the plan), but I'm also careful, for the first time, about how much I tell him. I'm definitely not going to say anything about Fabian, for example, and how I found myself looking up famous keyboardists, just so I'd know better what he does. I can't say, either, how by Thursday, Eli and Fabian already have most of the old songs nailed down and are ready to plunge forward. Which means I also feel weird about mentioning the new songs I'm writing, which is terrible because we used to work on those together.

Mainly I avoid writing about the band at all, and emphasize other things. (Lish-bashing takes up a lot of space.) In the periphery of the rest of my life, Darby and Gretchen fight and Gretchen spends most of her evenings over at her boyfriend's house. I walk home by myself again one afternoon, just because I know I can. Hannah makes dinner. Dad comes home and tells us funny stories he heard from his clients. Jilly sends me an email. It's a pretty regular week.

Regular, that is, until third period Friday, when Dr. Campbell hands out another take-home test for us to finish by Monday.

"Aw god," I groan to Benji, who's waiting for me outside of class.

"No sweat." He tries to take my arm, but I pretend I'm reaching for something in my bag. "So, after school? Or tomorrow maybe? What do you want to do?"

"Is it cheating," I ask him, genuinely unsure, "if we work on it together?"

He stops walking, stares after me in disbelief.

"Sugarcakes," he says, "Campbell doesn't care how we find the answers. He knows these tests are both easy and impossible. He just wants to see if we can do it. That's the game to him—*if* we can do it. He doesn't care how."

I consider this. Consider the delighted look on Benji's face while he talks.

"That doesn't really seem like, you know, real teaching, if you ask me." I head toward my locker.

Benji follows. "Man's got a PhD. He doesn't care."

"So I should not at all feel guilty that I'm about to agree to collaborate with you?"

I open my locker, and Benji sticks his head around the edge.

"Of course not. The real thing you need to be thinking about is: your place or mine?"

I roll my eyes, grab my lunch, and try to catch the side of his face as I slam the metal door shut.

He sniffs. "What's for lunch? I love sushi."

"You're disgusting." I'd elbow him too, but something makes me feel like he'd just enjoy it. So I keep walking to the cafeteria and the table by the Coke machines where I've been sitting to avoid an unusually-bitchy-this-week Whitney. I always look busy sitting here—mostly because I am. Usually writing in the notebook to Trip. Like about how I discovered that Lish must've switched her schedule, because now she has lunch this period too.

She was walking out to the parking lot to go off campus with D'Shelle the other day. Which is maybe another reason why I'm not joining Oliver out by his car right now.

"Don't you have class?" I ask Benji.

"Eventually." He shrugs, not caring about the bell ringing over our heads.

"Well, I have practice on Saturday," I say, to say something.

"I'm free this afternoon." He blinks. "And practice for what?"

"Practice for none-of-your-business is what." But I can't help grinning at him a little. "This afternoon, though, I could do."

He offers a charming little bow. "I love a woman who doesn't make me wait."

I wonder, *Why doesn't Trip like him?* while Benji salutes and says, "See you at the last bell."

Chapter Five

On Monday, Trip gives me back the notebook, but reading what he's written is like trying to decipher the scrawls of a crazy person. Turns out he was at a party Friday at Chris Monroe's and spent a good portion of the time in some corner, criticizing the entire thing for my benefit. He also seems to have had an entire bottle of peach schnapps or Jägermeister during the process, because his writing is a mess and he eventually trails off, trying to describe different couples making out around him. His last entry is about how he woke up on the floor in what he figured was Chris's dad's study, made his way out, and drove himself home, slept off his hangover most of Saturday. Sunday he watched Bruce Lee movies with his dad.

"You're drinking too much," I tell him when I see him after lunch period. "It makes me worry."

"Thanks for the input, Straight Edge."

"I am not straight edge. I'm just not a *lush.*"

"I'm sorry." He concedes, but he's put off. "Isn't that what I'm supposed to be doing at this age? I think it's in the manual."

I frown at him. "You're supposed to be working on new music. Like I am."

His eyebrows go up. "You are?"

His genuine surprise makes me feel sheepish about not telling him before. I let the long slant of my bangs fall between us. "What did you think?"

"I just didn't think—I mean . . ." He recovers a little: "I didn't know you were." He looks startlingly solemn. "But maybe I need a break from all that."

"It's fine if you need a break," I growl. "But the rest of us are going ahead."

He looks at me with that serious blankness, and I immediately regret what I've said. I start to put my hand on his arm, to apologize and tell him what I really want is for us to still be talking about songs and music, that I don't want everything to be so weird. But he steps away from the wall, away from me.

"I gotta go," he says.

When I slide into my desk, the only thing that's worse than discovering I only finished five of the ten questions we had to answer for today is realizing I also didn't give the notebook back to Trip.

"I can't make it to practice this afternoon," I tell Oliver outside of psych.

He is immediately annoyed. "Why not?"

"Well, I just—to be honest, I need time to write. I'm just not used to having to do this, you know, on demand. By myself."

He jerks open the classroom door so that he doesn't have to look at me. He waits, holding it. I have no other choice than to walk past him into the room.

I hate Oliver being in a mood. I hate *anyone* being in a mood, really. Trip was enough for one day. I need to turn this around, for both of us.

"It was easier for me when this was just, you know, a hobby. And not some actual, really happening rock band that is going to rocket to immediate glamour and fame. It's hard to write when I'm all busy going, 'What will Coldplay be like when they open for Sad Jackal?'" I'm tapping my finger against my chin, gazing at the ceiling dreamily. Making myself the fool is the only thing that works in this situation.

And it does. Work. He twists a reluctant grin at me. "Coldplay's lame."

"Maybe it'll be easier when I can write in my limo. Or on the tour bus."

"Shut up, Spider." But he is chuckling.

"You guys should just have some get-to-know-you time, anyway, without a girl around." I lower my voice as Ms. Neff comes in, balancing a big stack of folders and her ever-present travel mug of coffee.

He slits those blue eyes at me, sly-grinning. "*Are* you a girl?"

"Enough of one for Whitney to be jealous," I retort.

Oliver's lips puff out, sighing at the mention of his girlfriend. "That girl, man."

I don't say anything back. I don't have to.

"I thought you were riding with Oliver today," Gretchen says when I catch her at the car after school. "You've been so attached lately. I feel like I've barely seen you." We stand together against the back of the car, waiting for Darby to finish saying good-bye to all her fellow freshmen. I want to point out that the reason Gretchen's barely seen me is that she's been with her boyfriend, and that I'm not any more attached to Oliver than I was this summer, but since she's being nice, I decide to be, too.

"The band's been practicing a lot for the Halloween dance."

She's impressed. "Oliver and them are playing?"

I nod, trying to be cool about it.

She whistles. "Now I really have to get Max to go."

"Where is he, by the way?" I ask, making sure to sound neutral.

She groans. "Wrestling's started."

She launches into all the reasons why she thinks wrestling is completely stupid, but I only half listen. Instead I'm scanning the parking lot crowd: kids hanging out in groups around each other's cars, other bunches of them walking away together, up to the square. I don't see Lish but I do see her friend Kiaya with Bronwyn, walking together, probably up to the Yogurt Tap. Far off, near the back fence, I see Trip, too. Beside him Chris Monroe is laughing, both of them surrounded by several other people I'm not sure I know. The way Trip just walked off like that today, the way he wasn't there before psych—it burns in me. *Fine*, I beam in laser thoughts toward him. *Smoke and drink with your new friends, you big asshole. Waste your potential for all I—*

And then there's Benji's clattering Volvo, slowing down. He's got one hand draped over the steering wheel, a cigarette between his fingers.

"'Sup, Coastal," he says, winking at me.

I feel Gretchen beside me, suddenly curious.

"Coastal?" I challenge, not moving from my spot against the trunk of the car.

He shrugs. "Just a thing I'm testing out. See how it fits." The sun behind me is making him squint. I can't quite tell where he's looking, exactly.

"You let me know how that works out for you."

"I will do that."

He rolls off without waiting for me to reply, that hand of his saluting.

Gretchen snorts beside me. "*He* certainly thinks he's cool."

"He certainly does," I agree.

When we get home, Darby and Gretchen and I take out the chicken divan left over from the other night and eat it at the counter, cold, straight from the pan. When Jilly was here, we grouped together in pairs: me and her, and then the two of them. We were all mostly tolerant housemates of each other, not really intermixing much. Hanging out with them like this now is actually nice.

After we eat, though, Gretchen goes upstairs to their room and Darby goes straight to her best friend, Facebook. It's not even four o'clock. I need to do what I said I was going to do and work on some songs, but the fight with Trip makes it hard to focus. Working on the songs right now will make me think about *not* working on them with him, and not seeing Fabian, either. Maybe I should just walk over there now. I can show up late. But Oliver's expecting new songs, and I'm certainly not going to get much writing done there.

But ultimately I decide I can work on Sad Jackal later, when I'm not so distracted. I take some time to email my sister about everything instead.

Chapter Six

Four important things happen between Monday afternoon and rehearsal on Thursday:

1. Benji gets an A on his 20th Cen. test, while I get a B+. How we didn't earn the same exact grade, I don't know, but I don't care, because at least this is an improvement. We make plans to study again Friday afternoon. It crosses my mind that afterward we could go to the movies or something, though I'm not really sure what Benji would want to see or why I would want to sit alone in the dark with him.

2. I get the postcard for Mom's upcoming art show. It is glossy and sleek. Her name is on it and everything. I think about calling Jilly, but just text her instead.

3. Thanks to Gretchen's loud and painful breakup with the Wrestler, I come up with the lyrics to two new songs: "You're Ugly, Too" and "Just Hang Up." A third one, "Foreign Tongue," comes from looking at pictures Jilly took when her chorus went to Berlin to sing with a German choir there. None are quite as good as "Disappear," but they'll do.

4. Trip tells me he's signed up for martial arts classes at the new aikido place that just opened. "To get Dad off my back," he says. "And to give myself some structure." I try to be supportive, but I thought the whole reason for quitting Sad Jackal was so he could work on his own material, not quit music altogether. That night he plays two songs for me: "Kung Fu Fighting" (to make me laugh) and this other really cute Japanese pop song. I can't help but wonder if he heard the second one from Chris Monroe.

After school on Thursday, my jaw is going crazy again, knowing I'm about to see Fabian. Why this wasn't my first thought upon waking, why I stayed snoozing until the absolute last possible minute and left myself with my standard fifteen minutes to get ready for school, I don't know. I mean, sure, yes, he already saw me in a schlumpy outfit when we first met, but I shouldn't be sabotaging myself for a few extra minutes of sleep.

When he arrives at practice, though, it's not like he really notices. He smiles at me, but he smiles at everybody. Which makes me *really* wish I had a better outfit on. Something that might stand out.

Irritated, I take my seat on the couch as they start, warming up with "Afterlight," since that's the simplest. As usual, it takes Oliver a few verses to get into it. But Abe, emboldened by Eli and Fabian, is trying something different with the drums. It makes up for Oliver's twitchiness, and when they finish, I tell Abe how good he sounds. He gives me a pleased thumbs-up, and I want, stupidly, for Fabian to notice.

"We need to work on the new ones," Oliver says, sounding irritated, too.

"Do 'Cage Time,'" Eli says, thumbing a few strings. "Charlotte hasn't heard what we did with it yet."

The new song begins with a twangy riff. At first it's just Oliver playing, but then Fabian joins in with some eerie ghost chords, giving it more depth. Soon Eli starts, moving his hand slowly up the neck of his bass. Abe is still quiet, listening, waiting, his head cocked toward the others like he's lost in the woods and just heard a stick snap.

"A bag of peanuts in your hand," Oliver sings, low and quiet, leaning into the mic. *"Looking for something you used to understand."*

A wave of unexpected pleasure sweeps over me, and I hunch down farther into the cushions, not wanting anyone to see if they look up. This is my song—this sad, lame, weird thing I wrote, this mysterious thing that came out of me—and they've made it into *something*.

When Oliver starts the chorus, though, something's wrong. The band sounds fine, but Oliver's doing this screeching thing with his voice: an angry, squalling sound that's awful. I know it's a song about the zoo, but I'm not sure howler monkey is what we're going for. I grit my teeth, wait for Oliver to drop back into crooning for the next verse.

It goes fine from there, until he comes back to the chorus: *"You put me in this cage, now you want me out of it; You're enlivened by this rage, now you want to stifle it."* Apparently I can't contain my grimace anymore, because Oliver stops, seeing me, and goes, "What?"

He has never halted mid-song like this. Not even with Trip.

I'm aware, immediately, of all four guys looking at me. Of my face turning what must be an excruciating shade of red.

"It's just—" I clear my throat. "I'm just not sure the, you know, *angry* sound is the best way to go." I try to make this sound like an apology.

"*You're* enlivened *by this rage.*" Oliver holds his hand out like I'm dumb.

"I know it's talking about being angry, but the point, kind of, is that she—I mean, the speaker—is . . . over it. Like, 'You used to love it when I got all dramatic, but I've been held down by you for so long that I'm not sure I can work myself up anymore.'"

A memory comes into my head: Dad and Mom fighting, the tired sound of Dad's voice, simply not wanting to engage with her. I didn't know that's what the song was about.

"Melancholy," Eli says, nodding. "Tired."

Oliver's face clenches. "Well, *you* sing it, then," he says to me.

Clearly this is too much criticism from me. But also, Oliver suspects I'm right. He's holding the mic out, but in a way that means he doesn't want me to take it.

"No, you just—" I start, but at the same time Fabian goes, "Show us, Charlotte. Please?"

I cannot possibly be any more uncomfortable. Not only Oliver, but Abe, Eli, and Fabian are staring. They want me to sing for them. And I'm not going to. It's just too weird. And yet, *now you want to stifle it* rings between my ears just as clear as Jilly's voice.

"Charlotte," Fabian says, "it's your song, right? Just show us."

His voice is like Trip's: a gentle combination of praise and understanding. He's acknowledging my fear but wants to help me get past it.

I look at Oliver, whose face is a mixture of things. Frustration. Unwilling need. Embarrassment. Resignation.

I force myself to stand up.

"Okay." I wipe my sweaty hands on my jeans before I take the mic from Oliver. "The buildup to the chorus." My voice is wavering. "I won't sing it, but you know."

Oliver's off to the side amid a ton of cords and black boxes on the floor. He watches Abe for the count. Around me the music starts up. I hear the last lines of the first verse in my head: *Will you look at the real me? When will you see enough?*

Somehow the chorus unfolds out of me: careful, apologetic, worn. *"You put me in this cage, now you want me out of it; You're enlivened by this rage, now you want to stifle it."*

Eli stops, with the others drifting to a halt soon after.

"Do it again," he says to me. He has kind of a scowl on his face, but I can tell he's just thinking. To Abe and Fabian he says, "There, then slow."

Fabian nods, knowing what he means. He gives me an encouraging look. Oliver's jaw tightens. They start up again. I hear the song all around us, feel the way Eli's altering the rhythm—slowing it, only slightly but still noticeable. It comes out of me, again, stronger: *"You put me in this cage, now you want me out of it; You're enlivened by this rage, now you want to stifle it."*

"Keep going," Eli hollers. I don't want to, but I do. Charging through the second verse, taking up the chorus again, slowing down, feeling how their music supports my voice—it's easier to relax. I close my eyes, sing: *"Stare and stare and stare all day / Bent and crushed under all this weight."* I've only heard Oliver do the melody once, but thanks to Fabian, it's easy enough to hear basically where I'm supposed to be. I don't mess up too much, even when we go into the bridge and the key changes. At the end, Eli and Fabian just keep playing, so I start repeating *"Walking away from me,"* quieter and quieter. Getting to stand there and alter the song myself while it's being played, hearing how the words can be shifted, is actually pretty cool.

Not that I want to do it again. As soon as it's over I hold the mic out for Oliver. He won't look me in the eye.

"Okay, well, how about we start at the beginning and I'll—" he tries.

"Can you do 'Disappear' like that?" Eli says to me, paying no attention to Oliver.

My eyes dart to Abe. He shrugs, like *It's fine with me.* Oliver's looking at him too, but Abe just clunks around on his drums.

"I'm not sure I—"

"We should go forward with the new stuff, don't you think?" Oliver says over me.

This is all feeling very, very weird. And not good. In absolutely no way am I going to sing for Sad Jackal. Oliver doesn't need to be so flustered and stiff. I am no kind of threat to him at all.

But Eli is unfazed. "You've been sitting here," he says, pointing at Oliver and Abe, and then me, with the head of his bass, "on this amazing nut of a girl this whole time, and you haven't even cracked her open, seen what she can really do? Think about what it could mean, being big enough to switch it up from time to time. Having two singers in this group."

Oliver's holding my gaze and not letting go. He's mad. But he's also hearing what Eli's trying to say.

"Do you want to?" he asks me, eyes unwavering. Stern.

"No. Absolutely not. I'm no singer." I move closer to the safety of the couch.

"Oh, you're not, are you?" says Eli. "That's not what it sounded like to me."

This is making me blush with outrage and embarrassment, especially because, if I'm honest, it feels good to have someone as talented as Eli say something like that to me, even if he is being kind of mean about it. It's hard to keep staring him down, keep my chin up high.

"Why don't you just let us hear it?" Fabian asks, nicer. "Just so we can, you know, get a different perspective. I thought it was very helpful, actually, your singing. If nothing else, it might improve our warmth."

I check over at Oliver again. He is glaring at poor Abe, who is still fiddling, saying nothing. Maybe Oliver's wondering if the wrong person left the band. Maybe he thinks Trip would back him up and would also back me up in my desire not to sing.

Picturing the two of them agreeing I shouldn't be anywhere near the mic does something funny inside me, though. There's this kind of click in my throat, and I feel my spine straighten. It's not that I *can't* sing, I just—

"Just think about how it increases our demographic, man," Eli says to Oliver. "You get a hot chick up there and—"

Oliver makes a pointedly scoffing noise, and it's like I've been slapped. I didn't think my embarrassment and anger could get worse, but there you go.

"It *would* open up some more options, man," Abe says quietly.

Oliver's looking back at me again. But this time without so much venom. Again he says, "Do you want to?"

"Not 'Disappear,'" I hear myself saying. "That one is Oliver's. He just does it too well. But maybe 'Every Kind of Kindness.'"

"We could do some covers, too," Eli says, squinting around

his thought. "And I like the idea of Oliver playing something besides guitar. Recorder or something. My mom's got one of those old Autoharp things. You know, the ones we'd play in, like, elementary school? That could be cool."

Oliver is clearly embarrassed and furious. He is not going to play some elementary school instrument. And he's not going to let some crazy-haired bassist take over his band, either. If I'm going to be singing, Oliver has to make it look like it's his idea too. I can see all this in his face. And I hate knowing this about him right now.

"I never thought you wanted to before," he says to me. "I mean, you were always so weird about it with your sister and everything, so. But if you're game now, if you want to be more a part of it, we can give it a try."

It's unfair how he's making it seem like this whole time I've been holding back, even though it's also not surprising. I'm not going to fight with him, but I'm not going to give in, either. I still hear that nasty sound he made when Eli called me hot.

"What about 'Too Close to See'?" I say to Eli and Eli only, making it clear to Oliver that I don't care about his opinion right now.

"Sure," Fabian agrees. "Saturday we should probably lay down the tunes for the new songs, decide who will sing them. At least a rough idea."

Again Oliver's jaw tightens, but he nods.

"I'll work with you on the tunes if you want," I offer to Oliver, trying to move us toward some kind of truce, just so we can go forward with practice. Once we both get our heads out of our asses this afternoon, collaborating might even be great. For now I guess he still needs to be mad, though, because he keeps his face stone.

"Let's go back to this cage song," Eli decides. "Get it really good. We can focus on the other stuff as it comes. Oliver, now that you're not in front of the mic, don't be afraid to trust me, and experiment a little."

It's not so bad, seeing Oliver being taken down a notch for once.

We do the song over. And over. And then over and over again. Each time, it progresses and solidifies. By the end, I've forgotten to be embarrassed about singing. Forgotten, even, about me and Oliver being at odds.

While the guys pack up their stuff, I carry cups and plates back upstairs, mainly to avoid hovering around. I load the dishwasher for Mrs. Drake and wipe the counters (even though they don't need it) until the guys start coming up the stairs.

"So we decided," Oliver says to me, amiable once again, "we should meet earlier on Saturday, to get more time in with the new songs. Can you be here at noon?"

"Can you be *up* at noon?"

Abe hoots at this. I expect Oliver to get pissed again, but he makes a cuckoo face at me and says, "Sh-yuuh."

"I think Fabian needs a hand," Eli says. Talking to me.

Obediently I go downstairs, though the request is a little odd.

"Hi," he says. His equipment is all packed up.

"Hi," I say back. *I am downstairs with Fabian. By myself. And he wanted to talk to me. Alone.* My heart races, flips, stutters.

"You're really excellent, you know. Eli and I both think so."

I can barely move. Plus my face is probably scarlet.

"So you don't have to, you know, hold back or anything. Around us."

I wonder what they said to Oliver and Abe while I was upstairs. Or each other.

"Oliver and I have been friends since fifth grade." As though that's some kind of explanation for—whatever.

Fabian's just looking at me, waiting.

"And—" I feel at a loss. I don't know what we're really talking about. "This band is incredibly important to him. He doesn't . . . get . . . excited about things, I guess. Not this way. Maybe you can't tell, but he is astonishingly serious about all this."

"No, that's clear."

"So I just don't want to—"

"You're not going to ruin anything by being more involved in the band, Charlotte. You're going to make it *better*."

Walking home, I let the whole afternoon spin in my head: the looseness of the music around and in me, standing up there, leading the song. The incubating dimness of Oliver's rec room. Fabian telling me that I'm excellent. When I get back to the house, I still need to tell someone about it. I need to call Trip.

I'm surprised when he actually answers.

"What're you doing?"

"Same thing you should be doing," he answers. "Homework."

"How do you know I'm *not* doing homework, smarty?"

"Didn't you guys have practice?"

"Well, true."

"So how was it?"

"What, my homework?" I'm grinning.

"You're not doing homework, dummy. How's practice coming?"

I blurt it out: "They want me to sing. I mean, I'm singing. I'm going to sing a couple of the songs."

There is a bunch of quiet on the other side of the phone.

Then, "Huh."

"What's that supposed to mean?"

"I just mean 'huh.'"

"Huh, what?"

"I just . . ." More quiet. "I'm proud of you, I guess. I didn't know you'd ever want to do something like that."

"Yeah, I didn't think so either. And believe me, Oliver did not want me to."

"I bet he didn't."

"Which was part of what made me want to do it, you know?"

"Yeah, I know."

"But when I got up there, it felt really good, and now we've got to plan out the other three songs, and Eli wants me to do some more, and Oliver might play the xylophone or something."

"The xylophone?"

"Or Autoharp. Or whatever. So, but, I mean, isn't it great?"

"I said it was great."

"No you didn't. You said you were *proud*." I'm so glad to be telling someone who will actually understand what a big deal this is for me, that I'm on the verge of giggly.

"Well, I do think it's great."

"Okay, good. Hey—your Jujitsu start yet?"

"Aikido. And no. But I'm going to watch the tournament on Saturday. Meet the instructors. Dad's coming."

"Well, good." I don't know what more to say to this. I want him to joke about it, or say something more about my singing.

Mainly I want him to play a song for us.

"Hey, listen," he says. "I've kind of got to go."

"Oh. Okay, then." I try not to sound surprised. Or hurt.

"But good work with the band. I hope I'll get to see you."

"Well, you will, silly. The dance is in just a few weeks."

"Indeed." Nothing else.

When we hang up, I'm a balloon with all the air squashed out. There are plenty of other things I could and should be doing, but I don't want to do any of them. I end up downstairs on the family computer, watching music videos and feeling nowhere near as cool as anyone on the screen.

Chapter Seven

In the morning, Trip hands over the notebook as usual, though he's barely written in it. Certainly nothing about my singing. He just tells me who will be at Chris's party tonight (no one I know) and ends with *Yeah sometime you should hang out, I mean, if you have time.* And that's it.

Third period and I still haven't responded, mostly because I don't know what to say. Chris Monroe's? I still don't know what Trip sees in him. So instead of faking interest, I write notes back and forth to Benji about where we should study this afternoon. He wants to go to the bleachers by the soccer field again, probably so he can smoke, but I think we're more productive in the library, like last week. He teases that if I need his brain, I should go for the studying-out-of-doors thing, because it's proven science that fresh air and oxygen increase brain function. *Not if the fresh air you're inhaling is tainted with herb*, I write back. *Nature hater*, he replies. We decide to just meet at his car and make up our minds after school.

I'm on my way to psych at the end of the day when Oliver rushes up to me like he's on fire and I'm holding a bucket of water.

"What is it?"

"I need you for the songs." He's practically panting.

"What, now?"

He ignores me. "I tried last night but I just can't get it and I have to have something for tomorrow."

I'm trying not to laugh at how dramatic he's being, so I hold the door open for him instead. I follow him into class, to our desks. Maybe it's still a little bit of payback for the way he acted about me getting behind the mic yesterday, but something in me wants to make him sort of beg. Or, at least, make him feel bad for what a tool he was.

I make my face a challenge. "You really okay with me singing?"

He flushes. "It just threw me off, man. I thought you were mortified to get up in front of people. I mean, whenever you have to speak in class . . . like I said, I was just surprised."

I can see in his eyes that he is sincere and, in his own way, apologetic. He wants to make things okay between us. He is, after all, my friend.

"So you can come over? Straight after school?"

"I have a study thing. 20th Cen.," I tell him.

"Campbell's such a douche."

"I know. But not everybody can handle your superexcel course load," I tease.

"Shut up, man. But seriously, you can't just get the notes from someone?"

I could, I guess, go meet Benji at his car, get his notes, and borrow them for the weekend. It's not like we're working on a test; this was mainly for my benefit. But it seems a little uncool, canceling at the last minute. I feel like I would owe him something.

"It's that bad?" I ask Oliver. He hasn't ever had trouble with the music before. Though before, he also always had Trip.

Ms. Neff comes in, bringing class to start, but not before Oliver leans over the edge of his desk, whispers, "You have no idea."

After class we walk together out to the parking lot with the stream of everyone else. I see Lish hanging out by some volleyball girl's SUV.

Whatever.

I work my way between cars to Benji's old brown Volvo. He's in that army jacket and his aviator sunglasses, leaning against the door, watching me.

"Hey, Coastal," he says.

"You know I really don't get where that comes from." I try to sound irritated, mainly because I'm perplexed by how sort of thrilling it is, Benji having a nickname for me. Even a nonsense one.

He smiles with one side of his mouth. "You'll get it eventually" is all he says.

"Listen—"

"What, you got better plans?" He gestures over toward Oliver, who's watching both of us, this expectant little look on his face.

"It's not like that," I clip. "I just—we just need to work on something for this weekend. It can't wait."

Benji lifts his hand in casual dismissal. "I feel you."

"So I know it's uncool for me to cancel, but I was wondering if I could—"

He opens the passenger door of his car. When he turns back to me he's handing over his notes.

"Really?"

He shrugs. "I don't much need them."

I reach out. "Do you—want to see mine? I mean, I can—"

"It's cool."

He's still looking at me in that detached, amused way. It

makes me stumble over myself. "Well, it's really great of you and—"

"Calm down, Coastal. It's all good. I'll just see you Monday. No big."

His binder is heavy in my hand. I still feel guilty, even though it doesn't seem like Benji really cares.

"Good luck with your project. Better hurry along, by the looks."

He gestures again toward Oliver, who's talking to a few other guys but still glancing obsessively over at us.

"Well, thanks. I mean it."

"You're good," he says, reaching out to squeeze me, once, on the arm. Under his hand, I'm aware how squishy I am.

"Thanks again." I hurry off then, mainly because I don't want Benji to see how flustered that whole exchange has made me.

"Everything okay?" Oliver wants to know when I get to his car.

"Let's just go," I tell him, getting in and slamming the door, hard.

When we get to the house, I realize we didn't give Whitney a ride home from school today, that she wasn't even at Oliver's car this afternoon.

"What up with Whitney?" I try to be casual.

Oliver shrugs and opens the fridge to find us something to eat. "I told her we had to practice." He's so blasé about it.

"And she was okay with that?"

"Sure," he says, in a way that makes me think Whitney doesn't know, exactly, who "we" is today. But whatever.

We heat up some Hot Pockets in the microwave, pour big glasses of Coke, and take them downstairs, where Oliver's two guitars are set up on their stands. I'm surprised to see the acoustic one out.

"You really were experimenting last night, huh?"

He bites off about a quarter of his Hot Pocket and talks around it. "Just trying a few things out."

While we eat, he takes out my lyric sheets and spreads them between us on the couch. We look at the words, talk about what sort of tone we think each song should have. It's strange to be talking to Oliver like this, but also wonderful. He and Trip were always the frontmen, and I was just the girl who ran around covering the details. Now I'm in Trip's seat. *I'm* here making Sad Jackal what it is. It's kind of awesome. But at the same time, I know I need to prove myself. So I try to remember what Trip's taught me about music, to think like he might, and picture the songs as sound pieces and not just thoughts in my head.

"'You're Ugly, Too' can be your angry-sounding one, if you want," I say.

Oliver's face is not sure I will be much help, after all. "I don't want angry."

"Oh. Well, I just thought that you were going for—"

"That was just playing around. Most of it was Eli's idea."

"Got it." I'm not going to push it further. "At any rate, this one should be faster. Frustrated. But 'Foreign Tongue' has got to sound dark and European."

"No matter what Eli says, I am not playing the accordion."

We both laugh at this.

"You don't have to. But you know what I mean." I let my bangs drop toward my face, pretend I'm inhaling deeply from a cigarette, and make my eyes sultry. "Moody."

"Moody I can do."

This is a joke, kind of. When Oliver's mom first heard them play, she pursed her Mary Kay'ed lips together, smiled, and said, "Why, it's so *moody*, honey."

"It's called *Sad* Jackal, Ma," Oliver had said.

And true to the name—which Oliver and Abe and Trip just came up with; I'm still not sure what it's supposed to mean—the band's sound is mostly that: moody. It occurs to me that maybe this is part of why Oliver wanted new members, to at least bring in another emotion or two.

He goes for his electric. "Let me show you what I was thinking for that."

I watch him plug in, mess around a little, sing. He's just showing me the rough lines of the sound, but it's still good. I tell him, when he's finished, to do it again, so that I can listen for alternate paths the melody might take. He nods and starts right in, sings a little more seriously. Whatever happened yesterday at practice, he's already let it go, and so should I.

It's hard to concentrate, though, because while he's singing, Oliver's phone bings next to me on the coffee table, with about ten incoming texts. When he finishes playing he turns it off. I'm sure it's Whitney, but I don't ask.

We move on to "You're Ugly, Too," and after an hour—Mr. and Mrs. Drake leave for a benefit dinner in the meantime—end up changing the entire third verse, making it into more of a kick-in-the-throat song than a pathetic attempt at an insult.

"Fabian's going to like messing around with that one," I say from nowhere.

"He's good, right?"

I nod. Oliver saying Fabian is talented gives me a little thrill inside. But I can't let Oliver of all people see that, so I keep my face even. "Really good."

Working out "Just Hang Up" is harder. The chords Oliver's trying are all wrong.

"Stop playing and close your eyes," I finally tell him. I'm sitting on the floor in front of him, legs crossed.

He does, and his placid, trusting face is startlingly sweet.

"Think about a girl—a girl who's desperate to get the last

word in. A girl trying her very hardest to hurt the dickhead boyfriend on the other end of the phone. She has no way of knowing she'll never succeed. Because he doesn't really care and is just doing all this for some kind of twisted amusement. But she keeps trying. She won't let go. She's like some kind of pit bull."

He opens his eyes. "A pit bull hanging on to a dead man." The way he says it, there's some personal experience behind his words.

"Exactly. We should even put that in."

"Okay, here—"

He tries another progression of chords, these definitely darker. I test out a few lines along with him. We sketch out a melody and for a second try some harmony but just end up scrunching our faces at each other and laughing.

It isn't perfect. We have to go back, change some things, but we do it. Together. No egos and no awkwardness. Just me and him, working to make these songs the best we can.

Which is why I don't realize how late it is. "Oh, shit," I say, squinting at the digital clock on his elaborate entertainment console: 11:23. "Is that clock right?"

"Looks like it," he says, turning on his phone and holding it up for me to see.

"Damn. I've got to go. Like, right now."

He stands up. "It'll be quicker if I drive you."

Which is another good thing about Oliver: he is totally respectful when it comes to parents and their demands. Chores, groundings, curfews, family dinners, whatever, he understands it. He doesn't tease you or say, "Screw your parents, man," or anything like that. So when I jump up from the floor, all he does is switch off the power on his equipment, and then he's behind me up the stairs, grabbing his jacket, out the door.

We make it back to my house at 11:28.

"Thanks, man," I breathe.

"No, thank *you*. That was . . . enormous."

"It was kinda, yeah." I nod. "I mean, it was cool, working with you that way."

The wide, no-teeth, *I see you for real* smile fills up his face. For a minute I say a little silent *fuck you* to Whitney and all the girls who glare at me when I hang out around Oliver. He never smiles at them this way, I know. Or, at least, maybe not as often.

When I shut the car door I wave at him, and he waves jauntily back. Walking up to my house, somebody might accuse me of bouncing or something, and that'd be okay. Because tonight I feel really, completely, deep-down, all-around happy and good.

The feeling continues on Saturday. Oliver plays the new songs for the guys, and they get them almost right away. Even Abe throws in some truly inspired drumming, and it's just amazing to see how quickly Fabian can follow—and then play with, and then add to—whatever it is Oliver's doing. It makes my *Oh my god I dig you so much* feeling accelerate about fifty times.

While Oliver's singing "Foreign Tongue," I forget myself and start singing some harmonies, which are easier to find with Fabian playing along. Eli likes it so much we decide I'll do it for real. When I sneak a glance at Fabian, we both break into grins.

After practice, Trip texts to see if I want to go catch a movie or something. Surprised but thrilled, I negotiate with Gretchen and even get the car. Trip and I decide to see the new zombie apocalypse one, mostly because there isn't that much else playing. We laugh our heads off during most of the gory scenes (much to the annoyance of the people in front of us, who actually get up and move seats), and afterward we go to Java Monkey and crack ourselves up again, practically acting the entire movie out for each other.

When I drop him off, he reminds me about aikido starting this week, that his practices and my practices are going to dictate our lives. I suggest we plan to hang out every Saturday night, then, because this was so great. He smiles at this, and I do too. When we wrap each other in another good-night hug, I can't remember why I ever thought anything might go wrong.

Chapter Eight

I t's Thursday when things get bizarre.

First of all, when Oliver and I get into his car to head to rehearsal after school, he goes, "Just so you know, Whitney and I are finished."

"Wait, what?"

He jerks one shoulder up around his ear in response. So that's why we were walking so fast after school—he didn't want to chance running into her.

"When?"

"This morning."

"Hang on. You broke up with Whitney this *morning*? Why?"

"Why are you freaking, Spider? You hated her. Everyone did."

I hadn't realized I was that unsubtle. "I didn't hate her. I just—"

"You did and it's cool. She's an albatross, anyway. I just got sick of her shit."

"Her usual shit, or extra shit? I mean, is it about the band?"

He lets out a long, irritated sigh. "Just *shit*, man. She's not my girlfriend anymore, so I don't see why we need to talk about her any further."

This is one of the extremely irritating aspects of being friends with boys: their utter refusal, or perhaps inability, to divulge any kind of important information when it comes to matters like this. Whenever Lish broke up with someone (and when Clay finally dumped me last year)—we went over every single "he said" and "I said" and "then he," not to mention analyzed every heartbroken (or angry) text that came after that. But boys, they're just so maddeningly unresponsive. Oliver dumping Whitney before school is a perfect example. Even though I can't stand Whitney, that is complete and total *ouch*. A girl would have thought for days about exactly how, when, and where to do it. And she would've been a little more considerate. But maybe Whitney did something in the parking lot that pissed Oliver off and he just snapped? Who knows, since we're not allowed, apparently, to talk about it. Still, I can't wait for rehearsal to start so I can text Trip the news.

That Oliver wants the subject to be dropped, however, doesn't seem to matter much to Whitney, because about twenty minutes into practice, Mrs. Drake comes to the top of the rec room stairs and tells Oliver he has a guest.

"I'm practicing," he says in that pouty way he has with his mom.

"Yes, dear, I can see that. But if you could just—"

I love Mrs. Drake, because she is so perfect and polite all the time, but you still can tell when there's something she dislikes. I picture Whitney at the door, makeup dripping down her cheeks. Oliver's mom would definitely find that unpleasant.

Abe and I swap smirks behind Oliver's back.

"What's that about?" Eli wants to know as soon as Oliver's gone.

Abe shrugs. "Ex-girlfriend hysteria."

Eli shakes his head. "Bitches, dude. You can't keep them around long or they go sour on you, you know? Oh—" He glances at me. "Sorry, Charlotte."

But I think it's funny. "No, I hear you. It's all eggs and milk in here, and those have expiration dates, so."

Abe barks out a surprised laugh.

"No you didn't." Eli's jaw drops around an impressed smile.

I shift my eyes to Fabian, see if he's laughing too. When he's not, the pride and delight I just felt dissipates a little. Fitting in with Eli and the other guys is important, but not if it's going to make Fabian think I'm gross.

"She's probably pretty upset," I switch. "I mean, he did it before school."

"That's the best time, dude." Eli thumbs a string. "That way, they can't be calling you every five minutes. Gives it a chance to sink in. Once you've gone through the whole day, it's a sealed deal. She can't do anything about it. You're gone."

"Well, Whitney's a little more . . ."

"Difficult?" Abe offers. But then his face becomes totally inexpressive and he straightens up, as Oliver thumps back down the stairs.

"You okay?" I ask, automatic.

He rakes his fingers through his bangs a few times but that's it. "'Just Hang Up'" is all he says, counting off before his guitar is even back around his neck. I know the rest of the guys know that it's a breakup song, but I'm not sure they get, as much as I do, how badly Oliver needs that song right now.

Whitney crashing practice isn't even the most bizarre thing that happens, though. I'm gathering chip bags and stuff to take upstairs when Fabian, who has been taking an unusually long amount of time getting his equipment together, asks me from nowhere, "Charlotte, would you be interested in going to hear a band this weekend?"

It's all I can do to not drop the glasses I'm carrying.

"Um, who is it?" Like that would matter. Like I wouldn't go hear klezmer polka with him if he asked me.

"This band called Unkind. They're from Chicago, I think. I don't know who's opening."

Above us we hear the other guys coming back down the stairs.

"Um, sure," I say fast.

"Great." He smiles. I do too. And then, because I'm stupid and don't know what to do with myself, I bolt upstairs to give myself a few minutes to completely hyperventilate. I stay there in the kitchen, going, *Ohmygod ohmygod ohmygod ohmygod,* and sucking these little breaths in between closed teeth, just to try to calm down enough to face him coolly and without squealing.

When it's time to go, I'm a little calmer. At least I hope so. But then my heart accelerates again and I grind my teeth together to keep my jaw from doing that obnoxious popping thing when Fabian offers me a ride home.

"That'd be great, man," Oliver says for me. "I gotta get a jump on studying." To me he says, "You mind?"

"Uh." I am so dumb. I mean, literally, dumb. I think I am even breathing out of my mouth. "Okay."

The inside of Fabian's car is shockingly clean. There's barely anything on the floor mats, even, and it smells like a Febreze commercial.

"Your car is so clean," I say. Idiot.

"That was part of the deal," he tells me. "Which way?" His fingers point over the edge of his steering wheel, and I think, *I love his knuckles so much.*

"Oh. Sorry. Up to the stop sign and then right. It's not very far, really."

"You usually walk, right?"

"Yeah, or Oliver drives."

He nods and looks over, smiles in just a little curve.

"Um, so . . . the deal?" I ask.

His eyebrows scrunch together.

"You said keeping everything clean was part of the deal? Past the gas station up here, take the first left."

He's confused for a second. "Oh, yes. For the car. My parents agreed to the hybrid only if I promised to not trash it up like my brother did his first car. They didn't think I could do it. My dad sneaks out after dinner to look in the windows, see if I've slipped up. It's become kind of a fun game between us, actually. For me, anyway."

I am trying not to stare at him. At his face lighting up with impish playfulness.

"Um, you're going to turn right up here. Not this street but the next one."

"You're a very good directions-giver."

The back of my head, neck, turn golden under his compliment.

"It's this one. On the left. The one with the green door."

"Most people with white houses have red doors," he remarks. "Have you noticed that?"

"Yeah, that's actually why we don't. It's a folk thing, I think, to paint the door red. It says that your house is a place of refuge or something. Which is nice, right? But my stepmom, Hannah, she *hates* the red-door trend. She says that people just do it because they saw it in *Southern Living*." I realize I'm talking too much, but I'm halfway through the story and can't stop now. "She thinks most people don't understand the meaning at all and would never give refuge to anyone they didn't know—especially not anyone, god forbid, *foreign* or *homeless*—and so she doesn't want to be associated with that at all. Also, she says, it's not like we're running an Elizabeth Arden spa. So, our front door is green."

"Your stepmom sounds like a cool person."

And this would maybe be unflattering, but I feel it in the most admiring way when it strikes me that Fabian sounds, a little, like Kermit the Frog. Also, I haven't really thought of Hannah as cool before, but coming out of Fabian's mouth, it seems right.

"She's pretty cool, I guess. But I suggest you reserve judgment on my stepsisters until you actually meet them."

Which makes me blush to say. Fabian meeting Gretchen and

Darby. Meeting my family. I have got to get out of this car now before I say anything even more stupid.

I clear my throat to make my voice not wobble. "So, this show?"

"Yeah." Fabian reaches around, takes his iPhone out of his back pocket. "Tell me your number?"

"You actually have it, I think. From when I texted you? About the auditions?"

"Oh yeah, right." This looks like it surprises him. In a happy way.

He fiddles around with the screen a little more.

"Are you the 9061 number?"

"That's me." I've taken out my phone too. "Which one are you?"

"2277."

"Well, that's easy to remember."

Digits resaved in our respective devices, we smile at each other again.

"The show's at, I think, eight. I can pick you up?"

"What night is it?"

"Oh, yes. Right." He shakes his head a little, embarrassed by himself. It is wildly endearing, and kind of a relief, that I'm not the only one who's flibberty. "Saturday. At the Masquerade. Have you been?"

"Isn't that, like . . ." I feel like an incredible baby. "A bar?"

"But the shows are all ages on Saturdays. It's cool. You'll see."

"Sounds like it."

God. More stupid shit. I have to get out of this car now.

"Hey, thanks for the ride."

"Can I get back to Ponce from here?"

"Oh, right." I try to explain where he'll be going, but it ends up being too many streets so I just take out a piece of paper and draw him a map.

"You're good at maps, too." He holds it up. "I'll hang on to this."

"Okay, well." I practically stumble, getting out so fast, the idea of my stupid map staying in his car, being something maybe he'll refer to so often he won't need to anymore. I turn around and wave to him as he's backing out, but I don't think he sees.

As soon as I'm safely inside the house, I holler for Darby. She appears at the top of the stairs, mad at being interrupted, but also cautious, like she might be in trouble. "What?"

"I'm going to need your help," I gush. I know this is an intra-band relationship no-no I'd frown on with anyone else, but I don't care this second. "I, apparently, have got a date on Saturday night."

Chapter Nine

My excitement about going out with Fabian—fueled, in part, by Darby's crazed enthusiasm and our little What Not to Wear exercise after dinner—dissipates the next morning as soon as I read the notebook from Trip. The cartoons about Whitney doing all these awful things because Oliver broke up with her are hilarious, but the second part catches my laugh in my throat: *POTENTIAL SATURDAY-NIGHT PROJECTS*, the top of the next page reads. *BETWEEN ONE DEMPSEY "TRIP" BREWER AND ANOTHER CHARLOTTE ANNE AUGUSTINE.* Under that Trip has written out a list, some actual contenders (*Take MARTA to the airport and back, documenting the crazy conversations overheard during the trip),* some ridiculous (*Don formal attire and gallivant around Little Five Points, documenting the number of times people ask if we've just gone to prom).* There are at least twenty ideas here. Maybe more.

Crap.

After lunch I still haven't had the heart to write back to him. I don't want, for one thing, my date with Fabian to be recorded yet. And even though I told Darby, it still feels like something that's just mine. Secondly, I can't make myself write it—can't say, *I can't do Saturday night because I'm going out. With a boy.* Though Trip is my friend, it still sucks for me to stand him up. I know too well how it feels to be replaced by someone else, even for only one weekend. Though I'll make it up to him next Saturday for sure, it's still depressing. And he would probably have a thing or two to say about me dating someone in the band.

But Trip can see something's wrong as I head down the hall to meet him.

"You okay?"

"I can't do Saturday night," I tell him straight-out. Rip off the Band-Aid. That always feels better, right?

When his face falls, it doesn't. Feel better. He tries to recover fast, though. "Everything okay?"

"Yes, it's fine. I just . . . there's something . . . with a guy . . . He asked me to—"

"Who? Benji?" he asks, sharp.

"What? No. God." A solution occurs to me. Not a great one—and not one I really want—but one that might smooth things out. "Maybe you want to come? There's this band at the Masquerade and I don't know anything about them, but—"

"Um, no thanks."

"Wait. I mean, why not?"

Behind the gold rims of his glasses, his eyes are steady, flat. "Are you forgetting that tricycles are the only things that function well with three wheels? And I'm a little tall for those now." His fingers flute out to illustrate his complete height.

"It's not like that. I mean—" But, of course, it is. I didn't really want him to say yes, anyway. "Okay. You're right. I'm sorry. I can cancel with him. Let me study this crazy awesome list a bit more and—"

"No, don't cancel." He backs away from me, getting ready to head down the hall to his class. "Do your thing. It sounds cool. And you should probably be out hearing new bands, anyway, now that you're in one."

He turns and disappears down the hall before I can say anything; before I can say, for example, *Well, tonight's Friday—what about that?* And also before I can tell, really, if he's being sincere and supportive, or if it's supposed to sound as mean as it does.

• • •

When Trip isn't waiting for me later—when he doesn't show up after about two minutes of my just standing there, looking for him in the hallway—I guess I have my answer. I finally wrote him this long thing about how we could've done something tonight if he'd stuck around, how he completely, unfairly over-reacted, and how friends are supposed to be *glad* for each other when they get asked out by people they like, even if it's compli-cated, but that makes me stop writing, because, well, there's the whole not-wanting-to-put-Fabian-in-writing-yet thing.

I end up ripping up my little rant and tossing it in the trash outside of class. I'm going to try to catch Trip in the parking lot before he takes off after school, ask him about tonight in person. But when I get there he's nowhere to be seen. Since Benji and I aren't studying together this week either, I head home with my stepsisters.

It's not until eleven o'clock that Trip responds to my *Where did you go?* text.

With Chris is all it says.

I fling my phone down onto a pile of dirty laundry.

Saturday I can't worry about Trip anymore, because we have rehearsal. Instead I'm thinking—maybe for the first time—about my clothes. Normally, I'd pull on jeans and a Salvation Army sweater—maybe put my hair in a ponytail, maybe not—and walk over to Oliver's, start helping Mrs. Drake with the snacks. But this Saturday is different. I want to try at least a little harder today.

But as I stand in front of my dresser, hating everything I own, it also occurs to me that Fabian's already asked me out, even though he's mostly seen me in costumes befitting a stay-at-home dad. Trying too hard today might be obvious, or silly. And anyway, I want to dress up tonight, and for him to notice, so maybe I should wear what I normally wear to rehearsal. I consider calling Darby in for consultation or, better, Gretchen, who's actually *been* in a relationship, but then, that's ridiculous because it'll just bring even more attention to the whole thing.

It's just rehearsal, I tell myself. I put on my favorite jeans for comfort and a black turtleneck for the chic factor, pull my hair back, and throw in some earrings for good measure—call it a compromise.

Dressing normal for rehearsal doesn't make me feel any more normal, though. Abe comes in, then Eli arrives, and finally Fabian. *You're always last to rehearsal*, I want to say to him in some teasing way. But then it would seem like I was waiting. Which I was, but still. Instead I just smile, try to be aloof, and make sure I walk behind him down the stairs so he doesn't see my flushed face.

"I gotta leave at four, man," Eli says, jerking his thumb in the direction of the stairs. Immense relief and gratitude sweep through me. Darby has some pre-date regimen she wants me to go through, and I've accepted mostly because it will help to have someone distracting me from being so nervous. Now we'll actually have time for it.

"Let's go over the new material again, then," Oliver says. "And then if there's time, a few of the old hits, just to keep ourselves limber. Spider?"

"Huh?" I think my mouth is open. "I mean, yes?"

Oliver's eyes squinch a little. "You okay? With starting?"

"Oh, um. Sure? But maybe can we do 'Foreign Tongue' first? Since I'm just backup?" I clear my throat. "I haven't warmed up or anything."

Oliver nods. Abe nods. Eli nods. Fabian nods. Why my entire body is swimming with heat, I don't know. I've sung in front of Fabian before. He thinks I'm excellent.

But that's what makes it harder to sing now. He thinks I'm so excellent that he wants to spend more time with me. On our own. Together. Tonight. Only about six hours from now, he and I will be driving in his superclean car together to go listen to music that he wants me to hear and—

But I have to sing now. And I can't let Oliver suspect a thing, anyway.

"Listen, listen, sssshhhhhhh . . ." I half murmur behind Oliver's line.

Everything comes out properly, though my "sshhhhh" is sloppy: surprised and wet. The next part, *"Tell me, tell me, sssshh-hhhh,"* comes out better. I am not looking at Fabian. Or Oliver. I am trying to sing honest. Excellent. *"Tell me. Tell me."*

The rest of rehearsal, I force myself to focus on the music, to not wonder what we'll talk about tonight in the car, what the club will be like, if we'll go out on the floor to dance and if his hand will somehow come in contact with mine when we do. The end of the night—the potential kissing, even though we shouldn't—makes me press my eyes closed and my thighs together at the same time.

At four on the dot, Eli slings his bass into his case and splits. Abe looks like he's going to stick around, maybe play some video games with Oliver awhile, and I can't tell what Fabian's in the mood for because I'm trying not to look at him. I jerk my thumb in Eli's wake, explain I should be heading off too.

"Oh," Fabian says, surprised.

"Yeah." I pause. *Does he want me to stay?* "Got some . . . cleaning up . . . I need to do at home. I mean, around the house, before we . . ."

Is it me? Or are Oliver and Abe suddenly paying careful attention?

Fabian holds up his hand. A wave? A dismissal? A stop-before-you-say-too-much-because-this-is-a-secret? "I'll see you then."

Um. Okay. "Okay. I'll see you."

I give as normal a good-bye to Oliver and Abe as I can, and then get myself up the stairs and out the door as fast as humanly possible.

"You're so late!" Darby hisses when I make it safely to my house. She is halfway down the staircase, holding a plastic tray loaded with nail polish and cotton balls and several small, silver, plucky-looking tools.

I shut the door, hang up my jacket, and head upstairs, knowing she'll follow. I'm still jittery from trying to act normal around the guys, and Darby's pressure doesn't help. "He's not going to be here until, like, eight."

"Which means we need to hurry. You need to shower *and* shampoo"—her eyes narrow—"so that your hair can air dry completely before we fix it. And then lotion, and we'll do your nails, and I guess you'll have to eat before you get dressed so you don't spill anything. But you're not going to be that hungry, right? We could skip dinner. You could do some sit-ups instead."

"I am not going out on an empty stomach. And you're not doing my nails, either."

"Gah, Charlotte. I'm trying to help you, you know. You said you wanted."

"I know. And I do appreciate it. I do. But I think it'll be a little suspicious if I look like Powder Puff Princess all of a sudden."

"True." She assesses me. "But you do still need to shower."

"Agreed."

"Here." Darby hands me a glittery bottle.

"What is this?" I try to read the girly cursive label.

"Exfoliating wash. Scrub it over everywhere, especially your feet, elbows, and knees, before you do your regular soap-up."

"This doesn't smell like baby powder or anything, does it?" I pop open the cap, take a whiff.

"No, creep. It's Shalimar shea. You'll smell like a sexy queen."

"Sexy queen, huh?" I reach for my bathrobe, hanging on the back of my door.

"And don't forget to shave, for god's sake!" she screams after me down the hall.

Seven thirty, and Fabian's texted twice, letting me know when he's left his place and when he should arrive at mine. It's reassuring that he seems as anxious about tonight as I am. Getting ready so early has given me way too much time to think about it, though. For one thing, I've realized that going to hear a band at a club isn't exactly the same intimacy as going to dinner and a movie. It's not like we'll be able to talk much. Which makes me think, maybe he doesn't *want* to talk much, and instead just wants me along—like Lish used to do sometimes—so he doesn't have to go somewhere alone. But, then again, he doesn't seem like the kind of guy who would mind going somewhere alone. He probably has friends he'd meet up with, anyway, right? I mean, he's been there before, so this isn't some new experience for him. Maybe he *does* want my company.

But this could just be about wanting to get to know the members of the band more, right? *So then why didn't he invite Oliver and Abe, too?* I snap back in my head. I almost want to ask Darby about all of this—really, I want to ask *Trip*, but he's obviously not interested in discussing my plans this evening. Or anything, for that matter, since he's neither called nor texted all day. Jerk.

At 7:54, I'm letting Darby fuss with my hair some more, just to give us both something to look at until Fabian gets here. She won't let me go downstairs and hang out in front of the TV.

"You have to come down the stairs, duh. And you have to make him wait a little."

"But then Dad will try to—"

"Risk you have to take," she says, her eyebrows and lips patronizing as hell. "Besides, if he's going to be doing this often, he better be comfortable with your dad, right?"

If he's going to be doing this often. I am still not even sure if this is really a date. I mean, it has most of the essential first-date ingredients, including my breath-catching interest in him. It's his interest in me that I'm not so overwhelmingly sure about.

I look at myself in the mirror. Darby and I went back and

forth quite a lot on the outfit. She wanted me to wear tighter-fitting jeans and a purple minidress of hers over them with a big giant belt across my middle, topped off with a yellow-and-white-striped cardigan and these giant dangling sparkly earrings. "See if Gretchen will let you borrow her slouchy boots, too," she said. But I just glared at her.

"If I'm wearing boots," I told her, "it's my combats."

She scrunched up her face. "Flats, at least?"

We ended up compromising okay. I'm in jeans I haven't worn since last winter, because I don't like the way they hug my butt and hips, but Darby insists that's how jeans are supposed to fit. I passed on the minidress but agreed to a loose, artsy top that she usually wears with leggings. I said no way to the belt.

Makeup was another fight, because I just don't wear any, and Darby had this entire kit of waxes and powders and concealers and who knows what else.

"Mascara and lip gloss and that's it," I growled at her.

But she talked me into some powder. And a tiny bit of bronzer on my cheeks, too.

The hair, I have to say, is really the best part. I don't want her to get too big a head, so I'm going to have to ask her carefully, but I really would like to know what she did. It's just nice and wavy, instead of the heavy, tangled mess it usually is.

"You look good." She smiles happily.

"Thanks." My own smile at her in the mirror turns quickly to pale horror when the doorbell rings. Instinctively I reach for her hand. She squeezes it back just as hard.

But I can't stand waiting upstairs for as long as Darby wants me to, mostly because I don't want Fabian to have to suffer Dad and all his dumb jokes and questions. Even if Fabian and I are just friends, Dad is a torture I can't subject anyone to too much.

When I get to the bottom of the stairs, both their eyebrows go up. Which is when Hannah comes in from the kitchen, where she's been staying out of the way. She smiles brightly at me, pleased to see Darby's makeover, but—my stepmom really is cool—she doesn't say anything.

"You look nice," Fabian says. Does he actually think so? Or is it just that I look different, and "nice" is the only polite substitute?

Dad makes a big deal about hugging me before we leave and making sure I have my phone, plus repeating my eleven thirty baby curfew about five times, which is hugely embarrassing, but Fabian doesn't seem to mind. He's polite and patient and even says, "I like your dad," when we get to the car.

"He's a dork, but thank you."

"My dad's a dork, too. It's okay."

His unself-consiousness makes me remember that he *asked* me to do this. He wants me here. So I don't have to be any different than I'd be in Oliver's rec room.

On the drive to the club, we talk together about the things we haven't been able to at rehearsal: school, family, college plans, all of that. I don't feel the slightest bit awkward telling him I'm pretty convinced I'm applying to Georgia Perimeter—*maybe* Mercer—because I already know I won't have a very competitive application. By then Dad and Hannah will have three girls in college, anyway, so I don't think they'll mind me ending up somewhere cheaper and closer to home.

"I might not even go at all, really," I go on. I've only ever told Trip this part before, but Fabian's understanding face makes it feel all right. "I figure it might end up being smarter for me to just, you know, get a job or something. Take some classes. Get to know myself a little more."

"That seems reasonable," Fabian says.

And it does. Even more so, now that he's said it. Maybe I should get Fabian to explain it to Jilly and Dad, so that they'll get off my back about having higher aspirations.

"What about you?" I ask.

"International relations, probably. I'm looking at Duke."

"Wait, not music?"

He shrugs. "They have that too. But I'm not sure this is a forever thing for me."

"But you're so . . ." *Excellent*, I want to say. But then we're at the Masquerade. Seeing it, I realize I've driven by it a ton of times without paying attention. It's a big, dark, almost burned-looking building next to a giant, fenced parking lot that is maybe two football fields of asphalt. We have to walk almost five minutes before we even get to the door, where a puffy-faced, dread-headed girl asks to see our IDs. I want to ask Fabian more about the international relations thing—like how many languages he knows–but finally being here is a little intimidating.

While I dig out my driver's license, I grab a ten to pay my cover, but Fabian waves it away, saying, "You might not like the band, after all."

More evidence that This Is Actually a Date. Yesss.

Inside the club, Fabian leans in close to my ear so I can hear him. "There are some people I want you to meet," he says.

A twinge hits the back of my mouth. Yes, Fabian's face is now so close to mine that I can feel the warmth coming off his skin, but him saying there are going to be other people here makes my heart sink with disappointment.

"Do you want anything before we go dance?" he asks, leading me up a dimly lit staircase to the second floor, where there's a bar-looking area on the left and another dance floor on the right.

Part of me wants to suggest we get a Coke and talk a little bit longer before these mysterious other people horn in, but I know that's just stalling the inevitable. I shake my head and try to smile. I follow him into the spinning blue glow.

At the guardrail, he stands quiet, looking down. I watch the dancers on the floor, letting my eyes go from one body to the next. I don't know who we're looking for, and I don't want to know. I don't want them to materialize, ever. On the stage is one lone DJ and his laptop. He isn't as cool as the turntable guys Trip has shown me before, but the people on the floor seem to like it.

Suddenly I'm knocked in the back by some girl. I'm about to say *What the hell?* when I realize she's run up to grab Fabian in a squealy hug. I watch as he lifts her off the ground, holding her in tight. Every bit of me knows, without question, that this is no date. My heart folds up somewhere deep inside my chest and shuts out the light. I would very much like to go home now and dissolve. I am, I guess, just too easy to hang out with. Just one of the guys.

But it's not like I can leave. Fabian shouts something into the huggy girl's ear and gestures in my direction. I see there's a second girl standing farther back, watching us. Now I wish Trip had come with me, or that I'd sounded more sincere asking him along. It would definitely make this part more bearable. I decide I'll text him when I get a chance, whether he answers back or not.

"Charlotte, this is Taryn," Fabian says, close to me again. This time there's no electric jolt. "And that's Sylvia."

Sylvia raises her hand in greeting, solemn like one of those wooden Indian statues they have outside of hokey country stores.

She is short, with pixie-cut black hair. The rest of her is dressed in black, too.

Taryn is blond and bouncy like a pinup girl—one of the sweet, pink-cheeked ones who always has her knees (and sometimes her underpants) tangled up in some dog's leash. She is happy and grabby, squeezing both my hands, pulling on Fabian's arm. She's adorable. Even though I don't like that they're here, I realize, begrudgingly, that I will probably like them both as people.

"This DJ is awful," Taryn yells, googling her eyes. She says something else in Fabian's ear. He nods, and motions for us to walk ahead of him to the neighboring bar. Taryn bounces ahead, pulling me along by the wrist. Guess I'll get my Coke, after all.

We order our drinks and take them over to a high, grungy table. This time I insist on giving Fabian my ten, even though I know it's too much for one soda. I don't have a lot of dignity, but I figure I've got to hold together whatever scraps I can.

Taryn beams at me. "So, Charlotte! You're in Fabian's new band!"

"Well, yes. Sort of. I mean, I write the songs."

"She sings," Fabian adds proudly.

"I can't wait to hear!" Taryn gushes. "Fabian always has the coolest projects. Remember that Chinese exchange kid? You were *boss* with him."

I know their answer will only make me even more jealous,

but I have to ask: "How long have you guys known each other?"

Taryn frowns over at Sylvia. "How long is it? We met Fabian in—"

"A year and a half," Sylvia says.

Taryn's frown deepens. "No, that can't be right." She turns and squints at Fabian. "Is it really only a year? Gosh. It feels like so much more."

"Taryn and Sylvia are also in a band," Fabian helps.

"It used to be Fabian's band too, until he got too cool for us."

"What kind of music?" I ask.

"Cunt rock," Sylvia says flatly.

I don't know how to arrange my face, hearing that. Is Sylvia being serious or is she just messing with me? I can't imagine what cunt rock would even sound like.

Taryn swats her playfully and turns to me. "It's just a bunch of, you know, girl songs. Powerful girl songs, though. Covers, mostly. We like old Liz Phair stuff a lot."

"*You* like Liz Phair," Sylvia growls.

"It's a good band," Fabian says to me. "We should hear them sometime."

Stupidly, the hope in me that just crashed over the dance floor railing flickers a tiny bit. Does this mean he'll take me out? Again? To hear them play? Is he introducing me to these friends so that they can help him decide if he and I should go for it, in spite of the

Sad Jackal thing? Maybe this *is* a date. A weird one, but still. I take a long drink of my Coke to keep the sudden smile I feel in check.

Now that I'm more motivated to make a good impression, I ask Sylvia and Taryn about what other bands they like, which morphs into a discussion about bands we hate, and then bands we wish we could see live. It's interesting, actually, talking to girls who really know music. Know more than the Top 40 hits that Lish and Darby listen to, anyway, or the musicals and standards that Jilly always played in the car. There are several bands Sylvia mentions that I want to follow up on. When I say some of the ones Trip has introduced me to, she seems pleasantly surprised.

Long after our sipped-down drinks have gotten watery, we head to the lower dance floor, where the band, Unkind, has already started. I'm a little bummed we missed their entrance, because I always like to watch how a band first presents itself to the audience. Mostly I like to see this for Oliver's sake—in case there's any advice I can give—but whatever. I can't watch anything too carefully onstage anyway, because Taryn is dragging the three of us across the dance floor. It's impossible not to jump up and down with her, partly because she is still hanging on to my arm, but also because that's what everyone else is doing, including Fabian.

Sylvia dances mostly by throbbing her head either back and forth or side to side, the whole time standing firm in one place. Taryn is up and down and all around and over. Fabian and I do a combo of both, I guess, mainly staying out of Taryn's way. Every time we make eye contact he gives me that pressed-lips smile, and my flickering hope becomes a steady glimmer.

On top of the thrill of being with Fabian, the whole thing is plain fun. I'm not sure how long it goes on, only that way too soon I see, on some guy's watch next to me, that it's almost eleven. I don't want to have to drag Fabian out of here, like some girl with a pumpkin waiting outside, but I also don't want Dad to pull his whole "He's not responsible enough" thing and keep me from doing this again. Because I would. Like to. Do this again with Fabian. Even with Taryn and Sylvia. And maybe if I get home on time now, I can ask for a later curfew.

Reluctantly, I catch Fabian's eye and point at my wrist. His eyes widen in surprise, but then he nods and leans in to say something to Taryn, who nearly clocks him in the face in the process. I watch him sign to her that we have to leave. But instead of letting us just slip away, Taryn grabs Sylvia by the lapel and they follow us out, give me their phone numbers, and program in mine.

"It was great meeting you," I tell them, honestly meaning it.

"We can't wait to hear your band!" Taryn hugs us both, then waves merrily.

When we're walking back to the car, I tell Fabian, "Your friends are cool."

"Thanks. I like them too."

"Do you miss playing cunt rock?"

"Ha. When I was playing with them, we used to do a lot more poppy stuff. But—Taryn had these ideas and Sylvia was tired of what we'd been doing anyway, so."

"Is that why you don't play with them anymore?"

"Kind of. But also, it just got a little complicated when Taryn started dating Molly. And then Rachel. And then Stella."

I try to keep the surprise off my face and my voice even. "Why was it complicated?"

He shrugs a tiny bit. "Sylvia's had a crush on Taryn since they met. And it just got, for me, a little hard to watch."

I don't want to be obvious. But this is also an opening and so—"I guess it's just too messy to mix music and romance."

"Oh, I wouldn't say that." He breezes along like nothing. "Lots of people can make it work. I just wanted a different environment to play in, I guess."

I nod and stay cool, but these words from him have made my hope-o-meter burst to the top and past the bell, shooting fireworks everywhere.

Confidence and helpless infatuation regained, I amp up my funny and we spend the ride home trying to list all the bands we can think of who have dramatically changed their sound. The best one cracks me up for almost a minute.

"Jesus, who even listens to Van Halen this century?" I gasp.

He shrugs in the cutest way. "My parents like to go to Atlantic City over the summer, what can I say?"

We're laughing when we get to my house. I'm struck by how even more amazing he is, now that I'm getting to really know him and not just crushing during practice. I hope he is feeling the same way. But as soon as the engine's off, my hands are sweating and I don't know where to look. We've been having a great time, but now I'm not sure what's going to happen.

"Thanks for asking me," I start.

"I'm glad you enjoyed it."

"I'd love to do it again sometime. I mean, if anyone good is playing."

"Absolutely."

I am caught up in his smile, until I catch myself staring.

"So . . . I guess I'll see you?" I blurt. "On Monday? And, I mean, thanks for getting me home on time."

"I can't believe we only have a couple more weeks until the dance."

I fake shudder. "Don't remind me. I'm already nervous enough."

"Don't be," he says. Which is a perfect time for him to lean in and . . .

But he doesn't. So I put my hand on the door handle, which is when he puts his hand on my shoulder, gives it a squeeze.

"I had a good time with you, Charlotte."

"Me too."

In his eyes I see . . . something. I can't tell what. But I can't sit here waiting for him to kiss me—he's not going to, right?—and I don't think I'm quite up to lunging at him yet. So I force myself to just get out of the car.

"Thanks again."

"Bye." He waves.

I stand in the yard and watch as he pulls away, in case he turns to give a final wave—or, better, jumps out of the car to slam me on the ground with a kiss. But he simply drives down to the stop sign and turns out of sight. You don't *have* to kiss on the first date. And even though he thinks it's okay for bandmates to be together (hooray, hooray, hooray), we should still be cautious. I don't know how I will tell Oliver about this, for example. Besides, not kissing on the first date is probably normal. My old boyfriend Clay was always so gropey; I had to shove him off me constantly. But the idea of Fabian waiting—of drawing things out—makes me glow in strange places, including my armpits.

And twenty minutes later? That glow goes even deeper, loops twice around my knees and back up over my head: *You r cool, Charlotte*, he texts. *Had fun 2night.*

Chapter Ten

Monday morning, Darby ransacks all three of our closets trying to find something for me to wear for school and rehearsal. She's clearly not happy with the corduroys and (cute) hoodie I finally end up with.

"You've got to *show* him, Charlotte," she huffs at me in the car. "Boys are pretty stupid. And if you don't throw it out there, there's going to be some other girl who does. Don't come crying to me when he picks her and not you."

Gretchen cackles and looks back at me in the rearview. "This," she says, "from the dating champion with—how many, Darby? Two kisses to your name?"

Darby hits Gretchen on the shoulder.

"Ow, dammit."

"Big talk from a girl who dates some jockstrap for seven months and then gets dumped," Darby says.

"I dumped him."

"Which time, heartbreaker?"

"How about we just say," I interrupt, "that I'll listen to all advice gratefully, but won't necessarily do anything different."

Darby pokes her finger at me, thin and sharp. "That's exactly your problem, Char. You're too 'oh, whatever' about things. That's why you have to say something to him today. I swear—"

"Leave off," Gretchen groans, as we finally park. "It's not going to do her any good to fake it. Then he'll just be disappointed when he finds out what she's really like."

"Thanks, Gretchen," I mutter.

"No problem," she breezes, not getting her own insult.

"Who are *you* going to be all yourself with now, then, Lady Know-It-All?" Darby bugs her sister, getting out of the car. With the attention briefly off me, I gather my bag, wave good-bye, and head off to catch Oliver and everybody before the bell. It doesn't matter what Darby says—I know I'm not letting Fabian do all the work. I'm just letting him be him and me be me, and eventually we'll be together and it will work out great.

I'm so lost in my Fabian-and-me fantasy that I barely register the rest of the parking lot as I walk through, until I catch sight of Trip's tall blond head, standing in a group about two car rows over. Trip, whose phone was off all day Sunday, and who I haven't really talked to in forever. For a second it's almost like he sees me and is maybe going to wave or smile or something, but then Chris Monroe punches him in the arm, and their friends laugh, and then Lily Jearnigen of all people snakes her arms around Trip's waist and stands on tiptoe to kiss his ear.

I don't know why it makes me mad. But it does, and I turn back toward the building, heading straight for my locker, forgetting Oliver and everyone else. I don't care if Trip's dating someone; I really don't. I'm dating someone myself, maybe. But I can't believe he got all touchy about me going out with Fabian, and then turned all stupid drooly over some tiny art fiend like Lily. And when did this happen? Is *she* why he's been hanging so much with Chris and his posse? He could've just told me what was really going on, instead of tiptoeing around like I'd act like some jealous girlfriend. God.

When first period starts, I'm glad I don't have the notebook with me—that he hogged it and never gave it back—because I'd definitely have a thing or two to say to him right now. He probably hasn't even written in it, though. Probably been too busy watching Lily eat a candy necklace or whatever. If he can just fall in with this stupid gang of cartoon character wannabes, then maybe I didn't really know him like I thought I did. Maybe he isn't any more special than any other guy.

But none of that really rings true, and it bums me out even more. All our talking on the phone, listening to music together— all the work we did on the songs, everything we've told each other in the notebook—me and him, we're *friends*. Real friends. Friends more than Lish and I were, for sure. More than even me and Oliver. "Friend" sometimes doesn't seem a big enough word, though I don't know which other one to use.

Which means, for friendship's sake, I have to tell him what I think. So after first period I hurry to our morning meeting point. I'm not sure he'll be there, after our weird sort-of-fight on Friday, his phone off all weekend, and now this Lily thing, but it's the first place to check, I guess. When he's not there after about thirty seconds, I cut around and wait outside his French class. He may be trying to avoid me, but I'm not going to let him. Of course, on the way, it occurs to me that his girlfriend might be with him—or that he's walking her to class now—but as I hesitate, considering what exactly to do, he lopes around the corner, alone.

"Hey," he says, surprised. "Where were—"

"You can't do this" comes out of me, straight.

It's like he's struck. "I can't do what?"

"You can't just go off and get a whole new group of friends, pretend you don't even remember the rest of us. You can't just leave—"

He backs up a little, scowls. "Who says you can tell me what I can and cannot *go off* and do? Last I checked, you were pretty busy with your own new friends."

But I'm expecting that. "Most of them are *our* friends, smart-ass. And the new ones would be your friends too if you would come around ever."

"Oh, you mean 'come around,' like on Saturday night?"

"I do mean on Saturday night. You would've liked them. It. The whole thing. Fabian had friends there. You could've brought Chris, even. I texted you. I tried to talk to you all weekend. It was really fun and I wanted you to—"

"Yeah, well, I had other things to do."

"Oh." I'm sharp and mean. "Like cut out paper dolls with Lily?"

He is glaring at me now. "Maybe. She's really good at stuff like that."

Here's where I should be able to say, all sarcastic, *I bet she's good with her hands*, or something like that, but I can't. Because how he says it—how he's so unapologetic, how it sounds like maybe he has already spent enough time with Lily to watch her do something as dumb as cutting out paper dolls—it kicks me in the stomach.

"I think you would really like Fabian if you gave him a chance," I try instead. "I want us all to do something. And I need your help with these new—"

The blank-mask look on his face stops me. He stares off down the hall, finally says, "This is just how it is now. Okay?"

All I can see are the straining tendons in his neck, the tight line of his chin. I see him squeeze his eyes shut as the late bell blares out over us both.

The hall is quiet. "So that's it?" I can't move. Can barely hear my own voice.

He finally looks at me. "I've got to get to class."

I watch him pull open the door, slip through the small space, and let it shut quietly behind him. I'm rooted there, dumbass of the world. I feel like I could just stay put, staring at the door until the bell rings again and he comes back out. I would try again. I wouldn't be so mean. *You're who made it okay*, I would try to explain. *Jilly being gone, and Lish, and everything. You're the one who knows me.* I thought he knew it already, but maybe I need to tell him. Maybe that would make a difference.

But maybe too—and this is what snaps me into action, makes me shuffle off to algebra, because I don't want to think it—maybe he does know how much he means to me. And maybe he's doing this anyway.

I don't register the rest of the school day, not even much of Dr. Campbell handing out another take-home test and Benji immediately writing me a note about getting together to work on it.

Practice this afternoon, I see myself scrawl on the paper. He doesn't answer back, and he doesn't try to walk out with me either.

As I sit in my other classes and move myself from room to room, I write. Constant scribblings that won't stop coming out. Usually I need something to trigger me, to get me going, but apparently not today. Today it's constant. Lines and lines. And unlike all the other times I've written, nothing my pen scrawls down is a mystery. It is, instead, exactly how I feel.

When school's finished, I want to go home, shut the door, and feel sorry for myself. All I can do is picture Trip and his bubbly, pink-haired glitter girl, feel his cold "This is just how it is now" pouring over me, and it's just too much like Mom driving away, Jilly leaving me for college, Lish disappearing. I don't want to go to rehearsal at Oliver's. I don't want Fabian to see me like this, and I don't want to hear whatever new idea Eli has. I don't want Abe to give me his I-see-you're-upset-so-I-will-avoid-eye-contact-with-you routine, or for Oliver to try to cheer me up. I'd rather be completely alone.

But we have to practice. The dance is in two weeks. So I follow Oliver out to his car. He must get that something's really wrong, because he talks nonstop. About Whitney, mostly: how she won't back off and let go, how he's thinking about changing his phone number but what a pain in the ass that would be. He's trying to get me to laugh or say something caustic—maybe just say anything—but all I can bring myself to do is mumble "damn" and "that sucks." I'm not sure who's more glad when we get to his house, him or me.

I try to make myself look at least kind of neutral, but I must not do a very good job, because Fabian asks if I feel okay the second he sees me.

And his noticing does make my insides warm up a little. I give him a small smile, say something about just being tired.

But I keep writing all my thoughts while the guys practice some of the songs I'm not in. Nothing forms into cohesive lines, but words are still coming out fast. Fragments of feeling. Scraps of lyrics. When it's my turn to sing, I pull the mic close to my mouth, try to drown out every thought of Trip.

After practice, Fabian comes over and gives me a one-armed hug. "Taryn says to say hi," he tells me. "She's cuckoo about you."

Mood I'm in, all I notice is that he doesn't add, *And I am too.*

Our Saturday night feels pretty far away right now.

Later, I lie on my bed and listen to my Trip playlist for over an hour. I still can't pull any of the writing nonsense into any one song or poem that makes much sense, so I've stopped. It's infuriating enough to be writing about Trip at all, since he's obviously not thinking about me one bit, but that all the stuff I'm feeling won't materialize into anything I can use against him—it's like he *wins* somehow. On top of that, neither Mom nor Jilly has called me back, and I feel like I really need to talk to somebody other than Darby or Dad. I know Oliver would listen and try to say something helpful, but it doesn't seem like he really cares that Trip isn't hanging around anymore. I think about calling Fabian, but sobbing about my best friend getting a girlfriend probably isn't the kind of "you've got to show him" that Darby was talking about. So instead I lie there, the music washing over me, filling me with tears that I refuse to let fall.

The next morning, I wake up in the same sludge of blah. Between first and second periods, I don't even pause by the spot where Trip and I used to meet. I just go straight to Algebra II, try to fake my way through some of last night's assignment before the bell.

Afterward, I'm still so entrenched in my own pitying gloom that Benji has to call my name three times before I even register it's him behind me on the way to 20th Cen.

In his hand is a yellow weed. He holds it out. "This bud's for you."

"What, you get that from a movie?"

He looks at the wilty thing. "No. From the PE field."

"No." I laugh a little. "Not the—never mind."

He holds it out again for me to take.

I lift it up to my nose, sniffing for something I already know isn't there. "What's this for?"

"You were pretty solemn in class yesterday. Better now?"

I sigh. "You should do the test yourself this time. I really won't be any help."

We're outside the classroom now. A few kids pretend not to watch us talking as they pass.

"All the more reason," he says.

I narrow my eyes at him, twirling the weed. "You'd be doing most of the work. I'd feel like I owed you something."

"Pizza date it is, then," he says, steering me into class with one arm lightly around my shoulder. This time, I don't try to duck out from under it.

After school at the car, I swear Darby's head is going to pop off. "What do you mean? You're going out with *another* guy this afternoon?"

"See, sis? Apparently being yourself is a total guy magnet." Gretchen's sarcasm is heavy and thick. "You should try it sometime."

"I'm not going out with him. We're just studying."

They both snort at the same time, and I glare at them.

"Benji McLaughlin, right?" Gretchen goes. "That kid you hung with before?"

"He's in my Twentieth Cen. class. Why?" It's dumb to get defensive with Gretchen, because she'll just pounce and use it against me, but whatever. I don't need her criticism on top of everything else.

But Gretchen doesn't answer, just whistles low and long.

I don't get a chance to ask her to elaborate, because Benji's Volvo clunks up behind Gretchen's car right as Darby whines, "But what about Fabian?"

"I'll be home before Dad and Hannah, don't worry" is all I tell them.

"Uh-huh," Gretchen says, not even pretending to hide her knowing look.

Benji watches them over the rims of his aviator glasses while I get in the car. "Hi, ladies," he says in that lazytag way.

Gretchen nods and Darby does some kind of bounce-wave that is accented by a strangled giggle.

"Gah, the two of them are so stupid," I grumble.

"What, you're not excited for you, too?" He smirks.

"Let's just get this finished." But I can't help a small grin. That was funny.

Fellini's isn't that far away, so I don't even try to talk over the pulse-shaking garage punk coming out of the stereo.

"You ever go to Saturday shows at the Masquerade?" I ask as we're walking in. Since he seems to like his music loud.

"Place is all right." The one-shoulder shrug. "Lot of freaks there, though."

"Oh, right. Because you're *so* not freaky at all."

"Good one, Coastal," he says, holding the glass door open.

"What is that Coastal thing about?"

"That's just you," he says. "Girl of the tides."

It's an oddly personal, oddly sweet, oddly observant thing for him to say, and it pulls me back into my regular self again a little. I small-smile at Benji in thanks, and we order our food before spreading out at a glossy booth by the window.

Two pizza slices each and two and a half hours later, we shut our books, tests completed. We've been joking and sassing each other the whole time, cracking each other up, and I feel a lot better. I might even get an A on this test.

"Thanks. I needed that," I tell him when we get back to my house.

"I know you did." Those jokey eyebrows.

I look at him, serious. "I'm saying, really, thanks."

He pushes back in his seat, peers out the windshield. "Sometimes your head is the last place you need to be, you know? Or your house, for that matter. Am I right?"

I take in his relaxed shoulders, his unself-conscious face. How he's so easy and fun to be around.

"Did you sneak a smoke or something while I was in the bathroom? Because you are getting kind of deep, my friend."

I'm looking at him over the tops of imaginary glasses.

He touches his fingers to his chest. "Ah, such great depths inside here, Coastal, waiting to be plumbed."

And even though his smirk makes that statement sound dirty, getting out of the car, I'm aware how actually true I'm finding that to be about him.

Chapter Eleven

Feeling a little clearer-headed, I go up to my room, try to make sense of all my crazy writings from yesterday. There's still nothing to hang a song on: just a pile of random images and wounded metaphors that don't fit together. Or, at least, not enough of them do. And looking at the pages makes the Cloud of Sadness move a little closer, which I don't want. I'd rather joke with Benji than think about Trip. I shove the papers into the back of a desk drawer, decide to decipher them—and my feelings—later.

When my phone rings, though, I rush to it, relieved, and ready to accept whatever apology he offers.

Except it's Jilly.

"Hey. Where've you been?" I ask.

"Sorry, it's been really crazy here." She sighs. "I called as soon as I got a chance."

"Well, how was Savannah?"

"Oh, fun. But it kind of made things even crazier."

Her answer makes my bad mood creep even closer, but I don't know why. I listen while she tells me about her roommates and something to do with waiters at a Mexican restaurant, a fake ID. But it's kind of like listening to someone else tell you a dream. It's only interesting to her.

"Did you get my email?" I try.

"Yeah, I did. And god, I'm really sorry I haven't had a chance to write you back. But I think it's amazing that you're singing. Really, I do. When is the dance?"

Not that email, I grumble inside. *The other one. About Fabian.* "It's the same weekend as Mom's show, actually."

"Oh?"

"Yeah, isn't that funny? Me and her getting famous at the same time."

I'm just kidding around, but I can hear the shift in her even before she says anything.

"Is that what she said?"

"Who, Mom?"

"That she was going to get famous."

"No, she didn't."

"Well, good."

I pause. "Jilly, don't you think that for once she might—"

"She might be a *flop*, is what she might. Just like always."

"You don't know."

She quiets down. "You're right." She sounds tired. "I don't know. And I don't care. Maybe that's the whole thing. Listen, I should really—"

"But we haven't even talked about—" Fabian. Or Trip. Or Benji, even.

"I have to get to the dining hall in the next ten minutes or I'm eating out of the vending machine for dinner. Okay? We can talk more this weekend, I swear. I just wanted to hear your voice real quick, say hey. It's really busy up here right now."

"You said that."

"Jesus, Charlotte," she huffs. "Could you please try to handle a few things on your own for once?"

Which is not fair of her. And out of the blue. "I *am* handling things on my own. I'm so on my own it's not even funny! But I guess you're too busy *not* being on your own to even care."

I expect her to fight back—to try to convince me I'm wrong, to apologize for being so self-absorbed—but instead she says, wrung out, "Look, I'll call you later. But I have to hang up now."

I don't even have the energy to throw my phone down after that. Instead I just fall onto my bed and cry into my pillows.

Aside from passing notes with Benji in class, and avoiding any place I might see Trip, all I can do Wednesday is look forward to Thursday. But Thursday is the same thing, except after my last class I get to walk with Oliver to his car, hang out with people there a little before we drive to practice.

Things perk up, though, when Fabian shows up at rehearsal, for one because he is particularly cute today, and for two, we are both wearing vests. When he comes down the stairs into the rec room, we laugh at our matchy-matchiness, and I try to suppress the utter delight welling up in me, being twins with him.

Eli takes it a little differently. "Just make sure you each wear your *own* clothes next Friday," he grumbles.

"Oh, come on," Fabian pokes. "Don't you think some kind of uniform would be fun?" He grabs the sides of his vest and straightens his spine. "We look dapper."

We. He said "we." We are a *we* now.

Abe looks from Eli to Oliver, biting his lip. "What *are* we going to wear, man?"

"You're pretty much looking at it, if you ask me." Eli indicates his own T-shirt and faded gray cords, held up by a thick black belt buckled one loop off to the side.

"We shouldn't, you know, wear jackets or something?" Abe.

"I might, I don't know," Oliver says, like he hasn't already thought about every detail of his outfit. "I think it's important to at least make an effort. It's annoying when you go to a concert and not even the band seems like they bothered."

He's trying to sound indifferent, but this is actually a huge point of contention for Oliver. He practically squirms with discomfort if he sees an *audience* member in Crocs or cargo shorts at a concert. And I have never seen a boy with so many accessories; he has more belts and shoes than I think even Darby.

"You want this one in a dress?" Eli jerks a thumb in my direction.

Oliver glances at me, looks away again.

My face gets hot for no reason. "I'm not wearing a dress."

"No," Oliver agrees, too fast.

Jerk.

"Everybody's going to look great," Fabian butts in cheerily. "Let's just agree that we won't show up like we're pig wrestlers, and everyone's personalities will come through naturally. It'll be good. Right?"

A sunbeam spreads inside me. Forget Trip. Truly.

Oliver turns to me. "We think you should do 'Disappear.'"

Um. *What?* And when did they talk about this? "But we only have, like, a week to practice left, and you're the—"

"It's the first one you wrote."

"Yeah, but I wrote it for *you* to sing."

"Yeah, but you're better than I am."

We stare at each other. It takes me a full minute to process what he's just said. I look at Fabian. He gives me an easygoing thumbs-up. Even Eli is nodding.

"Well, if that's what you want . . ."

And apparently that decides it. I take my place behind the mic. We practice the whole set list a couple of times, and by the end of rehearsal, it feels like we're actually going to be pretty good.

When Fabian offers me another ride home, it's more than the band that's good. Sparkle spreads along my spine, and going out to his car I think I bounce.

"You up for Saturday again?" he wants to know when we get in.

Sparkle. Sparkle. Sparkle. "Absolutely."

"Great, then. I'll call you, but it'll be around the same time. Taryn and Sylvia will be there again. They said to say hey."

And I don't know if it's being happy after feeling so awful, or that today we even *look* like we belong beside each other, or the dozen pleased looks I got from him while I was singing, or Darby nagging me to show him how I feel, or that he's so, so, so wonderful . . . but when we get to my house, before I climb out of the car, I unbuckle and half reach, half lunge around to squeeze him in a hug and plant a quick kiss on what could be construed as either the side of his mouth or the lower half of his cheek, depending. He kisses my cheek too (more my cheek than my mouth), and his freest arm goes around my back. I am lined with double rainbows. Diamonds from the blue. Glittering sunshine through my bones.

I don't know if it's the glitter-glow of Fabian, or just enough distance from my fight with Trip, but Friday things feel a lot more normal. Eli high-fives me when I walk past him on the way to Algebra II, and even Whitney smiles meekly at me in the hall. Looking up and making eye contact with other people, instead of being caught up in my self-pity and self-absorption, I realize things really aren't that bad. When Benji passes me a note wondering what I'm doing tonight, I don't even feel embarrassed telling him Hannah's decreed it Family Game Night.

Can I come? he wants to know.

No. You'll just hit on my stepsister.

The scrawny little one? Or the grouchy sarcastic one?

Probably both, knowing you.

Don't think so. Not my type.

I tell him maybe he'll have better luck finding one of his types at those Lake House parties I know he goes to.

Not unless you're there.
Ha hardy ha.

In the parking lot after school, while Gretchen and I wait for Darby to finish hugging good-bye to about thirty of her friends, I try not to see Trip going past in the front seat of Lily's car. Try not to see him not even looking for me.

So that really *is* how it is now.

But Saturday, I practically run to rehearsal. As soon as Fabian shows up, I'm hot-buttery warm all over again. I don't worry anymore does he notice me like I notice him. I *know* he does, because half the time when I look up, our eyes meet and we smile together.

"Pick you up around eight thirty?" he says after rehearsal is over.

"Sounds good to me" is all I say back, because it's all I need to say. For now.

I try to explain it to Darby while she's fussing over my hair again back at home.

"You mean, you don't get that *thrill* when you see him?"

"Of course I do, dummy. It's just . . . more like a spreading-out tingle than, you know, a sickening roller-coaster ride."

"Dump him," she says, twisting an end of my hair around her fat curling iron.

"Are you crazy? I like him. And we aren't even going out yet."

"All I know is," she sasses, holding up a hand, "if the tingle vanishes, I do too. I mean I am out. The. Door."

"You and how many boyfriends again?" I tease.

She jabs me in the back with her knee. "You and Gretchen don't know all my business."

I roll my eyes at her in the mirror. "I still get the thrill, don't worry. But this is even better. It's like I just want to be with him all the time. Doing—whatever. I would be happy just watching him eat a sandwich."

"Oh god," she groans, making a big production out of it.

"You'll see, tinglepants. It's not always just about sex."

"You and how many boyfriends again?" she drawls.

And we both crack up.

Darby's talk makes me all ultra-self-conscious about tonight, though. I'm obsessed with what she said about things tingling while we drive together. My thighs actually feel like they're on fire, wanting him to reach over and put his hand down on one of them. But it's not like I'm going to jump him. I don't care what Darby says; I'm not that kind of girl. Wouldn't matter if I were, because about three minutes after we peer over the railing to the dance floor, Taryn and Sylvia show up.

My whole body is so focused on Fabian while they talk, it's

like some kind of weird hallucination when I see, of all people, Benji walking past our table.

"Hang on just a second," I interrupt Sylvia. Seeing her confused face, I try over: "Sorry, I just—" I look farther back. "I think I just saw someone I know."

I arch my neck to get a better view. And then—yep—there he is. Looking straight at me and raising his glass. The surreal jarringness of seeing him here makes me flush. And now I have to go say hello.

I move to the back, sit down next to him. "What are you doing here?"

He slants his eyes at me. "You look nice."

It's very Lish of me, but I still feel it: the idea of Fabian maybe watching me talking to Benji, and maybe feeling a little jealous.

"I thought you were going to some party at the lake," I toss out.

Benji shrugs. "I know somebody in the band."

I'm surprised. "You do?"

But he clearly doesn't want to talk about it. "Girl I used to date. We're still friends, so."

I'm weirdly stunned. I wouldn't've thought, from what I've heard, that any girl Benji went out with would want to be his friend after, or vice versa. But then again, now that I know him, maybe it doesn't seem that far-fetched.

I grab the sleeve of his army jacket. "Come meet my friends."

"It's cool; I'll just hang out—"

"They're not going to bite you, dummy. Come on."

I lead Benji back to the table and introduce him to everyone. Fabian gives me a curious little brow furrow as we shift our stools around to make space. Within seconds, Benji is at ease with everyone. Seated beside two pretty girls (well, one pretty girl and one formidably *cool* one), he flirts and flatters into oblivion. At first I'm mad, a little, that he doesn't act even half into me, but then it's hilarious, his efforts, since neither Taryn nor Sylvia would be interested in him even if he were a girl. Fabian and I trade amused little looks, and at one point my knee bumps against his under the table. When he doesn't move away, I don't either.

After a few deadpan looks, Benji eventually figures out that Taryn and Sylvia aren't going to flirt back, so he switches to telling stories. He cracks Taryn up so bad she almost falls off her stool. And this, somehow, gets Sylvia into a joking mood too. Her wild laughing is something else.

After another round of "Hooo boys" from Sylvia, Taryn grabs me and Benji by the wrists. "The band!" she cries. "You have to see them! Come on! They're so fun!"

I remember that I am intensely curious to see this ex-girlfriend of Benji's, so we follow Taryn down to the dance floor, where—she's right—the band is good. It's a different sound than the group playing last weekend: better. They've got about seven members, all with different instruments, and they all rock. When a surprisingly muscled girl with a tattoo of a dragon wrapped around her shaved skull steps up to take the mic, Benji points. "That's her."

I look at her, then him, then her again.

"I can see why she dumped you." I try to sound funny.

The briefest wince crosses his face. "She didn't want anything serious."

I realize Benji might've actually been hurt by this girl, and it makes me immediately dislike her, no matter how righteous she is sounding right now.

So I change the subject, though I have to say it loud over the music: "You still friends enough with her to ask her how I can get Sad Jackal up on that stage?"

A crafty twinkle glimmers in his eyes. "Only if you pretend to be my girlfriend."

I laugh, glad to see him back to his joking self. "Guess she'd better see us dancing out here first, huh?"

"You said it!" he shouts, and starts thrashing around like a whacko.

I jump up and down alongside him. Taryn bounces closer, pulling Fabian over. We all smile and flail, inspired by Benji and the intensity of the band. They switch singers again—Benji's ex falls back to pick up a flute—and the new song rises around us. Swept up in the pulsing, I grab Fabian on the shoulder.

"This is fantastic!" I shout into his ear.

He squeezes my hand. And we stay dancing like that for the rest of the night.

"You mean you didn't kiss him *again*?" Darby groans at the end of my bed when I get home.

I yank a brush through my knotty hair. "Not everything has to be all hoochie and gross."

"Not everything has to be all old-fashioned and boring, either. What's his deal? Is he gay?"

I level my gaze at her through the mirror. "He is *not* gay. If he were, he'd've asked Oliver out and not me. And maybe I didn't even want him to kiss me at that point—did you think about that?"

"Maybe because you really like Benji instead."

"Benji and I are just friends."

"That's your problem, Char. You're friends with all these boys . . ."

I put down my brush. "Stop telling me what my problem is all the time. And besides, Fabian and I are more than friends."

"Oh yeah? Says who?"

"It just *feels* like more than friends," I rush. "I don't care what you think. When we look at each other, I just know. And I like that we're moving slowly. It's more romantic."

Darby makes a disgusted noise from deep in her throat.

"We're in the band together," I excuse. "It makes sense that he's being a little cautious. How would it be if we broke up?" Though really, I hope this doesn't prevent our hooking up for too much longer.

Darby raps her knuckles on my forehead. "How would it be if you *even got together first?*"

I swat her away.

"It will be *great,*" I tell her. "I know it's going to be just great."

Chapter Twelve

The week before the dance is both vomitously exciting and vomitously nerve-racking.

Monday after school, every single car in both the upper and lower lots has got a flyer tucked under its windshield, advertising the Halloween dance. The name of the DJ is bigger than ours, but we're still on there, making everything incredibly real.

At rehearsal that afternoon, we spend almost half an hour buzzing about the publicity, but once we start practicing, we nail every single song. We decide on the final lineup, then go through it, serious.

The whole time, even when I'm not singing, there's a thread

between Fabian and me—flowing through the music and binding us together. It feels so strong, I wonder if the other guys can see it. They definitely seem affected by *some* kind of excited magic. By the end of the first run-through, Eli is high-fiving Oliver and Abe, who are both arm-punching each other with pride. Fabian and Eli squeeze each other in a hug, and Abe does some kind of robot move that ends in a salute to me. We go through the set again, twice. At the end of practice, I leap up and hug all of them around the neck. But Fabian gets—and gives—the biggest hug of all.

Wednesday at lunch, I'm walking out to Oliver's car to hang with the guys when Lish and her friends drive past in a stupid hulking SUV. I see Bronwyn in the back, wearing these giant sunglasses that are identical to the ones Lish has on in the passenger's seat. I don't know if Lish sees me. I don't know if she cares. And I don't know if I care. I also don't know, climbing up to take a seat on the hood of Oliver's car, whether it's cool or weird that she doesn't know I'm really in Sad Jackal now and not just managing. She'll find out at the dance on Friday, I suppose. My stomach twists, unsure what she'll think. And why I'm wondering about it at all.

Late Thursday night, right after our last amazing rehearsal, a text shows up from Trip. *Good luck 2mrw*, it says. And I'm hit by how foreign it is, hearing from Trip, how not hearing from him has become my new normal. I text back *Thx*, and then wait. Nothing else. I decide, if he's not going to say any more, then neither am I.

It's Friday after school when the panic hits me.

"Gretchen, I need the car this afternoon," I tell her as she drives us home.

"Why?"

"Or take us over to Urban Outfitters. Please. I have, like, nothing to wear tonight."

Darby claps her hands and squeals. "Charlotte makeover, here we come!"

"I was going to go—" Gretchen starts.

I lean forward, grabbing the back of her seat. "Please, Gretchen, I'm begging you. I'll do all your chores for a week."

"Two weeks."

"Two weeks is no fair. But I'll—" I calculate exactly how much allowance I have stored away. "I'll get you whatever you want if we go. Under a hundred dollars," I say fast, because otherwise she'd pull out some two-hundred-dollar jacket she doesn't even need.

"Fine," she grudges, though I know she loves shopping.

Twenty minutes later we're at Urban Outfitters. And of course everything is awful and stupidly expensive.

"Here, Charlotte." Darby holds up some flowered thing.

"You must be joking," I growl at her.

I find some jeans I think might work, but when I try them on they are totally no way. Gretchen already has four different things that look awesome on her, and Darby's found this killer dress that's way on sale. I hate myself. I want to cry.

At the register, Darby's shocked. "You're not getting *any-thing*?"

"Whatever. I'll just be myself, right?" This is so incredibly depressing.

While I pay for Gretchen's stuff, I hear them murmuring together behind me. *Yeah, I know. Somebody just take me out into a field and shoot me.*

Maybe, I think, I can find something in our closet that Jilly didn't take with her to college. But the idea of wearing Jilly's rejects onstage is almost worse.

"Come on," Gretchen says when I hand off her bag. She hooks her arm in mine, and Darby takes the other side.

"Where are we going?"

"You're gonna be a rock star, sister. We've got to make sure you look like one."

"More importantly, *feel* like one," Gretchen adds, squeezing me a little.

• • •

They take me to this quiet, old-lady-seeming place in Avondale called Finders Keepers. I've never been in here, but Darby is convinced we're going to find a secret stash of something "truly knockout" that is also still me. The two of them are on a mission, pushing me toward the long-sleeve tops and flanking other racks themselves. When we reconvene, I'm surprised to have found two possibilities: one a dark-green vintage shirt that ties in a big bow at the neck, and the other a long, patchworky top.

Darby takes them out of my hands and places them back, making a face.

"Come with us," she orders. Both she and Gretchen are carrying huge piles.

It feels like I try on eighty things. Dresses and skirts and layered tops and jackets. Most of the time I think what they've chosen is ridiculous, and once I walk out of the dressing room to show them, they agree. But when I put on the sailor pants they found, under a houndstooth minidress, Darby purses her lips and presses her finger to her chin. Gretchen's brows are drawn together.

"With leggings, you think?" Gretchen says to Darby.

"And boots."

"Charlotte, take off the pants and go try that jacket on again over the dress. The frayed-up one."

I am not sure this will look any better than anything else, but I obey.

"Perfect," Darby says when I come back out. Gretchen is pleased too.

When I'm back in my regular clothes, Gretchen goes through everything and hands Darby the rejects while she takes out the keepers. It's like I'm hardly there.

"You'll wear the dress and the jacket, and I've got a scarf. Leggings underneath, and your combat boots."

"I told them I wasn't wearing a dress."

Darby looks stricken. "But it's cute, right? I mean, it's totally the best one."

"It is," I agree. "I didn't think it would be, but you're right. It's just funny, is all. Oliver's going to croak."

It takes us almost a half hour to get home in the traffic, which means I don't have much time to get ready, since we have to be at the school early for sound check. Darby hurries me into the shower and sets up her stuff in my room. While I'm rinsing out my hair, I try not to think about how nervous I feel. Try not to think about Fabian and what will happen between us tonight at the dance, try also not to think about all those people watching me sing, including Trip, there with Lily. It's weird that he's not going to be up onstage with us. He should be over at Oliver's right now, both of them getting ready. But if he were, I probably wouldn't be singing at all, would still be just a girl in the audience, cheering for her friends.

Once I'm out of the shower, Darby is all over me with her hair dryer, and then the straightening iron and the curling iron, not to mention brushes and blushes and gloss. Because there isn't time to even argue, I let her do this smoky eye shadow thing on me and consent to some red lipstick. Even this hastily done, it looks pretty good.

"Okay, be awesome," she says, squeezing me in a hug when Oliver honks out in the driveway. "And for god's sake, don't humiliate me."

She is partly joking, partly serious. I roll my eyes at her and head out the door.

I've been to school dances before, but certainly never early. Never when the gym is completely empty and there's only Mr. Cornell there, plus the school super making sure everything's unlocked. Picturing it, an hour from now, full of people, my anxiety wells up in me again. I think Oliver, Abe, and Eli are equally nervous, because while I help them bring in their equipment, not one of us says a word.

Fabian breaks the tense feeling in the air when he shows up on his own, doing a little jig step. I go straight to him and grab him in a hug.

"It's going to be great," he assures me, patting me on the back.

"You think so?"

"You look awesome," he says, stepping back. "You should wear dresses more."

I blush. Oliver said a similar thing (well, all he said was "Niiiiice," but still). I tell Fabian he looks good, too. *We* look good. Together. He goes to the stage, and I follow.

The guys fuss around a bit, trying to get the sound right, so I sit on the edge, swinging my legs and watching my knees. I take deep breaths, try to focus on the moment. So much has changed in the last several weeks, it's almost crazy. I wouldn't have believed it if someone told me, when school started, that this would be happening. And then the thought of things changing for the better makes me remember something I haven't thought about in days.

"Going to make a phone call," I tell the guys, heading outside. She doesn't answer, of course, but I leave a message.

"Hey, Mom, I just wanted to say good luck tonight. Big night for both of us, and I can't wait to tell you how my show goes and to hear all about yours, too. Call me tomorrow, okay? Bye."

Outside, on my own, the campus dark all around me but the sky still tinted indigo, I force myself to clear my mind of everything. But even after several deep breaths—after the nervousness subsides—I can't clear away the glow of being with Fabian tonight. The thought of him is the quiet, flickering spark that lights everything up, just before it all explodes.

Ten minutes until doors open, and we're trying not to be nervous wrecks. We've been hanging around the gym, attempting to not look anxious, all of us jerking our heads up whenever the door opens. We watch girls in the Platinum club come in to set up their ticket-taking table, and then load some other folding tables with soft drinks and two huge watercoolers. Finally, when the DJ arrives, Oliver goes up to shake his hand, tell him we're ready, but the guy hardly gives Oliver a glance. All he says to us is that he's going to play for about half an hour, forty-five minutes, to warm things up, and then we're on.

"You guys can hang out in the greenroom if you want," he says over his shoulder as he hops up the steps to the stage.

We don't really know where he's talking about until Mr. Cornell pauses with his wires and points somewhere back behind the curtains. We thank him and scurry—*be cool, be cool*—into the fluorescent-lit room, crowded with two couches and a scarred coffee table.

"When do you think we should go back out?" Abe asks Oliver. "Ten minutes? Fifteen?"

"I'm staying back here until we play, man."

I'm surprised. "But dancing's our favorite part."

He twists his mouth, jerks his head in a no. "Afterwards, yeah, but—"

"It's cooler if we're *revealed*," Eli agrees.

I wasn't planning on just sitting back here with them, only able to imagine people arriving and dancing. I was kind of relying on having something to *do*, but oh well. At least Eli has a pack of cards.

Eight o'clock, eight thirty, and we can hear more and more people arriving. Eight forty-five, and the DJ's still playing a steady stream of dance hits, trying to get everyone going. It's almost nine before Mr. Cornell comes back and tells us that the DJ is going to introduce us in about ten minutes. We've been concentrating so hard on playing spades—not talking except to call tricks—that when he comes in we all jump about an inch out of our seats.

"Thanks, Mr. Cornell." Oliver waves like butter wouldn't melt within an inch of him, even though his knee is thumping up and down.

"Okay, guys," Abe breathes, worried eyes glancing at all of us.

We nod back. Under the table, I reach over and grab Fabian's hand, squeeze it. He squeezes—strong and warm—right back.

Eli stretches, takes a flask out of his jacket. "Time for a good luck toast, then."

"What's in it?" Abe wants to know.

"Liquid courage." Eli hands it to him after taking his own big sip.

"To the beginning." Oliver takes his turn.

Fabian holds the flask up, toasting all of us, takes a swig.

I don't really drink alcohol, but I don't want to jinx our good luck, either. And besides, then my lips will be where Fabian's were.

"You boys are the best," I say, my eyes lingering on Fabian's just a moment before I tip the flask back. I nearly cough it all back up, though, when Taryn suddenly pokes her head around the door, waving like crazy.

"Here they are!" she squeals. She pulls Sylvia into the room, plus a tall, wavy-haired guy with giant black glasses. "We had to sneak around the back to get in here," she whispers, pretending to tiptoe like a spy. "Very tight security. You must be cool."

"What are you doing back here?" Fabian's face is full of delight. He moves right past Taryn, who's already hugging me. Over her shoulder, I watch as he puts his arms around the new guy. And then kisses him. On the lips.

Mr. Cornell is back in the doorway then. He's not happy to see the extra people, and I'm not sure Eli gets the flask into his back pocket fast enough. But I only sort of vaguely register this, him saying, "You're just about on."

Really, I can't see past the colossal wall of shock that's just hit me.

And then Fabian's there, next to me. "Don't worry, it's going to be great." He grabs my hand and waggles it around, trying to loosen me up. "*You're* great," he tells me, but it's like the end of an echo.

"Fabian's told me a lot about you," Lover Boy says. "I'm Drew."

Somehow my hand accepts his. Drew. *That* Drew. The one Fabian mentioned going to the movies with a few weekends ago. The Drew who, Fabian said, thought our Van Halen conversation was funny when Fabian repeated it for him. Drew, who I thought was just Fabian's *friend*.

"Nice to meet you," I manage.

"Okay, okay." Mr. Cornell beckons furiously from the doorway. "It's time."

I move into the dark hall, shuffling like Frankenstein. Behind me I hear Taryn squealing, Eli and Oliver high-fiving, Abe pounding Oliver's back. Under that, though, louder than anything, I hear good-looking, too-nice Drew murmuring something to Fabian. There's the distinct sound of their lips connecting again, and I feel myself sink. About ten feet away is the curtain, and beyond it are shouts and screams and applause as the DJ says, "—in a public debut you'll be glad to say you were at: Sad Jackal."

I know I am absolutely going to throw up.

But I don't. Instead I stand there, hovering in the wings, watching as Abe, Fabian, Eli, and Oliver play the first song. With the stage lights shining down on them, it's almost easy to forget I even know them.

From here, because the lights aren't shining straight in my eyes, I can also look out and see the audience—part of it, anyway.

Enough to see Taryn and Sylvia and Drew, right up front. I close my eyes. Darby had already guessed right, and I was too stupid to see it. Does everybody get to have someone else, except me? And why, on top of everything else, does Drew have to have better legs than me?

My misery makes the first song fly by. The notes fade out, applause fills the gym, and now it's my turn. Oliver looks into the wings for me, expectant, and gives me a triumphant smile. I feel myself stepping out under the lights to take his place at the mic. I can't even look at Fabian.

But I can't see anyone out in the crowd now either, which helps, a little. Of course I know right where Taryn, Sylvia, and Fabian's boyfriend are standing, but it doesn't matter. I shut my eyes, close out everything but the music starting behind me. The words spool out with more meaning than they've ever had: *"A bag of peanuts in your hand; searching for something you used to understand."*

The sounds from Fabian's synthesizer sweep up and over me, and it's like I don't even have to make an effort to sing the next part: *"Will you look at me? Will you really ever look at me? Will you look at the real me? When will you see enough?"*

Eli was wrong about performing. Being up here makes it *easier*, not harder. At Oliver's house I was still me, Charlotte—Oliver's oldest friend, the dumpy, amicable girl who manages the band. Now, up here, in front of this gaping blackness, the lights and the music holding me up, I can disappear from everything except the crushing sadness I feel. I don't know what the people out there are thinking—I don't know where Trip is, if he's even here; or how excellently Fabian thinks I'm doing—and I don't care. All I care about is how utterly broken I feel right this second. Up here, like this, the low singing in me can be the all of it.

I haul the last repeating lines from a deep, breathy part of my throat: *"Now all I see is you walking away from me. Walking away from me. Walking away . . ."*

I don't think anything has ever been more true.

When the final vibrations of "Cage Song" dissipate around us, an enormous wave of cheering washes over me. Oliver moves up beside me to take his place at the mic again, touches my elbow lightly. "Awesome, Spider," he whispers.

Since my voice is only decoration on "Foreign Tongue"— not carrying the whole message—I'm a lot more conscious of my surroundings. Of Abe, for example, never taking his eyes off Eli, and how Eli gives him signals with these funny little side-jerks of his head. Of Fabian's head bent in concentration, curved over like some kind of beautiful flower. I can't shut my eyes, so I turn them out into the audience. It seems that no one is dancing out there, at least not the few people that I can sort of see. Since this isn't really a song to dance to anyway, I'm not sure whether their stillness is a good or a bad thing.

The balloon of approving sound comes at us again when we finish, though. I don't sing on the next song, so I beeline to the safety of the wings, where I can press my hands to my face and swallow down the unforgiving lump in my throat.

But I can't cry yet, because I have to go back out there again in a couple of songs. For bravery, I fix my eyes on Oliver. He'll want to know, later, how he did, so I need to pay attention. Watching him so fiercely helps, some: noting how he stands away from the mic but leans his face close to it when he sings, how strong his hands look while he plays. For a brief moment I wonder how Whitney feels, watching her ex up there slaying everyone with his awesomeness.

But that leads to thoughts about Fabian's boyfriend probably thinking the same things about him. And what Lily would think, if Trip were up there now. I close my eyes against it, but all that swirls there is Fabian's smile, and those lips of his pressing on someone else's.

Soon enough, it's time for me to go back out, but before we start the last song, Oliver leans into the mic.

"We wanna thank you all for listening, for being such a great crowd for us. We're Sad Jackal, and I'm Oliver Drake. On the drums is Abe Wallace . . ." He goes around, introduces Eli, Fabian.

I can only press my lips together in what I hope somehow

represents a look of appreciation when he calls me out. Nothing is going to make me smile tonight. But beyond the lights—is it just me?—the sound of applause seems to get even louder as he says my name. I picture Benji putting his fingers between his teeth and whistling. It almost helps. But mainly I want this whole night to be finished.

The first chords for "Disappear" are crushing. They always have been for me; this is one of Sad Jackal's saddest, and best, songs. After hearing Oliver sing it so much—after losing myself in the depths of his voice, the way he makes it seem like it's a secret he's embarrassed by, but unable to keep from you—I'd forgotten, mostly, that it was actually my song. That these words came from somewhere inside me, and that all that feeling that comes out of him so well—it came out of me first.

Now, tonight, it could be no one else's.

"Would you help me disappear . . ."

I close my eyes, drop away into it.

And then it's over. The gym is roaring, we're taking our bows, and we're heading off the stage.

In the greenroom, Oliver and Abe are actually hugging. Eli gives Fabian a hearty handshake and pats everyone proudly on the back.

"And *you*," Eli says, coming over to me with open arms. I

stand there while he pounds me in a hug/thump. "Getting up there and stealing the show."

I try not to mutter. I am trying to be happy for them, for us. "You guys were the great ones. Really."

Now that we're done, though, it just means we have to go out there. See people. Hang out. Dance. There's no way I can stand it.

Eli's flask comes out again and everyone takes a swig except me. They debate how long we should wait back here, how much time will be cool but not too.

"I think I'm going to go, actually," I say.

"You okay?" Fabian asks. He hooks his arm around my neck. "You absolutely rocked, you know," he whispers to me, closer. The warmth of it—how I thought, just yesterday even, that this kind of thing meant something—makes me clench my jaw tight.

"Too much adrenaline or something," I say weakly. "I just don't feel—"

"You need some water? Here, sit down."

And I really can't stand it. This connection. Of *friends*. I shrug him off. "I'm going to go find Gretchen," I tell Oliver. "See if she can give me a ride home."

He looks confused, then let down, and then like he wants me to think he doesn't care. "Well, okay." But he's disappointed that I'm not going to revel in our success.

"I'll walk you out." Fabian.

"No, really." I hold up my hand. "You guys stay back here. Be cool. Make 'em wait. Tell Taryn and Sylvia I said bye, though, okay?"

I bolt. My held-in tears really just aren't going to stay put anymore.

When I find Gretchen, she's mashed in a giant throng of seniors near the center of the gym, all grinding along to the song the DJ's playing. I duck under arms and elbows, shoulders, find her hand, grab it. For a second she looks like she's going to slap me—maybe she thinks I'm the Wrestler—but then she registers my face and wraps me up in a giant congratulatory hug. All I can hear is her squealing, and the pulsing bass. I stand still, wait for her to stop.

It takes a couple of tries, but once I'm able to get Gretchen to understand that I think I'm sick to my stomach, I have to give her credit. She hugs her friends good-bye and guides me through the crowd.

While we're squeezing between dark clumps of people, look-ing for Darby, I'm aware of grinning faces nodding in my direc-tion, hands patting my shoulders and back. The heat and the sound and the closeness of everyone really is making me feel sick now—does one slug of whiskey really affect you that much?—so I stare down at the floor, into the dark.

Next thing I know we're outside. Darby wants to stay, and

will get a ride home from a friend. Being out in the cold, clean air feels amazing. The noise from the gym trails behind us and disappears, and then we're to the safety of the car.

"You're cool to do this," I tell Gretchen, leaning my head against the seat.

"Eh. If I stuck around I'd have to give about five drunk people a ride home. So, you saved me. Plus, Jilly's done it for me before. You'll do it for Darby too, I'm sure."

I'm curious about what, exactly, my big sister did for Gretchen, and when, but mostly I don't want to talk, or think, about anything. I roll down the window, lean out a little to watch the few stars that I can see overhead.

"You were incredible, by the way," Gretchen says beside me. "It was like I didn't even know you. I mean, I didn't know you could do that."

"Neither did I."

And all I know is, I never want to do it like that again.

Chapter Thirteen

"Ma, I'm not kidding, you would not believe how amazing they were," Darby says, twisting around in her chair at the kitchen table to talk to Hannah, who is making us pancakes. Gretchen is still asleep.

"Everyone was talking about it," Darby says. "No one could shut up about you, Char. You probably have, like, fifty friend requests this morning."

"Well, they'll be disappointed when they find out I'm barely ever on there."

"Nobody'll be disappointed," she says, "about anything. The mystery is great. It's like you're this incredibly complicated, deep, secret girl with all these powerhouse surprises. I mean, I've lived with you for two years and I had no idea. You shouldn't hide that shit under a—"

"Darby," Hannah warns from the stove.

"I'm just saying, Ma. Did you have any idea Charlotte was this mega rock star? That she could be this mind-blowingly *cool*?"

Hannah turns to look at me, spatula still in her hand. "I've always thought Charlotte was cool."

Nice of her, but apparently not an acceptable answer for Darby. "But I mean, don't you think she should—"

"Hello? Darby?" I wave my hand in front of her face. "Still in the room here."

"What I mean," she huffs, twisting around to face me, "is that you're so—I don't know. Removed. Always with your door closed and always writing in that notebook. When you got up onstage and sang like that, it was like you were shining out and pulling everyone in at the same time."

"I was not shining." I sink down in my own chair. "I was miserable up there." A pang, remembering Fabian and Drew. Kissing. Ugh.

"Well, whatever. Even your misery was compelling."

Hannah brings plates of steaming pancakes and puts them down in front of us. In the distraction of butter, syrup, taking our first bites, I consider this. *Even your misery was compelling.*

"Well, thanks. I mean, it's nice to hear."

"You're going to be hearing it a lot, girl." Darby stuffs a drippy bite into her mouth, then points at me with the empty tines of her fork. "Because I bet you SGA is already talking Winter Formal."

After breakfast I have four messages on my phone. Four messages. In a twelve hour period. I don't think I've had four messages all semester.

1. Taryn. Practically screaming into the phone. At midnight. I can hardly understand her but she's obviously happy. "I'm so glad I know you!" she shrieks at the end.

2. Fabian. On his way home from Oliver's house afterward. Telling me again how great I did. Asking me to call when I wake up.

3. A long stretch of only muffled sounds, at first. Then, in the background, the old recording we did of "For Your Face." From when Trip was in the band. Nobody says anything. The message cuts off.

4. Lish. Ten minutes ago. "Hey, you. Wow. I loved seeing you at the dance. I miss you! This semester is crazy! Call

me if you want to go off campus for lunch or something, okay?"

I have no idea which message to be most puzzled about, which one to respond to first, so I put down the phone and take a long, hot shower. I stand there, letting the water pound my skin and watching it disappear down the drain. When I'm out and dressed, I dial Taryn.

"Hi hi hi!" she says right away.

"Hi there."

"Are you better? We were all so bummed you had to leave."

"Yeah. I just, I don't know. Too much stimulation or something."

"Oh yeah, I understand that. Totally."

I have a hard time picturing anything overstimulating Taryn, but I don't say so.

"But you were so supercool up there on the stage. I couldn't believe your composure. So dramatic and affecting and just— uber-wow."

"Well, thanks. I was—"

"Which is why I want to ask you. Sylvia and I were talking afterwards and, well, anyway, I wanted to ask you just in case, because, you know, maybe you would want to, I don't know, but we're wondering if you might also want to sing with *our* little band."

It takes me a second to process what she's actually asking me.

"Gosh, that is really cool of you," I say.

"Well, we just think your energy is so good. And Fabian told us you wrote those songs? Incredible. I mean, you wouldn't have to do that for us, of course, but still knowing that you *can* . . ."

"It's just that I'm not sure I have enough time to—"

"We could absolutely work around you. Absolutely. We know how that is. I mean, you think college is awesome because you get to pick your schedule and everything, but they don't tell you that you still have a ton of work outside of class."

I'm surprised. I didn't realize Taryn and Sylvia were in college.

"What year are you?"

"Oh, this is my first semester. I'm not sure I'm going to keep going, actually, because maybe this isn't my thing. I might take some time off and work in a nonprofit for a while or something, maybe teach music lessons—"

Taryn's plan sounds like my plan, a little. But I still can't join them.

"Like I said, it's really nice of you to ask me," I tell her. "But I just don't think I can right now."

She's quiet a second. "Okay. Well, you can't say we didn't try, right? Let's go get smoothies or something sometime."

Smoothies? "That sounds like fun."

"All right. Well, I gotta tell Sylvia the bad news, I guess. Let me know if you change your mind, okay? Any. Time. Because you're really great."

"Thanks, Taryn. Really."

"Okay, well, bye!"

After that, it's a puzzle. I'm not sure, still, what to say to Fabian. And the strange no-message message was obviously from Trip, but I can't figure out how I feel about his call, let alone whether to call back. And I have no idea how to talk to Lish right now.

I text Oliver instead. *You are proud about last night, right?*

Right away: *Yes, you? Feel better?*

Was just nervous I think.

You didn't need to be.

Thx you neither.

He doesn't say anything else, so I abandon the phone and pull out my books. Every now and then, though, I catch myself gazing into space, thinking about what Taryn said about my being great.

When the doorbell rings at four o'clock, pulling me out of a cross-eyed black hole of reading, for a bizarre second I figure it must be Fabian at the door. Checking on me. Maybe even coming to explain that after last night he realized he really wants me, not Drew, but he just didn't get a chance to say it because I left so fast.

But then the giggling and shuffling around outside registers. With everything going on, I forgot that today is actually Halloween. Ridiculous, I know, because we just played the Halloween dance, but I guess I didn't think about it. I hear Hannah open the door, her exclamations of delight. "Trick or treat" is hollered, and miniature Milky Ways plunk into plastic pumpkins and pillowcases.

I consider going downstairs to help her. That used to be our job—mine and Jilly's—when she got too old for trick-or-treating and I didn't want to be anywhere that Jilly wasn't. I wonder if Jilly misses it today. Maybe she's dressing up tonight, or—more likely—spending today recovering from a big Halloween party last night on campus. She's probably glad not to be sitting at home, pretending to be scared by kids in werewolf costumes. The doorbell rings again, and I hear Hannah's laugh. Helping her just wouldn't be the same as doing it with Jilly. I text my sister *Happy Halloweiner!*, after one of our favorite picture books, but there's no reply. She's probably out, which makes staying in, without her, feel even worse.

Monday morning, Darby comes crashing into my room. "Come on, missy. We've got some work to do."

"What the hell?" I can barely open my eyes enough to glare at her. It can't be six thirty yet. "How are you even *up*?"

She yanks the quilt off me, squares her hands on her hips. "We've got forty-five minutes before we have to leave for your big entrance."

I pull my quilt back over my head. "You make the entrance. I'm sleeping."

"Come on," she whines, plopping down on the edge of my bed. "Everybody's been wondering about you all weekend. They're going to be paying attention this morning. Don't you want them to see you in something besides jeans and hoodies?"

I turn over, look at her squarely. "I'm not going to pretend. I'm not cool, and you need to live with that."

"You don't have to tell me twice," she snaps. But knowing she can't manipulate me with temper tantrums makes her recover quickly. "It's like they say on *What Not to Wear*," she tries again. "It's not *not* you. It's helping people actually see the real you."

"The real me is going to sleep for another ten minutes."

She slaps the edge of the bed. "Fine. But at least let me pick out your outfit."

She's not wrong, exactly, about people paying attention. When we get to school, I see Oliver already standing by his car. Abe is there, of course, and Eli, and a whole lot more kids than have ever been there before. So maybe I'm not sorry that Darby made me put on my new sailor pants and a navy striped sweater. Earrings.

"Okay, go get 'em, champ." She straightens the collar of my coat. I brush her hands away but hear her giggle when I stride off, swinging my hips in this exaggerated strut. For at least a few steps.

When I'm about ten yards away from Oliver's car, a girl in a red jacket and a chunky knit cap separates herself and heads toward me. It's Lish. Coming over to give me a hug. I can't remember the last time I even saw her, and now here she is.

"Wow, right?" she says, bringing me closer in. There are so many people, they spread around three other parking spaces. Who *are* they all?

"Did you get my call?" Lish tugs on my wrist.

"Yeah, I'm sorry I didn't get to call you back."

She slides past the outer rings of kids, pulling me with her into the inner circle, where Oliver and Eli are.

"So do you want to go to lunch? Mondays we usually go to Duck's."

I nod, but not because I'm agreeing to go. More like, in my processing the "we" in that sentence, I understand she doesn't mean just me and her.

Eli holds out his fist for me to bump it. "There's my girl," he says.

"This is Lish," I tell him. Because I don't know how else to introduce her.

"Yeah, we met."

She giggles. He watches her with an interested glimmer.

"I was telling Eli that you guys should totally get in touch with the guys at this place WonderRoot. They do all kinds of awesome shows," Lish gushes.

"You hang out there?" I try to sound casual but am mostly wondering how she knows a venue that I don't.

"Oh." She flicks her eyes at Eli but pretends she's just looking into the air, trying to remember. "Kiaya's brother knows some guys who do stuff there."

So you haven't actually been, have you? I want to say. But it's pointless to try to make her look bad, since Eli obviously doesn't think she does. Plus, standing so close, I'm not sure I'm even mad at her—or more like I can't remember why I was. Maybe we could check out this WonderRoot place. Maybe Fabian knows about it, and we could . . . But I'm still not ready to think about Fabian yet. Thank god we don't have rehearsal this afternoon.

While Eli and Lish talk—mostly to each other—I look around, taking in the number of seniors suddenly here. Some of them catch my eye, give me a friendly nod, like they know me. My initial shock is wearing off, and I'm starting to absorb every-thing, when I see Trip walking over. With Lily, of course. Trying to get closer to Oliver.

Immediately, I want to hear what he says. I tell Lish I'll be back.

When I reach them, Trip glances down at me, and I give him a *Hey it's good to see you* smile. Because it is. Good to see him. And since he called me Friday night, maybe he's ready for us to get back—

But he clears his throat, holds his hand out for Oliver to shake. "Just wanted to tell you good show, man. We should still jam sometime." He pulls Lily closer to him.

"You were so good," she says up at me. Her cheeks are brushed with glitter.

"Thank you. It was really a—"

But I don't finish, because Trip turns and leads her back toward her gang of friends. She gives me a cute little wave over her shoulder. It's hard not to stand there with my mouth open.

"Well, *that* was awkward." I try to recover, rolling my eyes at Oliver.

But he shrugs noncommittally. Maybe it's just because there's somebody else approaching to shake his hand.

"Nice, man," the good-looking senior says to him. "And you were beautiful." To me.

"Thanks," I manage. It is so stunningly strange to be accepting a compliment from a guy like him. "I'm really glad you enjoyed what we did."

I tune out while they talk, but snap back when I hear the guy ask Oliver how long it takes him to write and put together all those songs. I expect Oliver to look up, wave me over, and get me involved, but instead he scratches his chin. "I dunno," I hear him say. The second part I don't catch, and then ". . . getting the lyrics right, and then there's the tune, too. It's a long process for me. I'll just say that."

I'm so perplexed by his answer, when Lish charges across the circle, wanting to introduce me to a round of her new friends, all I do is follow, blind.

But it doesn't take long for me to forget Oliver's weirdness in the parking lot, because on the walk to my locker, and then to homeroom, first period, all these random people—people who haven't said hello to me since eighth grade—are paying me compliments and giving me looks of praise. It's crazy. But what feels even crazier is that I did it. I got up there and sang. They really are talking about *me*.

Don't forget who your real friends are, Captain Famous, Benji writes to me in third period, after Dr. Campbell tells us we have another take-home due Wednesday.

What's your name again? I write back.

He turns around, gives me a sly grin. I give one of my own right back to him.

• • •

I can't linger long after third period, though, because in the hub-bub of this morning I apparently did agree to meet Lish for lunch.

"Off-campus lunch, eh? Very uptown of you, Coastal," Benji says as we walk.

"It's just a bunch of girls. I hardly know them."

"Just wish I was going to be there to see it, is all."

"I bet you do. But there's that whole, you know, class thing you have."

"Yeah, well." He sighs. "You riding the pep squad bus with the volleyball crew after school now too?"

"They're not going to be my *friends*," I retort. Although I guess Lish, technically, is my friend. Sort of. Still? "Anyway, you know I can't do this test without you." I grab a bunch of his army jacket in my fist, make a begging face. "We don't have rehearsal today, so—after school okay?"

He brings two fingers up to his right eyebrow in a semi-salute. "You know where to find me."

"Awesome. And who knows. Maybe I'll skip to go off campus with you during second-session lunch sometime."

"Oh, very rock star of you, Coastal," he says over his shoulder, ambling off. "Very rock star. But hey—you were good. Sincerely."

This compliment from Benji is, for some reason, more power-ful than any other I've gotten today.

"I love you, Benji," I yell after him, making a few people turn and stare.

When he waves, embarrassed, I know I almost meant it.

Walking off on my own to the parking lot, though, everything becomes a little more muddled in my head. I told Benji it's no big deal, this going off campus for lunch, and I guess it isn't, but honestly, I am looking forward to being around Lish. Not so we can immediately jump into being best friends again or any- thing—I'm not *that* stupid—but because seeing her toothpaste- commercial smile this morning made me realize I've actually missed her. When she dropped away at the start of school, I guess I just sort of accepted it.

Seeing her waving to me when I'm still twenty yards away, how she comes up and tucks her arm into mine to walk me over to her other girlfriends, feels pretty . . . nice. Something about her giggly enthusiasm is contagious, I guess, and pil- ing into Kiaya's car with everyone else, laughing at something someone says—it feels good. I wonder if that's what's been missing for me lately—not only Lish but plain, old-fashioned girl *giddiness*.

At Duck's Cosmic Kitchen we order our food, and the girls fall into talking all around me. Not in a bad way, though. Just like I'm a part of it already. Like I don't need an introduction.

Most of it is drama from the dance. Things I missed by being up onstage and leaving early.

"—and it's just like, break up with him already, please."

"Yes, please."

"But she just spent the whole time, practically, on the bleachers, crying her mascara down her neck."

"So stupid."

"So lame."

"It doesn't even make sense because she didn't even like him that much in the first place. We had to, like, convince her to even go out with him."

"And now we can't convince her to break up with him."

I think of Gretchen and her saga with the Wrestler.

"I know how that is," I say.

Five faces whip in my direction, focused. The waitress brings the plates with our sandwiches. I wait until everyone's got their food to go on.

"I wrote a song about it, actually."

"That vanish song you sang?" Kiaya goes. Her eyes are fringed with the thickest black lashes I've ever seen. "God, that was *so* crush."

I shake my head. "No, the first one Oliver did, 'Just Hang Up.' I wrote it when my step—when someone I knew was going through something similar."

D'Shelle laughs with her mouth open. "That's what we should

tell her to do! Can we get you to go to her house and sing that song?"

"I could serenade her, sure." I giggle, and accept one of Lish's fries.

By the end of the school day, I almost feel like a different person. I don't even feel down anymore about Fabian. Yeah, he has a boyfriend. So, it sucks that we can't be something more. But we're good friends already, right? And it would be stupid to mess that up. Probably it's *good* that he has someone else, because it resolves the dating-in-the-band problem. I should call him this afternoon. I should be embarrassed for taking it all so seriously.

I forget about the whole Oliver-maybe-letting-people-think-he-writes-the-songs thing from this morning until psych. I'm late, and Oliver hasn't waited outside for me. But he sounds perfectly fine saying hey as I take my seat next to him and Ms. Neff starts up class.

After psych, though, he's walking so fast toward the parking lot, I have to trot to catch up with him.

"It's not like we got offered a record contract or anything," he grumbles when I ask how it feels being a real rock star.

"Fine," I huff. "Be cool about it. But I've got some ideas I want to—"

"The other guys should be in on it. We'll talk about it Thursday."

"Well, but what about you and me going to Java Monkey later tonight or Wednesday afternoon? We could—"

"Let's just see, okay, Spider? I've really got to get going."

And even though we're already out in the parking lot, though we can see his car from here, he practically jogs to it, leaving me behind. I stand there watching him, stunned. Is he seriously this mad about me leaving early on Friday night?

"The cool-mobile is this way, Coastal," Benji hollers behind me. I watch Oliver for about ten more seconds as he says hey to the people collected around his car. Some of them see me and give a small wave, but Oliver doesn't glance over even once.

Benji and I finish the test together faster than usual.

He shakes his head. "End of the semester, you're not going to need me anymore."

"Please. I don't even want to think about that exam yet."

"So what *do* you want to think about?"

I think he's making a lewd joke at first, but he isn't. Instead he's looking at me, open and curious.

"These girls asked me to be in their band," I tell him, from nowhere.

His eyebrows go up while the corners of his mouth go down. "Cool."

I sigh. "Yeah, it is cool. But it's not like I can quit Sad Jackal, obviously."

"Explain to me why you can't do both?"

I look at him like he's crazy. "Um, my grades are so bad I have to take an open-book test with a stoner beside me. Why do you *think*?"

"I'm not a stoner." He pouts, but his eyes are simmering with mischief. "I am an appreciator of the natural world."

"I'm not sure that'll hold up in court. And explaining that my grades have tanked because I'm too busy playing rock 'n' roll probably won't hold up with my dad, either."

He scratches the side of his neck. "Well, how often do you have to practice?"

"Three times a week now with the guys. And with Taryn and Sylvia—"

"Wait. Those girls from the Masquerade?" He is impressed now. "You should totally play with them. They're good."

"You've seen them?"

He smiles. "I been around."

"Still, there's no way I can swing it."

He touches his fingertips—barely—against the edge of my forearm. "All I'm saying, and I am not blowing smoke up your ass here, though that might be nice—"

"Gross. God."

His face is amused, then serious. "I'm just saying that you are quality. The talent's obviously *in* you, you know? So just . . . talk to Oliver and make it work. Maybe practice Sad Jackal twice a week. Two other nights, play with the girls."

I skip over the pleasure of Benji's compliment and think about his second point. It might be possible for me to handle two bands. It's not like I'm doing much of anything else, though with Lish coming back around, maybe.

"Besides." He leans back. "You can hire *me* to do your homework."

I snort. "And finance your appreciation of nature? No thanks."

"Just sayin', Coastal. The offer's always out there."

When Benji drops me off at the house, I'm still thinking about how cool it would be to play with Taryn and Sylvia. I want to talk to Jilly about it, to see if she has any advice about handling Dad. I'm about to call her when my phone rings, making me jump. Who it is surprises me even more.

"Mom, how are you doing?"

"Hi, honey," she breathes. "I thought I might just get your voice mail."

The way she says it, it's like she would've *preferred* to get my voice mail.

"Well, you've got me now. How did the opening go?"

"Oh, you know. Lots of people wearing turquoise jewelry. Lots of wine."

"You sell any pieces?"

"Not exactly. But listen, I only have a minute. Tell me about the dance!" Her voice is overbright.

"It was good. I mean, people liked us."

"That's so great, baby. Well, sorry, but I really need to go. I was just planning on leaving a message while I was driving in."

She still hasn't told me anything. And she's barely even asked, either.

But, like that, she's gone.

Things are way better when I finally get in touch with Jilly.

"I missed you on Halloween," she says. "It's weird not giving out candy or having a pumpkin."

I tell her how equally strange it was without her here.

"Speaking of, can you believe it's almost Thanksgiving? I'll be coming home in just a few weeks. If I survive my midterms."

Thanksgiving isn't really *that* close, but the idea of having Jilly home is so pleasing and warm that I almost don't need to say anything else. Almost.

"These two girls I know asked me to sing with them," I tell her. It's funny that this is what I have to talk to her about, when she never got the full story on Fabian.

"That's great!"

"Well, I don't know yet. Do you think I should?"

"Why wouldn't you?"

"I'm just not sure—"

"Oh, I'm so excited for you!" she squeals. "What a big weekend you had! And I just wore black leggings and cat ears, and stood around drinking some ungodly concoction that had actual candy corns dissolved in it."

"Gross. Hey, I talked to Mom today."

"Oh?"

I can practically hear the temperature drop on Jilly's side of the phone.

"I think her show went okay. It was hard to tell."

Jilly snorts. "Which means it *didn't* go well."

I don't know why this makes me feel defensive. "Why do you never give her a chance? She's really working out there and—"

"Oh. Right. Taking out the trash for a bunch of paint dribblers . . . that's work."

"I mean on her art."

"Her *art*?" Jilly's laugh could crack bones, which makes me hot-faced. Because it's like she's laughing at me.

"I don't see how you going to college to study music is that much different from—"

"Don't you dare compare me to her," she explodes. "I'm

actually doing something toward my career here. Don't you get it? If you want your talent to grow and develop, if you want it to become something that really matters, you have to *work* at it. All the time. Mom put her art on the shelf and thought she could just start right in again. Well, guess what? It's not like that. It just *isn't*."

I wait, to make sure she's really done. She's so angry I can hear her whole body trembling through the phone, and I don't want to set her off on another rant against *me*.

"Are you still there?" she says, quieter.

"Yes."

"Well, are you going to say anything?" She still has an edge to her voice, but she's calmer.

"I just didn't know you felt all that, I guess," I manage. Careful.

She laughs, bitter. "Yeah, well. I don't think I always did either. But"—I hear her take a deep breath—"it's not like it makes much difference."

Her breathing calmer helps me breathe calmer too.

"It makes a difference to me," I say. "I mean, I understand a lot better, actually. Why you're so—you know. You always got angry at what felt like nothing, before."

"Well, when she left, that's all I was. Angry. But Dad needed help and you had middle school to deal with, so I guess I didn't . . . I don't know."

I picture us back then: frozen dinners, learning how to do laundry, Jilly always having to make sure Dad actually got up. "Are you glad?"

"What?"

"Not to have to take care of us anymore?"

"It's not like that. I mean, there are other things to take care of now. Harder things, in a way. Different things. And besides, Dad is so much better, and look at you—singing in rock bands. Good *thing* I'm here in hard-core-musician land. It'll help me keep up with my baby sister."

Her joking means that everything is really okay now.

"I miss you."

"I miss you, too."

"But, hey, believe it or not, I've been hanging out with Darby and Gretchen more, and they've been pretty cool. Ever since Gretchen broke up with the Wrestler, she's much less bitchy."

"God, about time." Jilly half groans. "I should call her."

And it hits me that I'm not the only sibling who might be missing Jilly, or who Jilly might miss. So I catch her up on Darby and Gretchen, then tell her about Benji, how fun it is to joke with him, and the Fabian thing too, which she laughs about but says nobody could blame me for. About Trip she just groans and says it's annoying but pretty normal for a guy to ditch his girl friend when he gets a girlfriend.

When we hang up, I feel confident enough to call Taryn. It's just her voice mail, but I tell her that if we practice twice a week, I can probably do it. So long as Oliver doesn't kill me for cutting back on Sad Jackal.

Chapter Fourteen

There are slightly fewer people at Oliver's car in the morning, so there isn't as much jockeying for position. I'm glad, since yesterday was such a whirlwind on a lot of levels, and I'm ready to get back to normal. Oliver spends the whole time talking to a bunch of new guys hanging around, and Lish dominates my attention once again, so it's hard to tell what's up between me and him, but things seem okay. Later, when I meet Lish for lunch, we don't go off campus, but just hang out around Kiaya's car. One of the girls shoots video of everyone talking in fake accents, and it's fun, again, to be playing around with Lish like nothing happened.

But something has happened. Kind of. At least with me, and joining Taryn and Sylvia. So at the end of the day, I psyche myself up to tell Oliver about reducing my rehearsal time. Taryn called me back late last night, and she and Sylvia and I are getting together. So I need to tell him.

Like yesterday, however, Oliver's not waiting for me outside of psych. Instead, he sneaks into his desk ten seconds before the late bell. At the end of class, he's up and out like the building's on fire. I only catch up to him because some football player stops him in the hall to say he totally scored thanks to one of our songs Friday night.

"You got something after school?" I ask when Oliver turns to head out.

"Doctor," he grumbles.

"Okay, well, I'll walk you. I kind of need to talk."

He doesn't look at me.

"It's about the band. I need to cut back on rehearsal time."

I'm getting out of breath, trying to keep up with him.

"We'll figure it out." It's like he's a robot.

"Well, I know you need to go now, but call me later? So we can talk about it? I can still write and everything and it's not like . . ."

"Okay, Spider. But I really gotta go."

I stop where I am, since I've got to turn around and go to the lower lot, anyway. He shoots forward without waving or looking back, and all I can think is *What is it now?*

Wednesday morning, Oliver has neither called me nor responded to my *When can we talk?* text, but I let it go. I feel like I need as little drama going on today as possible. And at first it starts that way. We're almost late for school in the morning, so I don't see anyone first thing. During lunch, too, everything's normal—well, my new kind of normal, where I hang out with Lish and the other girls. I want to tell them, a little, about my thing with Taryn and Sylvia this afternoon, but decide not to, since I'm not sure how it will go. Instead I let myself relax and just enjoy myself. I forget, even, that we haven't been friends all semester.

But after fifth period, before psych, I find a note from Lish in my locker.

> Hey you! I didn't want to say anything in
> front of the other girls, and I still won't,
> but I just wanted you to know that I
> think it is really cool—and, hello? ABOUT
> TIME—about you and O. Of courz it's
> under wraps, but I'm just EEEEEEEE
> for you, you know? But like I said, your
> secret is safe with me as long as you

want it to be. We should talk more about
this though. Call me later!

Xoxoxox Lishfish

Um. *What?*

I read it again. If it weren't definitely in Lish's handwriting, I'd think it was a practical joke, though I'm not sure who would play this kind of joke on either me or Oliver. Why would anyone think we were together? Nothing even remotely romantic has ever happened between us.

But if Lish thinks something's up, that means someone else does too. She had to hear it from somewhere, right? So does that mean Oliver's heard it too? And is *that* why he's been so bizarre? God. He doesn't have to act like I'm a leper. This is so stupid.

Unless—my stomach crashes—he somehow thinks I want it to be true?

I shove the note into my bag and move in the direction of psych, though part of me considers skipping. The whole thing is stupid, obviously, except that Oliver clearly doesn't think so. If that's what he's being weird about. I mean, it could be something else. Maybe he doesn't even know. But he's obviously tweaked about something. I need to find out more about what Lish heard, and from whom. If it's not a big deal, then I shouldn't make a big deal out of it with him, because then it will just be more awkward for both of us.

So this time I'm the one who's unable to look over at his side of the room when I slip in just before the bell, because I don't know how to arrange my face. We continue ignoring each other during class, and when it's over I hover around Ms. Neff's desk, pretend I have a question for her, just so he doesn't have to work so hard at avoiding me this time. I don't like acting like this, and I don't like him acting like this, but I don't know how to fix it yet, so.

Speed walking to the lower lot, I text Lish, *CALL ME ASAP.* I probably won't get to talk to her until after practice. All I can do is pray she's not hanging out with Oliver and the guys after school. Even though she said my "secret" is safe, I can just picture her trying to let on to Oliver that she knows all about what's going on. If—god—she hasn't done that already.

It's not until I'm walking up the three short concrete steps of Sylvia and Taryn's house that the wave of nerves sweeps over me. I stand still a second, taking deep breaths. This is going to be completely different than singing with Sad Jackal, and I haven't had a lot of time to process it. These are cool girls who I barely know, not my best friend from fifth grade. What if I mess up? What if they decide they don't really like me as much as they thought they did? What if the stuff they do isn't something I can sing well?

But I can't stand here like an idiot. I press the doorbell.

Some girl I've never seen before answers. She's holding a giant plastic cup and sipping out of it with a bendy straw, which she talks around.

"Are you Charlotte?"

"Yes."

She holds open the door. "They're downstairs."

"Are you playing too?" I ask.

"I'm just part of the entourage."

She leads me to the dim kitchen, papered with vintage cookbook pages. On the opposite side, a door opens onto some stairs. Taryn's head appears at the bottom.

"Hey hey! We've been waiting for you!"

I head down and let Taryn hug me. Over her shoulder, I see her synthesizer set up. Sylvia's sitting on a stool, tuning her guitar.

"So, what do you think?" Taryn says, spreading her arms wide.

"This house is awesome. How many people live here?"

"Right now, four of us. Veronica you just met. There were five but Megan and Ginger broke up. Believe it or not, renting this place is cheaper than on-campus housing."

I pretend to follow what she's saying.

"You'll meet everyone in a little while. In fact, I don't know where they are." She squints at Sylvia.

"They went to get some food, remember?"

Taryn sighs, looking at me. "We have a lot of craziness in this house, if you couldn't tell."

I have no response to this.

"So . . . what is it you had in mind for us to play?" I ask.

"Mostly we do covers," Sylvia explains. "We're an homage band, really."

"But an homage to the *ladies*." Taryn's eyebrows go up and down.

I'm trying to remember what "homage" means, and also what cover songs I know. Probably Trip would strangle me for not thinking of any.

"Anyway," Sylvia says. "We only do songs sung by women, but we like to go all over the place with it. Dolly Parton. Rihanna. Neko Case. Katy Perry. Courtney Love. We wanted you on board because I can't sing worth a damn—"

"And apparently I can't either," Taryn finishes, "because we're not getting anywhere."

"Um, I don't think I can sing like Katy Perry," I say.

"You don't have to," Sylvia says. "The way we mix things up, you can barely recognize the original."

"Which is the beauty of it!" Taryn claps.

Sylvia stands up and brings a sheaf of papers over to me, along with a wireless mic. "Here's lyrics."

I flip through the pages. Over half the songs I've never even heard of. It is funny that there's a Taylor Swift one in there, though. And an eighties band Mom used to like.

"I might know this Heart one a little," I tell them. "Can we start there?"

"Let's see what you've got," Sylvia agrees.

When Taryn begins playing, it doesn't sound at all like the cheesy song I remember, but when Sylvia starts, I know a little better where I am.

My first line comes out raspy and unsure, so I take another deep breath, try to calm down. My brain is divided between the song and the memory of Mom singing along in the car, Jilly harmonizing, me pretending to play the guitar. The windows down, all three of us happy. When I get to the chorus, it's hard not to close my eyes, clench my fist, and squeeze the words out with deep passion, the way Mom would in the front seat.

Upstairs, there's the sound of people tromping in over our heads. I make myself keep singing. *These dreams,* I croon while the four of them come down and plop on the couches and watch me. One of them gives me a huge grin. Even though I'm still trying to concentrate, I can't help smiling back.

I get to the end. Taryn and Sylvia fade out. The girls on the couch applaud.

"That was terrific!" one chirps.

"Good call, TeeTee," another says to Taryn, but pointing at me.

Taryn is beaming at me. "That was *perfect.*"

"Don't hold back on the cheese, either," Sylvia says. "I saw you clench your fist at that one part. Follow that kind of instinct. That's the sort of thing we want."

Taryn bounces on her toes. "Can we please please please do 'Drown Soda' now?" She puts her hands together in prayer under her chin, batting her eyes at me.

"Okay, but I don't really know how it—"

"Just do it like you're talking, if you want. Or whatever. And remember we asked you to be here," Sylvia says.

The girls on the couch all encourage me too. They shift around, get more comfortable, draping arms or legs over each other, like a pack of kittens. Being here, among these girls, I feel this wild sense of abandon.

Taryn starts playing again, a bagpipe sound. Sylvia nods at me to come in, and I do: *"Oooh yeah, he wants to take you . . ."*

The next hour is absolutely great. The more I ham it up, the more the girls on the couch all cheer. By the end, I'm jutting my hip way out in the air and making emotional hand gestures. When we finish the last song, I take a deep bow, flinging my hair back over my head.

"You are an absolute doll," a freckle-faced girl squeals at me. "Come over here and tell us all about yourself."

"Yes, do." Taryn drapes her arm around my neck and leads me over to the couch. "It's so loud at the club, we never really get to talk."

I feel like I've got a head rush, the kind you have after a really good pillow fight. It's hard to know what to say.

"Well, what do you want to know?"

"Tell us about Sad Jackal. How did that start?" Taryn leans in.

I tell them about Abe and Oliver, and the three of us knowing each other since middle school. I tell them about Trip moving here last January, and how the three of them formed a group. About the poems I wrote for Mrs. Stenis, and Oliver wanting to use them for songs. Then me coming in to organize all the gigs this summer too.

"Wait now." Sylvia stops me. "He takes your lyrics? And sings them himself? Doesn't give you any credit?"

I shake my head. "It isn't like that. Oliver and I have just been friends for so long, and he knows I—"

Freckle Face tsks. Even Taryn looks like I've made some kind of mistake.

I stammer. "It—it's not like he tells people he wrote them."

"Not in front of you." Freckle Face snorts.

I think of Oliver's vague, not-wholly-true answer to that guy in the parking lot Monday. I have never once not trusted him.

But being surrounded by all these disapproving girls, a creepy feeling comes over me.

I don't want to turn traitor on my friend, though. My friend who's stuck around through all sorts of changes in our lives and could've ditched me at any point along the way, just like Lish did.

"Well, I sing with them now, so—"

"You sing great," Taryn says for what feels like the twelfth time. "I just think you shouldn't automatically give all your talent away like that."

"Especially not to a bunch of dumbass high school boys," one of the girls adds.

"Any boys." Sylvia.

"Boys aren't so bad," Taryn chirps. "We heart Fabian, right?"

Fabian, whom I still haven't had the nerve to call or text back. God, he must think I'm terrible.

"Fabian's different," roomate Veronica says. "Fabian is transcendent."

"There are plenty of good guys out there," Sylvia says, cutting off the chatter. "The thing is"—she turns to me—"you're acting like a sidekick to this Oliver guy. When, really, you are the superhero."

Sidekick. It's funny to hear that word in Sylvia's mouth. I've always thought of myself that way, with Oliver. Been proud of it, even. But now it sounds like a bad thing.

●　●　●

When I get home, I run up to my room to call Lish. She sent three texts while I was at practice, all of them saying, *Where R U?*

"I'm glad you're not at dinner," I tell her when she answers.

"No, but we're about to be, so I can't talk long. But, you know, ohmygod EEEEEE."

I have to pull the phone away from my head, she's so loud.

"Ohmygod EEEEE *nothing*. Who told you that we were?"

"You don't have to act innocent with me."

"I'm not acting innocent," I spit. "There isn't anything to be acting innocent about. We are not together. Never. No way."

"Please. I see how he practically walks away whenever you come over. I mean, you two are so far undercover that even Eli looked at me like I was crazy."

"You said something to Eli?" I try not to screech.

"I figured he already knew."

"And that's 'keeping my secret safe' how?"

"How am I supposed to know who knows what? *You* won't say anything."

"I'm telling you, there isn't anything to know."

"Oh crap, my mom's calling me. I gotta run."

She cannot hang up now. "Listen to me, Lish. You have to tell people that it's not true. Okay?"

"Well, that's gonna be a little hard." It's almost like she's laughing at me. "Everyone saw you two up there at the dance."

So that's it.

"Just because we sing together doesn't mean—"

"Listen, my mom is about to have an aneurysm. I'll be on later if you want to chat some more."

"I mean it, Lish. You have to help me out on this."

"Okay, but right now I gotta go."

She hangs up, and I know she still doesn't believe me.

I jet downstairs, where Darby is in her favorite position: hunched in front of the glowing computer.

"Have you heard anything about me around school in the last couple of days?"

She doesn't even look up. "What *haven't* I heard about you around school? I told you, everyone thinks you're boss now."

"I mean have you heard anything about me and Oliver being girlfriend and boyfriend?"

Now she turns around. She has the most evil grin. "I knew it. I *knew* it. I told Sadie she was full of shit, but man!" She pounds her thigh with her fist.

I grab her by the shoulders. "Whatever you've heard, whatever people are saying, it isn't true. Do you understand me? No way are me and Oliver together. He's like my brother or something. Even *thinking* about dating him is giving me the creeps. I know how he treats his girlfriends, for one."

She squints, weighing what I'm saying versus what she's

heard. "So . . . he didn't kick Trip out of the band in order to get you in?"

"What? God. No. I was there the whole time, anyway."

"And he didn't break up with Whitney because he couldn't resist you anymore?"

Jesus. Jesus. Jesus. "Absolutely not."

"So you aren't screwing each other's brains out in between rehearsing songs?"

My hands go up into my hair. "Is that what people are saying? No!"

Her mouth twists up and her eyes get a mischievous glimmer. "Well, that's not what probably half the school thinks at this point."

I slide down to the floor. "I know," I groan. "What I don't know is what we're going to do about it."

After dinner I try to call Oliver, but his phone isn't even on. Which means either he turned it off because he knew I was going to call him and he was too weirded out to talk about this, or he simply forgot to charge it again. I leave him a message that just says, "Don't ignore me," and then a text repeating the same thing.

Not even when I wake up in the morning has anything come in from him.

• • •

I still don't know how to handle the rumor when we get to school, but I know I need to keep as far away from Oliver as I can when other people are around. I head to the library, pretend to try to catch up on the Algebra II assignments I haven't done.

When the bell rings, I avoid eye contact with everybody in the halls. I have no idea how widely the rumor's spread. It feels like, as Darby said, everyone must know about it. I don't want a single person to have the opportunity to give me any kind of knowing look.

Not until third period, when Benji sidles up to me, holding our most recent test.

"One hundred percent," he says, flicking the paper to make a loud snap.

I go over to Dr. Campbell's desk and get my own test, moving in slow motion. Not because of the high test grade—which I can hardly believe when I see it—but because, suddenly, I know the answer to all my problems. If I can make it work.

Going back to my desk, everything about Benji is in high-def.

"Suck it, McLaughlin," I murmur to him. "You're not the only one getting A's."

He turns around, looks at the red letter at the top of my test.

"Good work, Coastal." He holds up his hand for a high five.

I meet his eye, but I'm not really seeing him. "Well, it wasn't all me."

"No." He winks, leaning in close. "I know it wasn't."

And I know I have to do this next thing. Do it for me. For Oliver. So, shaky-handed, while Dr. Campbell starts class, I write: *I don't know what I would do without you in here. If you don't have plans on Friday . . . would you want to go out? With me?*

A hot feeling crescendos up my chest and through my face as I slip the paper under Benji's elbow. It gets worse as I wait for him to respond. When I unfold the note he hands back to me, my hands are sweating so much I can actually see damp marks.

Would I? is all he's written. That, and his phone number.

Part one of my Plan to Make People Believe I Am Not Dating Oliver Drake is now in place.

"Where were you this morning?" Lish demands when I get to the parking lot at lunch. "I think Oliver was looking for you." Wink.

"He was not. Because we are *not* going out." I say this part loud enough for the girls around us to hear. "We're just friends. You know that."

She won't get that pleased little smile off her face. "Right."

I take her arm, pull her off to the side. "Listen, Lish. You have got to cut it out. It's not funny. Please tell me you have not been telling everyone that we're together."

"Not me." She holds up her hands. "I think it's cool that it's a secret."

"It's not a secret. It's not anything. I never think of Oliver that way."

She slits her eyes at me. "You expect me to believe that? I remember first semester last year, you know. It wasn't that long ago."

Which isn't fair. I mean, of course it's never been lost on me how good-looking Oliver is. And funny. And cool. And just awesome. But after that one week of wondering what it would be like if we ever got together, now all I can think is *No*. Kissing would do nothing but mess things up.

But Lish sees me pause, and pushes forward. "Whitney told us—"

"Since when do you talk to Whitney? You barely even know her. You weren't even around when they were going out."

"Oh sure, bring *that* up." She rolls her eyes.

"Bring what up? This isn't about you and me." Acknowledging our whole we-weren't-friends phase throws me off for a second, but I regain my clarity. "Look, Whitney Carroll is just psycho in general. She hates anyone who spends more time with Oliver than she does, including his mom."

No lie—I was there during that fight.

I push on. "Forgive me if it's just a little surprising that you, my *friend*"—I almost say "best" there, but we both hear the omission—"would believe some dumb thing she said, over believing me."

Lish's face gets even meaner. "Don't think I don't still know you, Charlotte Augustine. Don't think I don't know you're too cool for anything or anybody. Too cool to care."

Now I have no idea what she is talking about. Or why this conversation has gone in this direction.

"I do care! That's the thing. I care very much that you *believe me that Oliver and I are not together.*"

Half the parking lot is probably looking at us now. I seize the moment.

"Besides." I lower my voice just a little, so she'll think I'm telling her something special. "I'm going out with Benji."

"McLaughlin?" she says, too loud. Perfect.

"Mmm-hmm."

Lish gazes at me steadily, then tosses her head. "Okay, fine. You're not with Oliver. But I don't think it's *me* you should be standing here telling."

She means Whitney. And all her overdramatic friends.

"I'm not going to say one word to that girl. She'd probably beat me up."

"I'm surprised she hasn't tried already." Lish smiles, picturing it, then turns intense again, but in a gossipy way. "She was pretty upset at the dance, you know. You should've heard her in the bathroom. Super. Drama."

And suddenly, like that, we're back to normal.

"I thought she was going to throw up, she was crying so hard," D'Shelle says behind us, obviously having listened to the whole thing.

I shrug, not really looking at either of them. "I split after we played, so I didn't know. I didn't feel so good myself."

Bronwyn jumps in. "She probably would've clawed your face and ripped your hair out if you hadn't."

I lift my heavy ponytail. "Lots to choose from."

Everyone titters.

"I guess it was kind of stupid, huh?" Lish half apologizes.

"It's not surprising, I guess." I still can't look fully at her.

"Yeah, now that you're famous." She grabs my arm and shines her toothy smile on everyone. "The whole school wants to be in your business."

I'm counting on it, I think, but instead I just mutter, "Too bad for them, then," and change the subject to an easier topic: the guy Bronwyn likes in our Enviro class.

While Bronwyn dissects all the things he did and did not say to her today, I realize part two of my Plan to Make People Believe I Am Not Dating Oliver Drake has been executed with relative success. Now all I have to do is talk to Oliver.

• • •

School obviously isn't going to be the place for us to have any kind of conversation—people don't need to see us with our heads bowed together, that's for sure—but I wait for Oliver outside of psych anyway. When he sees me there, his face twitches a little in annoyance, but he does, at least, say hey.

I remind myself I have to act normal. That I'm the one who can fix this. I give him a punch on the arm. "You giving me a ride to practice this afternoon, bud?"

"I don't think—" he starts, but even he realizes how dumb that is. "Sure."

"Thanks" is all I say. We go into class.

During the entire walk to Oliver's car, we don't say a thing. I want to be telling him about Taryn and Sylvia and yesterday's rehearsal, but it's clear that until we get the whole I Know What People Are Saying business cleared up, I have to focus on getting *him* focused, first.

As soon as we shut the car doors, I turn in my seat and look at him. His fault, my fault, their fault—it doesn't matter. We have to deal.

"So, Whitney's continuing to be a bit of a problem, huh?" I start.

He looks at me, face unreadable. "You could say that."

I let myself exhale. But I can't hold his gaze while I say the rest. The weirdness of this conversation is made three-hundred-fold weirder because it's *Oliver*.

I'm quick. A Band-Aid torn off: "I heard what she's telling people."

He starts the car, doesn't say anything while he backs out. I wait. As we leave the lot, I see people's faces turned our way. I hope Oliver is trying as hard as I am not to care.

"I think it's better if we just act normal," I go on. "I mean, it's not true, obviously, and if we act like we're all bugged out about people thinking it's true . . ."

"Even *Eli* asked me about it, man."

"I know. That's Lish's fault."

He looks sideways at me. "Such a blabbermouth."

I sigh. "She is. But I talked to her today, so."

"Talking isn't going to be enough." Everything in him is frowning.

"I'm working on that. I mean, there are things in motion. Alternate . . . realities."

Oliver's eyebrows go up in surprise.

I cough. "Yeah, well, you're apparently not going to start making out with anyone in the parking lot, so . . ."

I pause. Because it occurs to me that he actually could. Make an effort. With another girl. There are certainly plenty he could have his pick of. It's surprising that he's stayed without a new one for so long. And it's beyond annoying that I'm the only one who thought about being with someone else.

"Who is it?" he asks, both dying to know and disbelieving.

"Don't worry your pretty head about it too much," I tell him, "but I think it will fix everything."

I hope so, anyway, I tell myself, not looking as we drive past Benji's car.

By the time we get to Oliver's, things are back to a relatively normal level of comfortableness between us. Which I guess should make it easier to face my next uncomfortable situation of the afternoon: Fabian.

It's not like I'm still all heartbroken, the way I was over the weekend. That pretty much dissipated after the roller coaster of this week. But it's not like, when he comes in, I don't still feel that sparkle, not like I'm not immediately happy just being in the same space with him. It's not like I don't still wish he felt for me what I *thought* he felt.

But now I have to deal with knowing that when he smiles at me, it means he likes me but doesn't Like me. And it's harder than I want it to be.

Luckily, we have Mrs. Drake's gourmet snacks to focus on at first, and the excitement of being back together, after the dance. Since this is the first time we've all been in one place since then, there's a lot to say. Including what to do next.

"I still say we work on some covers," Eli says, eyeing Oliver.

I'm in a new cover band, I almost pipe up. I'm not sure why I can't tell them—maybe because who I really want to tell is Trip—but it doesn't feel like a good idea. And maybe I want to have something that's all my own for a while.

"It's just that everybody does that," Oliver says, mouth still full of sandwich.

"Because that's what the people *like*," Eli insists.

"They liked what we did on Friday night," Oliver answers. "Or did you not hear? Have you not been there in the mornings, man? I'm still getting punks coming up to me, wanting to know where they can hear us next. Kid in my AP Physics class asked if we needed a *roadie*."

I don't know how the other guys feel about it, but Oliver's cockiness is actually making me wince. I want to tell him to tone it down a little.

He senses my squeamishness. "You writing more?" he asks.

I shrug, considering my own sandwich now. "Haven't yet, but I can."

Eli groans. "But it'll take *time* to put together new stuff. Covers we could learn in, like, a day. Me and Fabian already know a ton of shit, and it's not like Coldplay's bass is that hard to pick up."

I look at Oliver, barely able to hold in my laugh. When his closed-lip smile falls on me, I know everything's okay.

"Coldplay's lame," we both say at the same time.

"I'm just saying—" Eli goes on.

"Charlotte, what do *you* want to sing?" Fabian asks.

All I can think of is the stuff we messed around with at Taryn and Sylvia's. The wild feeling I got, singing something that had nothing to do with me.

"I think covers aren't a bad idea," I tell them. "If we can all agree on something good. I mean"—I turn to Oliver—"I can still write new material. But mixing it up a little—how could that not work?"

"Fine," he says. "Just . . . who do we do?"

Eli stretches and yawns. "I say we do some research, bring some things on Saturday." He points at me. "Including you."

Suddenly I'm a deer in headlights. "Um . . . I can't make it Saturday, guys."

All their eyes are immediately on me, needing an explanation. Oliver forgetting, I guess, our conversation earlier in the week about me cutting back.

And I could tell them then—I could. I *should* tell them about Taryn and Sylvia, I know, because this is my band. But for whatever reason, there's still this hesitation that pricks inside me.

"Dad's putting the pressure on me, gradewise," I lie, though after report cards tomorrow it's probably not going to be far from the truth.

"You can still send me new stuff, though, right?" Oliver says. "As soon as it's written."

I make myself look at him. "Mondays and Thursdays I'm still totally in, so of course. I just might not be able to work on the—"

"Settled, then." Eli claps. "Mondays and Thursdays it is for you. You crank out new material, and us guys will drum up some covers Saturday. When the gigs start rolling in, we'll be ready."

And that's that. Normality seems reestablished for everyone, which I guess is good. But lying to Oliver certainly isn't normal to me, and I don't like lying to Fabian, either. When he offers me a ride home, though, that's a normal thing that is pretty nice, even if trying to talk normally about his boyfriend might be a challenge.

"Taryn told me you're singing with them," he says, straight-out, when we get in the car. Though it feels accusatory, I can see he's glad for me.

"Yeah." I shrug. "I mean, we'll see how it goes."

"Is that why you didn't say anything?" He flicks his hand, indicating Oliver's house behind us.

I fumble. "A lot of the time I don't like to say things out loud until they're an actuality. And this feels kind of like that."

His face is understanding, which is a relief.

"If either band takes off, though, you'll have to decide."

I'm aware of his hands on the steering wheel—hands that won't ever be on me.

"I mean," he goes on, "you and Oliver are really close, right?"

"We are," I concede.

"And I don't know him as well as you do, but from what I do know, it seems it could hurt his feelings if you weren't totally dedicated to this project."

I didn't think Oliver was so transparent to everyone else, and I almost say so. But I've honestly had enough of thinking about what Oliver needs for one afternoon.

"Maybe I don't *want* to always just attach myself to Oliver. Maybe I want to do something different." I realize I sound pouty and stupid, but the way Sylvia said "sidekick" is in my head again.

"Maybe you do," he allows. "But then, why not be honest about it?"

He pulls up to the curb in front of my house, turns off the car.

"Being honest about what you want is part of getting what you want," he goes on.

I narrow my eyes at him. "You're a tough one, you know that?"

He reaches over to tousle my hair. "I just don't see much value in time spent deceiving yourself. Not to mention anyone else."

You mean how you deceived me? pops in my mind. But I know that's not fair.

"I'm glad you think it's a good idea," I tell him. "Me and Taryn and Sylvia."

We agree to do the Masquerade again on Saturday night, and it's all somehow okay again with him and me. While he drives away, I flash on the events of the day—Lish, Benji, lying to the guys, talking to Fabian—and a lingering sense sneaks in that while everything feels fixed, nothing is. Not really.

Chapter Fifteen

In homeroom the next morning, everything else disappears behind the immediate crisis of my report card: three C's, one D, and two B's means a total GPA of Absolute Flop. Even though I can smile about the B in 20th Cen., I know that Dad won't be smiling about any of it. I'm not the greatest student ever, but usually I only have two C's, not three, and I swore I would never get another D after the Algebra II incident last year. Dad is going to flip.

I'm so distracted, I almost don't see Trip walking toward me in the hall between homeroom and first period. Though our homerooms are just a few doors away from each other, our paths don't cross around here anymore. It's almost like he came this direction today on purpose. And, seeing him, my whole body feels how badly I could use one of his hugs right now. But probably he's only taking a faster route to meet Lily, or Chris. I'm not going to even make eye contact with him, but then at the last second I can't help it. And it's like he's waiting for me to. He lifts his own report card, and his eyebrows—just barely—go up in sympathy. I almost stop. I almost do. But then we both keep walking and the moment is over.

I obsess about it through first and second periods, thinking of all the things I'd say to him if I had the notebook right now. But there are other things I probably *wouldn't* be telling him about—namely Benji and our date tonight. Though he'll probably hear the rumors anyway.

This makes me more nervous to see Benji than I want to be, so I walk slow to 20th Cen., barely making it in before the bell. As I pass his desk to get to mine, Benji holds his fist up for me to bump.

For once I'm glad when Dr. Campbell lurches up to the overhead to start class.

Afterward, Benji and I walk out together, and I talk just loud enough so that the kids going past us can hear.

"Where should we meet tonight?"

"I'll pick you up," he says, fast and a little defensive. Which is odd.

"Do you need directions?"

"Have you moved?"

"No."

This should be a joke or something, but we've both turned strangely formal.

"What time?" I ask.

"Seven?"

"Seven is good." I smile, because tonight could be really fun. And also because it's kind of funny how serious he's being.

"Okay, then. Text me if, you know, you need more time or something."

I want to tease him for that, as well. But I don't. Instead I tell him I'm looking forward to it. He says that he is too.

Lish must still be pretty much choked with shock about me and Benji, though, because she hardly says anything at lunch while the other girls tell wilder and wilder stories they've heard about things Benji's done to and with different girls. They talk on top of each other, and I try to ignore the overwhelming hot feeling I get, wondering what Benji might want to do to and with me tonight. And what—wave of warmth—I might want to do back. I try to focus instead on how, after this weekend, the whole me-and-Oliver thing will surely be very old news. Maybe one date is all it's going to take.

When Gretchen, Darby, and I roll out of the lot at the end of the day, headed for the weekend, we drive past Lily's car. Trip's opening the door, about to get in the front seat. He looks up, straight at me. And this time he acts like I'm not even there.

I don't want to think about Trip, though, so I fully submerge myself in Darby's pre-date routine: bubble bath, painted nails, hair blowout, sparkly lip gloss, short dress with leggings, boots. As Darby works, she chatters all around me, but I'm hardly listening.

When Lish calls, though, I have to answer.

"We're having dinner, but I don't know where," I tell her when she asks. "A movie. Regular date things."

"Well, it was a shock." She tries to say it in a British accent.

I'm not sure which part is a shock: me going out with Benji or me going out with anyone. Either way it's irritating.

"Benji's cool when you get to know him. He's smart. And hilarious."

"I think *Eli*'s pretty cool," Lish says.

I can't help snorting. "Eli just gets weirder the more you know him, believe me. And if you think Benji has a rep with girls, you should hear how Eli talks about them."

"Except you, of course."

"Except me." I chuckle. But then I realize she wasn't trying to be funny.

She sighs. "Well, let me know if you want to hang out tomorrow night."

"Can't," I say quick. "Sorry. I've got plans with a guy in the band."

"Oliver?" She perks up.

"No. God." I want to hit her. "You can come with us if you want."

Wait. What did I just say? I don't want Lish hanging out with me and Fabian. And Taryn is sure to blab to Lish about our new band, which means Oliver—and the whole school—will know about it in ten seconds. Too late now, though.

"Where are you going?" Lish wants to know.

"The Masquerade."

"Isn't that, like, a bar?"

"Most of their shows are all ages."

"Huh. Well, Miss Cool and Popular."

It's stupid that she says this, and especially stupid how jealous she sounds.

"People suddenly recognizing me in the hall, after years of near invisibility, does not make me popular."

"You were never invisible before," she says. "Only now you're more visible to more important people."

This whole conversation has been awful, but now it's especially so.

"Look, I gotta go."

Which is true, because Darby is glaring at me, powder brush in hand.

"Okay, well. Have fun tonight," she sings. "Text me later, 'kay?"

"Okay."

But I know, without a doubt, I won't.

Dad gets home twenty minutes before Benji's supposed to arrive, and immediately wants to see our report cards.

The three of us stand with him in the kitchen, waiting for his response, while he looks at them. Gretchen and Darby both get quick approval, but I have to shift uncomfortably while he stares at mine for a full minute. When his eyes come back up at me— and my perfumey sparkle gloss—they aren't happy.

"You going out?" he wants to know.

I nod.

"All right," he says, quiet. "We'll talk in the morning."

And that's all. But it's enough. It's more than enough.

And then the doorbell rings and Benji's there.

He stands in our living room, shakes hands with Dad, and tells me that I look nice. The expression on his face makes me believe I really do. And I have to admit, he looks pretty good himself.

"So, how's it going with the *lesband*?" he asks once we're together in the car.

A surprised guffaw comes out of me. "How'd you know Taryn and Sylvia are gay?"

He sideways glances at me. "Um, I have a pulse?"

You flirted with them plenty last weekend, I want to sass. But that doesn't seem like Benji-and-Charlotte-sitting-in-a-tree behavior.

"It's definitely different," I say. "I'm not used to singing with them yet, but it could be good."

"I bet they're glad to have you."

His sincerity catches me off guard and makes me blush. "So, what's this dinner place again?" I say to cover it up.

"You'll see," he says. "But it's not far."

I notice there's some kind of bossa nova jazz coming out of his stereo, instead of the usual sound track.

"A little mood music?" I snark before I think.

His right shoulder raises in this shy way. "You know."

Which is when I remember that Benji's actually on a date too. The understanding renders me mostly silent for the rest of the ride. Because, until this minute, I didn't honestly think of Benji as actual boyfriend material. And now it's the only thing I can think.

But Benji doesn't seem to notice. We find a parking place behind a small Decatur restaurant, and on the way up to the door he puts his arm around me—loose, like he's testing it out. His hand is a white-hot thing against my shoulder.

Inside, the restaurant is warm plank tables and a big chalkboard menu. The lighting is dim but cozy. Benji grabs a paper menu from a wire basket. We squint over it together. I can barely read a thing, but it's clear all they've got here is hamburgers.

"You're not vegetarian, are you?" he murmurs.

The urge to joke with him takes over. "Um, actually . . ." I bite my lip, feign disappointment.

He jumps. "We can totally go somewhere else." He's pulling me toward the door, uncool and awkward in a way I've never seen. "I mean, I couldn't remember and I'm really sorry."

Which makes me feel awful, but also surprised he couldn't tell I was joking.

"I'm kidding. It's okay, really." I hook my arm around his, squeeze myself closer—to reassure him, but also because now I'm curious what being Girlfriend Girl with him might feel like.

We step up to order our burgers and some fries to share. There are too many toppings on this menu, so I stick to the basics: onions, tomato, lettuce, and cheese. And then, at the last second, I remember no onions. Because probably we are going to kiss.

As we take our seats, Benji's eyebrows toggle up and down. "Big slice of meat, eh?"

Which makes me laugh, for real.

While we wait for our food, and then after it arrives, we talk nonstop. About music, our families, people at school. I find out that he, like me, has a sister who's in college, though his is older than Jilly. He tells me about the book he's reading. I tell him about writing songs. We keep talking on the way to the movie, the jokes and the back-and-forth continue, and as we walk up to the theater, I link my arm through his again. A group of people from school are coming out of an earlier showing, and when we see them we wave. All of it is perfect, in every way.

Until we step up for our tickets, and I reach for my wallet. Benji puts a hand out to stop me.

"You paid for dinner," I protest.

"I got this." He frowns, like I've insulted him.

I want to tell him he's being stubborn and stupid, but instead I say, "Thank you," both of us awkward again.

We decide to skip snacks. Taking our seats, Lish's squealy voice careens through my head, but I squash it. While I'm kind of excited, the brief formality of getting our tickets makes me realize there's no going back to being just friends after this. Even if Benji's the type who can be friends with his exes, there will never not have been this between us. I will never be able to see him and not think, *I kissed that mouth. He put his hands*— But at the same time, I'm not totally sure I don't want to find out what kissing him is like, whether it kills the Oliver rumor or not.

As the movie starts, I push my hesitation aside and execute proper I Like You behavior: leaving my arm conveniently on the armrest between us, my hand dangling down so that it's almost touching his knee. When the movie gets intense, I let my fingers clutch at his sleeve. Eventually his hand is entwined in mine, and then our palms are pressed together—warm and close.

But we don't kiss. After what I heard at lunch today, I'm pretty surprised, actually. I don't know if it's because we both get into the movie, or because Benji's nervous too, or because he doesn't want to kiss me, or what, but it doesn't happen.

"So . . . it was funny, right?" he asks in the car back to my house.

I look at him. "You mean the part where he realized his best friend killed his dad? Or the part where his girlfriend drowned?"

He frowns. "Well, not those parts. But . . . you know . . ."

I don't.

"It wasn't anything like the comic," he tries again.

"I didn't know it was a comic," I admit.

So he dissects the differences between the two for me. While he talks, I nod as though he's right, even though I don't really read comics.

"I thought the fight scene at the end was cool," I say when he's done.

We are both polite, considerate of each other's points of view.

We are both afraid to make the other think we might be laughing—in the wrong way—at anything the other one says. It's a completely different dynamic, and it makes me realize that kissing him is probably not worth it if it turns us into *this*.

By the time we make it back to my house, I feel like this was a bad idea. But leaping out of the car at this point probably wouldn't improve anything.

I touch the top of his sleeve. "Thank you for everything."

"You going to the Masquerade tomorrow night?" he wants to know.

I nod. But then I remember Dad. "Unless I'm grounded for the rest of my life."

"Report card?"

"Yeah," I admit. "Though you saved my Twentieth Cen. grade, that's for sure. I don't know what I would have done without you."

And I do mean it. Mean it so much that when he says, soft brown eyes focused directly on my lips, "You're welcome," I'm suddenly not afraid of what will happen.

He moves close enough for me to lean in too. Our mouths meet. And it doesn't feel at all awkward or fake. His lips are half parted, and mine don't land quite squarely on his at first, but it's sweet. There's some pecking, a poke or two of tongue. Nice.

"I'll text you," I say, pulling back and trying to sound normal, "about Masquerade. It'd be great if we could go."

There's an expression on his face that I can't read. "Sure."

"I'm glad we did this," I tell him.

"My pleasure," he says softly.

And because I don't know what else to do, I get out of the car.

Though my date with Benji was confusing, there's nothing unclear about Dad's disappointment down in the kitchen the next morning.

"So," he says, lowering the screen of his laptop.

I pour a bowl of Corn Pops at the counter. I'm not hungry, but I want to keep my back to him. I know my grades are bad. I don't need his disapproval on top of it.

"Just say what it is you have to say, Dad," I grumble.

"Well, obviously I'm not pleased with the report card you brought home yesterday."

I lean against the counter, facing him, decide I'll eat my Corn Pops standing up.

"And I think it's plain that you're not spending enough time or energy on your studies," he goes on.

"I've had practice. You never got on to Jilly about that kind of thing."

"That's because Jilly never let her after-school activities interfere with her grades." He frowns at the table. "I've tried to be supportive. But obviously you've let things slip."

The calm, slow way he handles everything is maddening.

"It's not like I decided to, Dad. I just lost track. I've had a lot going on."

"I understand that you have. Hannah and I can hardly keep up with all the fellows lately. Which is why you obviously need us to step in now and reduce the number of things you're involved in."

The tiny amount of sarcasm he uses when he says "fellows" like that just sends me over the edge. I see my life the way he and Hannah must: three afternoons a week at Oliver's house, plus long phone calls with Trip, and then Fabian showing up with rides home and what they could only interpret as Saturday-night dates. And now this business with Benji. That Dad thinks, like everyone else, I'm *dating* all these boys—that not even my own father understands it isn't like that—well, it makes me furious.

But because screaming is Jilly's jurisdiction, I try to start out as calm as him.

"Maybe I am distracted, Dad." I breathe through my nose. "But it isn't like you think. The rehearsal I have this afternoon? That I'm going to no matter what you say? It's with *girls*. Girls who think I'm cool. And did you even know that I'm singing with Sad Jackal now?"

His face is surprised, but I don't pause.

"No, you didn't. Because you were too busy counting how many guys were coming in and out of here to pay attention to your own daughter. Well, I am. I'm singing. Me. So yeah, I'm a little distracted—I'm distracted doing something I love, something I want to do more of."

"And we support that. Just not at the demise of your other—"

"I'm never going to be good in school!" I shout. "It's not my friends that are the problem; it's that I'm just not *Jilly*."

"That's a silly card to try to play right now, don't you think?"

His being right makes my anger even more uncontrollable.

"This is something I'm good at," I holler, on the verge of tears. "And I'm not going to let you keep me from doing it. I'm not going to let you hold me back, the way you held back Mom."

It's like somebody turns all the sound off in the room. I can't hear the coffee machine, the hum of the refrigerator—nothing. My eyes can't make themselves blink.

But then Dad clears his throat and the ability to move returns to us. He looks down at his hands, now both flat on the table. "I wasn't aware that was how you felt."

I wasn't aware that was how I felt, either, until it was out. And now that I've said it like that, I'm not exactly sure it is how I feel. But this isn't a piece of paper I can crumple up and throw away. They aren't words I can cross out to start over. Now they're out, and I know they'll hang here, between us, maybe forever.

"Taryn and Sylvia want me to come over at two," I say. "They can come get me if I can't have the car. And if, you know, I can still go."

"Have you checked with Gretchen?" he asks, still looking at his hands.

"No, but I can."

"If you two can work something out, it's fine."

"Dad—"

He lifts the edges of his fingertips, just barely, to stop me. "I think we should be done talking to each other for right now."

Which is worse than the yelling. Worse than getting privileges taken away. Worse than anything. If he would just let me say I'm sorry . . .

But he won't look at me. So I walk out of the kitchen, upstairs, to see if Gretchen's awake yet. I leave my cereal bowl on the counter. I'll clean up the soggy remnants later, when I know Dad has left.

Gretchen's still asleep, though, and who knows when she'll get up. I go ahead and call Taryn, ask her for a ride to rehearsal.

Since there's time to kill before she arrives, I think about texting Benji, but Darby would probably tell me that I'm supposed to make him text me first. The thought of him, last night, both the yes and the no of it . . . I decide to examine the wreckage of my schoolwork instead. I pull out my folders, all the random assignment sheets and notes, and start to make a list of what I need to make up, what's coming next week, and what it's too late to really do much about. While I'm doing this, I hear Dad and Hannah talking downstairs, and then him leaving for his clients. I pause, frozen at my desk, to see if he hollers up the stairs to say good-bye, but he doesn't.

It's not until almost three fifteen when the doorbell rings. I've brought my psych reading downstairs, so I can be ready as soon as my ride arrives, but it's been hard to concentrate, checking my phone every few minutes to see if anyone's called or texted—even though they haven't—not Taryn, about being late, and also still no Benji, which bums me out more than I expect.

When I open the door, it's Sylvia.

"Sorry," she says, only half sounding it. "Taryn didn't tell me you needed a ride until I was on the way back from the farmers' market. And her directions weren't exactly the best."

It's annoying, but I can see Sylvia already feels that way. "It's okay. I had homework anyway."

"Yeah, I've got a paper too," she says.

As we drive through Decatur and over toward Emory I ask her what she's working on, the classes she's in. I've never heard of sociology before, but by the time we get back to their house she's told me enough to make me curious. It might be something I'll want to take, if I can get in anywhere. I help Sylvia with her grocery bags, and when we go inside, there's an amazing smell coming from the kitchen. Taryn, their roommate Veronica, and Freckle Face from the other day are in there, talking. Taryn's in a ruffled apron, bending over the open oven.

"Perfect timing!" she says, pulling out a tin of blueberry muffins.

"Those smell fantastic," I say.

"I thought we didn't have any food." Sylvia holds up the grocery bags.

"I found some blueberries in the freezer!" Taryn chirps.

"Great," Sylvia grumbles, unloading her bags.

Taryn puts the muffins on a plate, and we take them downstairs to eat while we practice.

"Let's start with the stuff we sang Wednesday," Sylvia says, picking up her guitar. "So at least we have that down."

"I found that new one, though," Taryn says. "Wait, let me get the CD." She runs back up the stairs. We can hear her bouncing all the way to the second floor.

"Super," Sylvia says under her breath.

"Do you not want to do it?" I ask.

She shakes her head. "Tee just gets excitable sometimes."

Taryn comes pounding back down, waving pages over her head.

"Lyrics." She pats me on the head. I see that this is a song I actually know.

But I don't want Sylvia in a bad mood during practice.

"What if we do one from the other day first," I try, glancing at Sylvia, "to warm up?"

Taryn pokes out her lips for a second. But then, just like that, she grins. "Okay!"

The bagpipes from Taryn's synth begin. Veronica and Freckle Face come down to listen, parking themselves on the couch and tucking their legs underneath them.

I lean forward, start.

For the most part, it goes pretty well. Before we can do it again, though, a phone starts bleeping from the big glass coffee table. Taryn lunges for it.

"Sorry, I just . . ."

She looks at the screen, holds it so Sylvia can see. "It's Erin. I really need to take this but just for a sec, I promise." She doesn't even wait for Sylvia or me to answer, just presses something and says, "Hey," real quiet. We watch as she puts her finger to her other ear, goes up the steps.

Veronica rolls her eyes. "We're going to take off, then."

Sylvia hardly nods at them.

"Bye, guys," I say, waving.

Freckle Face points her thumb in the direction Taryn just went. "Have fun."

"Who's Erin?" I ask Sylvia when they're gone.

She shrugs. "New girlfriend of Taryn's. Who seems fairly needy."

I glance at the clock over the washing machine. It's already closer to five o'clock than four.

Sylvia sees me. "Why don't we go over some of these others together?"

It's another hour before Taryn comes back down. She startles us both with a big *"God!"* at the top of the stairs.

"Sorry about that." She throws up her hands. I think she's going to explain, but she just goes, "Drama," as if that's enough. She moves to her keyboard, walking a wider-than-necessary path around Sylvia. "So, should we just pick up where we left off?"

"If you want." Sylvia shrugs.

"I actually—" I look at the clock again, not wanting to. "Am going to have to go at six thirty." This is already way later than I thought I was going to be over here. I'm supposed to go out with Fabian tonight, but the clock hands—and my fight with Dad this morning—tell me that's not going to happen. I'm not actually grounded yet, and maybe I won't be, because of the mean thing I said—the way I hurt him out of being angry—but I don't really want to flaunt that in his face.

The gleam goes out of Taryn. "Well, why don't we work a

little longer, at least. Show me a few you did, so I can catch up."

We go back through the songs Sylvia just taught me. Taryn's rhythms and loops mixed in make everything way different, but also a lot better. By the last song, even though I mess up a few times, I've still got that kind of giddy feeling I had the other day. I like what we've done, and the warm spread of excitement pushes through me again.

"Come on, Little Bit," Taryn tells me, shutting down. "I'll take you home."

"Thanks for being so patient," I say to Sylvia.

"Well, keep working on it."

"Char's fabulous the way she is," Taryn clips, not looking at Sylvia and heading up the stairs.

I'm not looking forward to facing Dad, but whatever it is that's going on in this basement between these two, I'm ready to get away from.

Chapter Sixteen

After breakfast the next morning, Dad asks me to go on a walk. "I need the air," he says, patting his stomach. "Not to mention the exercise."

I could use the exercise too, but I wish, a little, that we'd stay in the house, so Hannah or at least Darby can be around for backup. What I really need to do, though, is just apologize and listen, so I suck it up, put on my sneakers, and go.

For a long way, he doesn't say anything. Ten minutes solid I'm tense, waiting for him to start discussing my punishment. But eventually it's nice, just walking together, me and him. It's like the grocery store, which we haven't done in forever.

We're about two blocks away from the house again when he breaks the silence.

"I want you to pursue your talents," he goes. "But you have a responsibility to your schoolwork too, for more than one reason."

I tell him I know. I tell him I'm not going to do anything but homework today. That I promise to be focused, and I'm sorry for what I said.

He hugs me in the driveway. "Maybe I'll get to come see you sing sometime. I mean, I'd like to." And it feels good, thinking that when he does, I'll make him proud.

When we get back, I've finally got a text from Benji: *Slept late but woke up still thinking abt Friday. Thx for giving me something to smile abt this wknd.*

It's sweet, but also a little weird. And late. While I'm glad he's thinking about me, I wish he'd been more like Fabian and left it at *Friday was cool.* And sent it yesterday.

Hope your day keeps you smiling, I text back, my own cheesiness making me wince too.

I spend the rest of the afternoon making good on my promise to Dad, but after dinner, I'm itching to work on a new song for Sad Jackal. At first I think I might write about friends turning into—what, sweethearts? Lovers? Something with benefits?—but

I don't know what Benji is to me right now, and besides, if I do that, everyone will think it's really about Oliver and we'll be back where we started.

There's plenty else in my head, but none of it is right for a song either. What I really need—really, truly need—is the notebook. I need to write out all the jumbled-up things inside me about Oliver, Taryn and Sylvia, even Benji. And I need Trip's insight and understanding on the other end of it. I need his perfect balance of humor and seriousness. I need somebody who won't expect me to have all the answers right away, but who's interested in helping me find them.

I don't have the notebook, though, and I don't have Trip. What I do have is a deadline with Oliver and a duty to Sad Jackal. So I test out a few other ideas. *"We're just friends"* and *"Quit talking about us, you rejected bitch"* are the only things I can think of when it comes to Whitney or Oliver. Being surprised to find out that the guy you're crushing on is involved with someone else is out of the question, obviously, and *"I'm in two bands at the same time"* isn't a good way to break the news to Sad Jackal.

Frustrated, I open Jilly's iPhoto and flip through that, but it's all images I've looked through a ton of times before. One picture stands out this time—a crazy Hindu parade she walked into, coming out of the subway on a chorus trip to New York. But thinking about New York makes me think about what Taryn and Sylvia said about hipster girl bands and how they try so hard to be all detached and disinterested, lisping into the microphone in their little-girl voices. *Only a little girl crawls out of you*, I jot down, but that's as far as it gets. It's midnight and I need to go to bed.

On Monday, I'm not really sure what class Benji has before 20th Cen., but I wait for him by the double doors of the main building, because it seems like the right thing to do, for a couple of reasons. While I'm there, I picture not just today, but the next day, and the next, and maybe several more days or weeks after that—me waiting to meet him so we can hold hands on the way to class. I remember that flower he gave me and wonder what other surprises he might show up with, if I gave him the chance. How would it feel, leaving school every day in that Volvo of his, going—wherever we wanted?

When he sees me, he's pleased, and even more so when I take his hand. He doesn't say anything about it—just asks me about my weekend as we walk to class. Our fingers are entwined, loose and casual. It feels natural and yet also completely weird. After class, before we separate, he kisses me, quick, on the lips, and I think, *Yeah, maybe I could get used to this.*

Maybe.

•   •   •

The girls and I go to Duck's for lunch, and they want to know all about my date. "Is he a good kisser?" And "Did he try to drug you?" And other stupid things like that. I tell them how Benji acts all tough but is this terrific guy inside—which is true. What I can't say is that part of me is still thinking, *Benji and me? Really?* But by the time we head back to school, half the girls seem in love with Benji themselves, even Lish. I barely have to say anything about what kissing him was like; they all swoon just hearing how sweet he was about it.

It's hard to tell what Oliver thinks, though. About anything. I thought he and I were okay after last week, but when he sees me waiting outside psych, he doesn't stop to chat. Instead he opens the door, holds it for me, and then follows me in, barely lifting the corners of his mouth. The only thing he says when we're in our desks is did I bring the new song. And he isn't happy when I can only look back at him, biting on my lip.

Whatever. I've been busy and I'll have the new songs soon. I hope.

Even though he's sullen, we have rehearsal, so I hang out for a while by his car after school, making sure to stand nowhere near him. That is until I remember Lish's comment about how hard we try to look like we're not together. There's no winning in this situation. It's stupid.

What's also stupid is that when Oliver's ready to go, he simply glances my way and jerks his head toward his car. A wave of irritation sweeps over me. Again.

What I want to say is, *What the hell?* But instead I go for predictably normal and calm: "So, how was your weekend? Feel better?"

"I should ask you the same thing." His caustic tone fills the car.

"What's that supposed to mean?"

"Have a good time with McLaughlin?" He laughs a little. "Contract any horrible diseases we should know about?"

I'm burning. He cannot make a dig at Benji, not like that. "I don't see how that has anything to do with you, and how your weekend was, or how you're feeling, which is what I asked."

He shrugs. "I still don't like the cover idea."

"Yeah." I look straight out the windshield. "Well, it's not just your decision to make."

"People are still staring," he mutters as we pull out of the lot.

"Ignore them, then. God." *Why would it be so terrible if people did think we were going out, anyway?* I want to add. Absolute total no, of course, but his making such a big deal about it is verging on mean.

"Covers are lame," he goes on. "It's like, *Really? You couldn't come up with anything else?*"

Covers aren't lame. They're fun. And so, so, so much easier.

He sighs. "But what we really need are some new songs."

"I'm working on it, okay?" I snap. "If it's so unbearably urgent, why don't *you* write them? Instead of letting everyone *think* you do?"

I watch him from the corner of my eye, to see how he reacts to this.

"That's not what happened."

"Yeah, well, that's how it sounded."

"Maybe Trip should come back," he says, half to himself, as we get to his house.

Which makes me want to punch him. I mean, I was the one who told him not to let go of Trip in the first place. And Trip clearly has no interest in playing with us or anyone anymore, no matter how bad we miss him, because he's obviously too deeply entrenched in his new group of friends. His new girlfriend. Also, I don't *want* to be in a band with someone who doesn't want to be friends anymore. Oliver's moodiness is bad enough. I don't need to be in rehearsal, avoiding standing too close to Trip, too.

I don't get a chance to say any of this to Oliver, though, because Eli's already at the house, waiting. I glare at Oliver's back as he goes inside, then drop down on the rec room couch to watch them race on the PS3. When Abe and Fabian arrive, I am still gloomy and unhelpful. They play some songs, but I don't comment. I sing "Cage Song" and "Disappear," with as little luster as possible. I think Oliver and Fabian can tell, but they don't say anything. But it's not just me. No one seems very energized at all. It is nothing like practicing with Taryn and Sylvia.

When we finally wrap up, Fabian asks if I need a lift home. I glance at Oliver and tell Fabian no, thanks. I'm sick of Oliver's crap. He and I need to have a real talk.

But once the guys have all left, Oliver's obstinate on the couch, his acoustic draped across his lap. He messes around, playing one thing, then another.

"So, what's up?" he says, not making eye contact.

I sink down into the chair across from him, so that if he does look up, he'll have to look straight at me. "I should ask you the same thing."

"I don't know what *that* was." He points his thumb to the practice area.

Normally I would tell him we're merely on a low after a big high, that the energy will pick up, but instead I just look at him. None of us were that great this afternoon, but neither was he. So he can't act like he's the only one who doesn't have a problem.

"We need to get out there more," he says. "Make some more connections. Look for new venues. Spend some time recording." He rubs his bangs, frowns. "What we really need is some new material."

That does it. He can't treat me however he wants and then expect me to do everything for him. And it occurs to me: I don't have to.

"You said that before. About nineteen times. I get it. But maybe for once you're going to have to find someone else to help you."

His blue eyes jump up at me, widen. It almost scares me too.

"What do you mean?"

Part of me backs down. But another part, a new part, feels glad to see him this way: panicked that I might not be around.

"I'm not just your lackey," I tell him. "You can't snap your fingers and expect me to do your bidding. I have a life outside of you, you know. And in my real life, my grades are horrible and there's all this stuff going on, and I'm sorry if it means I'm not good enough for you, but I don't know if I can keep it up, to be honest. Or if I want to."

That last part lingers between us. The me not wanting to. Do this. Anymore.

His eyes move away from me, back down to his guitar. "You don't have to be here," he says.

It stings, how simply he says it. How detached. But I know he's right. I don't have to be here. I think of Taryn cheering me on, telling me how fantastic I am. How Oliver can barely stand it to give me half a smile sometimes, how pissy he's been since the dance. How I've crazily gotten into pretending to date—and then maybe wanting to date—Benji, all for Oliver's ego. I have a flash, then, of Trip. Nobody else in the world could possibly understand how infuriating Oliver's being right now. And I wonder if this is how he felt before he left the band.

But, like him, I understand I don't have to stay.

So I say it: "Well, maybe I won't, then."

I expect Oliver to at least look up after that, but he stares at his guitar, fingers barely making any sound over the strings.

I stand up.

He doesn't move.

I go upstairs and let myself out.

Getting out of the warm closeness of Oliver's rec room and into the clean, cold, darkening air is like a physical manifestation of truly making a break. But it also feels sharp and terrible, leaving him that way. I'm not sure, ten yards away from Oliver's house, that I've actually done what I've done. I need to say it out loud to make it real. And since Trip is not an option, I call the only person I can think of at this point who I know will answer for sure.

"I quit the band," I tell Benji as soon as he picks up.

"Which one?"

This makes me laugh. "Oliver's. Sad Jackal. I quit. I think."

"You think? Or you know?"

I tell him about telling Oliver I don't want to do it anymore, how tired I am, doing his bidding with almost zero appreciation.

"You okay?" he asks.

I'm honest. "I'm not sure."

"You need me to come over? Give you a little . . . comfort?"

"Shut up," I retort, before I realize this isn't the old Benji talking. "I mean, I think I'm okay. But that's sweet of you."

"I didn't mean it like that," he says.

"I'm okay, really." But I think of psych tomorrow and having to be in the same room as Oliver. Of Lish at lunch, pestering me about why I quit. Do I tell people? Or just let them find out? Am I honestly not going back? And how in the world am I going to tell Fabian?

"Listen," I say with seriousness. "You've been so incredible to me. And I appreciate it. I mean, thanks."

"My pleasure."

It's not enough, but it will have to do.

I let myself into the house quietly and tiptoe upstairs to my room. Since I promised I would, I figure I should try to get some more homework done before Dad and Hannah get home. But almost as soon as I shut the door behind me, Darby bursts in.

"Did you hear?" she squeals, ignoring my comment about, you know, *knocking*. She grabs my hairbrush and starts singing into it like a microphone, popping her hips and pointing a glittery fingernail at me. "You. Are gonna. Be playing at. Winter Formal!"

The blood drops out of my face and into my stomach. "No."

"Yes! I was just online with Alicia, whose sister is in SGA, and she said at their meeting this afternoon it was *unanimous* that they want Sad Jackal. Even, like, the director agreed." She juts her hand over her head in rock star victory. "So, what do you think about that, huh?"

"I think that's great," I groan. "That's really . . . great."

I don't tell Darby about my quitting Sad Jackal. Partly because she'd freak, and I don't want to deal, but also because, thinking about it a little more after dinner and the next morning, I'm not sure I have technically quit. I only said *maybe* I don't want to be a part of the band. And Oliver said I didn't *have* to be there. Which means, if I want to, I can be. And the idea of Winter Formal makes me think I still might. I mean, Winter Formal is huge. And it will also be fun. But I'm still mad at Oliver. He'll need to say something to me about it first, and apologize for yesterday. For all of it.

I thought he'd call me last night, actually, to tell me the news. But when he didn't, I figured he doesn't know yet. Just because Darby got hot gossip, that doesn't mean SGA has reached out to Sad Jackal. They'll probably call him, to be all official. maybe I'm not even supposed to know. I figure I'll wait Oliver out, see what he does.

It's hard not to tell Benji about it, though, when I meet him to walk to 20th Cen. He gives me a peck on the lips that's so quick I hardly know it's happened, and we walk to class, holding hands. Though I don't feel very girlfriendy toward him right now, it's still nice.

It's nice too when, as soon as Dr. Campbell announces we'll have another take-home test to pick up at the end of class, Benji turns and winks at me. Probably I don't need his help anymore, but I like it that this is now our thing. Whether kissing is involved or not.

At lunch I keep waiting for Winter Formal to come up, but it seems the weekend is the main topic of conversation. Benji and I are old news; everybody's busy talking about the new movie that's opening, where we're spending the night, what time we'll go to the show, et cetera. Not even Lish mentions Sad Jackal, or my new boyfriend.

After lunch I try to focus on my next two classes, but mostly I'm thinking about Oliver. He's going to be *stoked*, whenever he finds out, and even though I'm mad at him, it will be great to see his face.

But I meant what I said yesterday and, more than that, I meant what I felt. I won't go running back to him because he needs me. This isn't like seventh grade, when all it took was for him to wait long enough after I started giving him the Silent Treatment for me to break down, and we'd go back to normal after a joke before school. Just telling me about Winter Formal and asking about new material—even if he has that really panicked look on his face—isn't going to be enough. He needs to show me that he really understands, on every level. Because probably to get ready for this gig, I will have to quit singing with Taryn and Sylvia, and the way Oliver's been acting, working with them is way more fun. Oliver's going to need to—well, maybe not *beg*, but definitely do something more than act like nothing happened, like he usually does. Being asked to do the most important formal at school besides prom (and maybe after Winter Formal we will get asked to do prom) doesn't mean good old reliable Spider will jump in like always, help him make everything work.

So I don't wait for him outside of psych. When he comes in, my eyes don't waver from my reading. After Ms. Neff begins her lecture, I face forward the whole time.

When the bell rings at the end of the day, I take my time putting my notebook in my bag. But when I look up, he's already gone. And he isn't waiting for me outside, either.

Who *is* waiting for me, however, talking to Gretchen by the car, is Benji.

"Hey there," he says when I walk up.

"Hey."

He leans in, gives me one of those quick kisses again. Gretchen looks away.

"I've got practice this afternoon," I tell him.

"I know." He smiles up under his bangs. "I thought—" He puts his arm over my shoulder, trying to be casual. He watches the people walking past us, clears his throat. I see Gretchen not-looking at us again. I lean back into his arm, try to make it feel a little more normal. But we aren't talking, and he doesn't say anything to Gretchen either. We stand there, waiting for take-forever Darby. Every minute that passes, his arm gets heavier on my shoulder.

"So, then," he says when my stepsister finally strolls up.

I get myself out from under his arm. "So, tomorrow? After school? For the test?"

"Should I call you later?"

"I'll probably be at Taryn and Sylvia's right up until dinner," I dodge. "And then I have a ton of homework and some songwriting to do probably. So, tomorrow?"

He nods. But I see the trace of a frown on his face.

"I'll see you in my dreams," I try to joke, but I sound weird and stiff too.

"Sure thing." He gives me that crooked salute and strides off toward the upper lot. I realize he must've hustled out of last period to make sure to find me down here before I left. It's pretty perfect boyfriend behavior, to be honest. But not perfect me-and-Benji behavior, which is what I'm starting to miss.

Taryn's supposed to pick me up at three thirty for our practice, but as four o'clock and then four thirty pass, I realize I'm waiting for nothing. I'm stranded at home with no car, and neither Taryn nor Sylvia is responding. After five, Taryn sends a text: *SHOOT! WE HAD A MTG 2DAY I 4GOT. MAKE IT UP SAT? XOXOXO.*

In my frustration I'm tempted to call Fabian, but complaining to him about the friends he introduced me to seems uncool, and telling him about my fight with Oliver is unnecessary, since we'll make up any minute now. I put some bagel pizzas in the toaster oven and email Jilly. I write and write—not knowing I had so much to say. I tell her how enthusiastic Taryn and Sylvia are. How Lish has resurfaced and that I'm looking forward to hanging out this weekend with her and the other girls. That I sort of quit Sad Jackal, but I know Oliver's going to ask me back, and ultimately this is a good thing for us to go through. I tell her about Benji, too, and in doing so think maybe I should call him, since I'm not at practice. But we left it that we'd talk tomorrow and for some reason that's what I want to do—think about him, and the rest of it, tomorrow.

• • •

I'm at my locker between first and second the next morning when Lish comes crashing into me, throwing her arms around my neck and squealing indecipherably into my hair.

When she steps back her face is lit up like a birthday cake. One with lots of pink roses. "I can't believe it. I can't! Winter Formal? Oh my god! You are so cool!"

She's grinning so hard I could pluck the tendons on her neck and play a song.

So, I guess the word is out.

Now that I know Oliver knows, I'm dying to see him. All he has to do is apologize, really. I mean, he is one of my oldest friends, and this is my band too.

I'm so caught up in thinking about it, I can barely concentrate in 20th Cen. When it's over, I almost don't know why Benji's taking my hand and leading me out the door.

"You still want to do the test this afternoon?" he asks me after a minute.

His uncertain tone catches me off guard enough to pull me out of my mental whirl. "Of course, duh. Why? Don't you want to?"

"Wasn't sure if you needed me anymore is all."

"Of course I need you. You don't think that?"

"It's up to you," he says, not smiling.

I stop, since I'm going out to the parking lot to meet Lish, but he keeps walking. "Hey," I holler. "After school, yeah? Parking lot? We're cool, right? I really, really, really need you!"

His hand raises up, but he doesn't turn around.

I don't wait for Oliver outside of psych, but I do look up when he comes into class. He doesn't look at me at all, and it twinges a little, but this is how it usually works with us. I glance over at him a couple of times before the bell, but he's got his back to me, talking to the kid on his other side. It's immature, but I can take it. Our friendship and the band are both bigger than this, and so am I.

After Ms. Neff gets us settled into our timed writing, I tear off a corner of notebook paper and write on it, *Great news about Winter Formal.* I slip it across to him, tucking it under his elbow. For just a second, his head jerks up in my direction, but then he frowns at his paper and writes with more purpose. When I look back, the note's on the floor. A strange shock rises in me, understanding that he actually pushed it there on purpose. Without even looking at it.

We write for the entirety of class. Half-focused on my essay, I can't help but sneak looks every now and then at my scrap there on the floor, right by his shoe. Maybe he didn't see it fall. Maybe he doesn't even know I slipped it over.

But I know he saw me. I know he lifted his head.

When the bell rings, he moves coldly and quickly away from me. So now I also know that Sad Jackal is going to play Winter Formal without me.

The stun of absolute rejection from Oliver numbs me. I can move—I'm plodding out of class, into the hall, up the ramp, and through the doors, out to the parking lot—but I can't feel myself doing it. I walk, lifting the corners of my mouth in recognition when other people wave hello. I squint in the cold, bright sunshine. I find Benji's car, see him resting his forearms and elbows on the roof, watching me through his sunglasses. I know I do this. But I can't feel how.

"Hey," I say, closing the gap between us.

I watch myself reach for the door handle, feel my muscles pull it open. I hear his fingers drum against the roof of the car. Hear, "All right, then," over me as I drop down into the passenger's seat.

"You okay?" he wants to know, appearing in the seat next to me.

"I'm okay."

I can't tell him. Can't explain, because I can't fully wrap my head around what's happened. Also, I'm not sure I can get the words out.

"Good to see you," he says, leaning across to kiss my cheek.

I don't even feel it. "Let's go."

"Pizza day?" He checks the rearview.

"Uh-huh."

He touches some buttons on the stereo, and the music explodes around us. For once I am not wishing he would change it. We say nothing on the way to Fellini's. I am so glad that we drive this short distance instead of walk.

We are out of the car. Walking inside. Benji holds open the door for me. At the counter, words come out of my mouth: a white slice, a Coke. Benji orders something, gives the cashier money. I pay attention to the echo of ice, the harsh hiss of the soda falling into my cup.

We sit across from each other by the window. Benji's aviator glasses are off. His eyebrows are furrowed.

"So, you gonna tell me, or what?" he says.

Utterly against my will, I start crying.

"Hey, hey, hey." He half stands up, leaning toward me, like I've spilled a soda across the table. It's awkward for both of us.

His hand is on my wrist. It is warm. And heavy.

"He just won't even talk to me," I croak, as though that explains anything. "Usually when I get mad at him he just blows me off a couple of days and then . . . But this time . . . I mean, I tried, and then he just . . ."

"Who? Oliver?"

I nod, still not able to look at him.

Benji's hand leaves mine. He falls back against the wooden booth.

"Dude," he says, waiting a second, hoping I'll look up. When I don't, he finishes: "That guy is a goob."

"He's not a goob," I say, automatic. I can't take my hand away from my face to frown at him. I have no idea what I look like. I kind of don't care.

"He is. I've thought so since ninth grade, man. An utter, old-fashioned, emo-boy, no-one-cares-anymore *goob*. Those sweater-vests and jackets? What is that? And tell me, really—because I know you know—how long does it take for him to get his hair like that? Strand-by-strand sculpting? Or more of a sleep-on-your-face kind of thing?"

In spite of myself, I laugh. I can feel the itchy cloak of my tears still on my cheeks, but I am laughing.

"I can't reveal his dressing room secrets," I choke out. "Not even to you."

He hunches down, leans closer, squinting. "But you know, don't you? You do know."

"There are secret formulas I may be privy to," I concede. My voice is thick, but I finally lift my face.

"So why you want to hang with a homey like that, yo?" He makes some stupid gang sign, squeaking his voice.

"I've known him since fifth grade," I eke out. "We've always been together. He's a jerk sometimes, but I understand him. It's the way it works."

"Unless it doesn't work," he says gently.

My eyes connect with his. We don't say anything. I know I'm a mess. But that I've made such a surprising friend like Benji fills my heart with gratitude. Simultaneously, knowing how I've used him fills the rest of me with shame. I understand, very clearly now, that my feelings for Benji don't go beyond friendship. And it's time for me to tell him.

"I don't think this whole dating thing is really . . . going to work," I say.

He looks away, says quietly, "Well, that's not the response I was looking for."

Ugh. Ugh. Ugh. Ugh.

"I know. And I'm sorry. And I honestly thought it was going to work for a while. I mean, I wanted it to."

He doesn't say anything for a minute. I feel horrible.

"I guess I'm not very good at relationships." He finally looks at me.

"No, that's not it." I grab his hand. "You do everything great. I'm too stupid to appreciate you that way, is all."

"Huh. Well, that's mature-sounding of you."

God. He's really hurt. Ugh. "Benji, I so don't want to lose you as a friend."

He shakes his head. "Oh, you won't." His voice is bitter. "It just puts me in an awkward position for a little while, but . . . I'll get over it. It's what I do."

It's selfish of me, but I'm relieved. And am also trying not to laugh.

"You said 'position.'" I leer at him from across the table.

His hand goes up, maybe a little irritated, but slowly he smiles. "Well."

I clear my throat, looking at him. "I used you, kinda." It's uncomfortable to say.

He shrugs. "I let you. And, you know . . ." He leans closer, making it hard to see anything but the pointy gleam of his longer-than-the-other canine tooth. "I liked it. At first."

Perfect timing for the server to come with paper plates bending under the greasy weight of our pizza slices. We thank him, sip our drinks, clear our throats, try again.

"Which section do you want to tackle first?" He reaches for his 20th Cen. textbook and the test tucked inside.

"How 'bout you take front page, I take back page?"

"Sounds like a plan."

"And hey, Benji, thanks."

His eyes are still sad-looking, but he bops me on the head with his pencil and gives me a wink. "Just goin' with the tide, Coastal."

• • •

I know my breakup with Benji has the potential to disintegrate quickly from fine to horrible, so I'm nervous all night and the next day, when I meet him before third period, as I've been doing. We don't hold hands, and there's notably no kiss, but we get through it okay. It actually makes me think maybe Oliver and I can still fix things, eventually, if given the opportunity. But then the idea of fixing things makes me picture Trip, and when I do, I'm not sure whether I could be as forgiving as Benji in his case. Or if he would care.

Sixth-period psych, and Oliver's clearly not in a forgiving mood either, because he's not looking at me again. I examine him across the row. He is wearing—ha-ha—another sweater-vest today. Those stupid skinny jeans, those wing tips. If I didn't know him so well, maybe I'd see him the way Benji does. *You are a goob*, I try in my head. It almost sticks.

But the end of class is a little harder. I have to give myself a reason to not get up to leave when he does, so that we're not walking out at the same time and I don't have to see him not looking at me. Ms. Neff's handed back our timed writing, so I make myself have questions about mine. Even without looking, I hear Oliver walk out. He's heading to practice. Maybe this afternoon they'll test some new songs he wrote. Even though I don't want to be scurrying after him, I don't like not being a part of his project—our project—anymore.

By the time Darby, Gretchen, and I get home, I'm bummed enough about losing Sad Jackal that Darby easily talks me into helping her with Spanish flash cards. I lie on her bed, holding up card after card, correcting her or saying "yes" or "try again" for almost two hours. I'm trying not to look at the clock. I'm trying not to listen for my phone in the next room, in case Fabian calls to find out why I wasn't at rehearsal or to say they missed me. Or, better, that he, Abe, and Eli all rebelled when Oliver told them the news, and they're demanding I come back.

But my phone, like so often, is silent.

Miraculously, Friday does have its own special kind of levity. On the drive to school, I find myself looking forward to lunch, to gossiping with Lish and the other girls, just laughing about nothing and finalizing plans for tonight. We're all going to the movies, then spending the night at D'Shelle's house, since her mom doesn't care what anyone does, and supplies, from time to time, a bottle of pink champagne for sleepover parties. Also, Fabian texted very first thing this morning, saying: *Damn about the band. Saturday night still?*

Buoyed by hearing from him, by the beautiful, crisp November sunshine and another good encounter with Benji in third period, I'm a lot happier walking out to the parking lot at lunch. I remember me and Lish skipping arm in arm down the halls last year, for no real reason, cackling and not caring what anyone thought.

I see her up ahead, leaning against D'Shelle's car, arms crossed, and I'm about to say, "We should've skipped out here," when I realize she's frowning.

"What's up?" I'm breathless.

"So annoying," she huffs, shaking her head. The other girls are gathered together a few cars down, huddled around the open driver's side of someone's truck. One of them looks back in our direction. Not, I notice, for very long.

"Well, report cards." She holds up an exasperated hand.

"Those were last week."

"I know." She tosses her head. "Which is why it's even more annoying that now D'Shelle's mom is all, 'You're not going to improve these grades if you're staying up all night every weekend with your friends.'" She makes her voice tight and grating, like I guess D'Shelle's mom must sound.

"But that's easy to fix; we'll promise to sleep."

"I know, right? But they had some other fight or something this week, and whatever, and so . . . we can't tonight."

"We could do it at Bronwyn's. Or yours. I'd say mine, but Darby's so annoying—"

Brief displeasure clenches her face, and her hand flicks in the air again. "It's too late for that. Everybody's parents checking with everyone else's. You know how it is."

It'd take five minutes, I want to say. But then I catch, in the corner of my eye, Bronwyn looking over at us, a wisp of her long brown hair catching across her lip. Something in her face—I don't know what it is, exactly—makes me understand this isn't about report cards. Déjà vu creeps up my spine. I've had this conversation, or something like it, with Lish before, back when she couldn't give me a ride to school. I don't know what I did to be uncool then, but I understand what I did this time. Lish must've heard from Eli about my not being in Sad Jackal.

But instead of being crushed and sad the way I was on Wednesday when Oliver pushed my note onto the floor, this whole Lish thing simply makes me *mad*. I squint at her, realizing what a stupid poseur she is. She has no idea about me anymore. She may have been my best friend for a couple of years, but she didn't truly understand me, and I didn't really understand her. Now I do, but she's still in the dark. Besides, I've dealt with her ditching me before. She has no idea how over her I can be.

It stings knowing all the other girls think I'm uncool too, knowing I'll be at home on a Friday night and eating lunch by myself from now on, but I don't want Lish on my coattails anymore. I don't know why I didn't see her this way before, but it doesn't matter. I will rise above her, and them, and all of this high school bullshit, and they'll realize what a mistake they made.

But I'm not going to give her the satisfaction of getting a rise out of me. "I see."

I turn around without saying anything else, not even when she calls after me, surprised.

Chapter Seventeen

Saturday, Taryn and Sylvia change our practice time five
times, and finally Gretchen has to drive me, but I don't
care about the details. I just want to be over there, singing
with them, having fun, forgetting.

In the car, Gretchen goes, "I heard."

"Heard about what?"

"Heard about you and Oliver."

I groan. "Jesus. We are not going out. I thought that died
already."

"No." Her mouth goes down in a line. "About how you had a
big fight. How you're not in the band anymore."

Huh.

"We didn't have a fight." I find myself echoing Trip. "It was just creative differences."

"Uh-huh," Gretchen grunts.

Whatever. I don't care what she thinks. What anyone thinks. I'm growing in new directions.

"Can we come?" Gretchen asks. "Whenever you play?"

"I guess so." I'm eager to get out now, to enter the basement of fun and escape.

"Good. Give me a call if you need a ride home. I'm not going out until later."

"Okay. And, you know, thanks."

She smiles at me, almost pitying. I get out and head to the house.

Taryn wraps me in a huge hug the second she opens the door. There's music blaring from the living room, and at least five other people are in there. Taryn introduces me to everyone, her arm wrapped tight around my shoulders.

"Hi, everybody." I wave to them.

"Charlotte is our secret weapon," Taryn says proudly. "We're going to win Earhorn next week, thanks to her."

"Um, what?" I say.

"We told you about that, right?"

I shake my head. *We're performing next* week?

"Oh." Taryn sneaks an *Oops* look at her friends. "Well, we do this amateur-night thing at this place sometimes and the winners get money and everything and I think maybe Jack Johnson got his start there. Or is it John Mayer? Or . . . well, I don't remember. I think John Mayer was Eddie's Attic, where of course we'd love to play too one day. But still, if you win you get paid and then every six months or so they have a show with all the winners and . . ." The last bit just comes out in a winded sigh: "We just think you would make us win."

Sylvia comes around the corner from the kitchen, wiping her hands on a towel. I'm still a little shocked that our first performance is coming up so soon and that they hadn't told me anything about it before, but the concept sounds fun and cool. I say so to both of them.

"Hooray hooray," Taryn cheers, leading me past everyone and down into the basement, where there are about a dozen candles lit around the room.

"We wanted, you know, some special ambiance," she explains, though I'm not really sure what for.

Her other friends tromp down the stairs behind us. I'm glad that there are other people here. It'll help me get ready for next week, singing in front of strangers.

"We found a couple new songs," Taryn says, shoving some pages into my hands.

I look down at the lyric sheets. I'm not sure it's a great idea for us to take on new material right before performing, but maybe she just wants to expand our options. Maybe she's thinking beyond next Saturday too.

"Well!" Taryn says. "Lots to work on. What should we start with?"

She's looking at me, not Sylvia. So is everyone else. I guess I really am their lucky charm.

"Well—" I think of Eli, and how important he thought it was to drill every song. "How about we warm up with the Heart song, since that's the one I know best."

Taryn looks at Sylvia. "But I really want to try a couple of these new ones."

Yeah, but we need to practice, I want to say, but it's clear Taryn doesn't think so. I figure starting with a new song or two won't kill me.

And so we start. The first one Taryn chooses is really too high for me, but it kind of doesn't matter, I guess, since we're just testing it out. After that, we run through song after song—some old, some new. But we never go through anything more than once. Taryn's nodding and encouraging me the whole time, and her friends on the couch are rolling their heads and tapping along, so I try to stop worrying, and just throw the notes out.

By the time we finish, it's after seven. I'm breathless and happy

and even Sylvia is bouncy, since the last song got everyone dancing around the basement. Taryn suggests we decide on Tuesday
what we'll perform at Earhorn, and then work on getting everything perfect. Since Sylvia agrees with everything Taryn says, I
don't let myself be bothered about it either. The whole afternoon
feels like a much-needed karaoke party.

"We should go to Earhorn!" Taryn holds her hands over her
head in victory.

"What, now?" Sylvia.

"No, not *now*, silly. We should get some grub first. Go, I
don't know, to the Righteous or something, and then head over
there. Check out the competition. Do some research." She rubs
her hands together like she's developing an evil plot.

"I have to check with my dad," I say. Stupid high school girl.
But nobody seems to care.

So I call Dad, ask him if it's okay if I go out to dinner with
the girls in the band, maybe hang out awhile after.

"Home by eleven thirty," he insists. "And I want to meet
these girls."

"You will, Dad. We're playing next Saturday. You can come."

"All right, then." His tone perks up, though he's trying to
mask it.

"All right."

When I tell everyone it's okay, they clap and cheer and argue about who's riding in which car with me. This is way better than Lish and her stupid slumber party, or Oliver and his moods.

The Righteous Room turns out to be a long, skinny bar full of tables crowded with hipsters and their cigarettes, plus a few regular construction-looking guys in baseball caps. Everyone talks around me about what they're going to eat, handing menus back and forth. While we wait I text Fabian, tell him I'm out with Taryn and Sylvia and that I can't do next Saturday night because we'll be playing (*!!!*). A menu finally gets passed to me, and I order the first thing that looks like it might be good.

We eat. We talk. They drink. Across from me, Taryn and a girl in a yellow hat are embroiled in some conversation about education for women in some country I haven't heard of. Sylvia sees me watching them, raises her beer in a sympathetic toast.

But I like it, being with them. I like being in this gaggle of women who have more to discuss than who is wearing what, who's dating whom, and who might be doing what with someone else. Sociology, indie bands, socialized medicine—whatever. It's energizing to be submerged in something so different.

We finish eating. I give Taryn the twelve dollars I have in my wallet and hope it's enough. Cards are handed across the table to her. Nobody else seems to know what they owe.

Into the cars again—I offer to drive, but Sylvia and Freckle

Face say they only had one beer and are okay—and then down through a bunch of streets I've never been on before and into the parking lot of what must be Earhorn. Looking at the plain warehouse front, you wouldn't know this was anywhere to be if you didn't know it was where to be. *Lish, you would die to see this* goes through my head as we walk up. *And you, too, Oliver. Both of you would fall down and die from the overwhelming coolness.*

Inside is amazing, and I wish, for a second, that I'd somehow known about this place back when Trip and I were friends, because he would totally flip over the whole Victorian vibe inside. The front room is dedicated to gallery space—all kinds of art on three walls, with flickering candles and a fireplace filling up the other one. A round velvet couch is in the middle. On and around it are a few girls in scarves, some boys in dark jeans, all of them holding plastic glasses I can only assume are filled with wine.

We all squeeze down a thin hallway to another room, this one even darker. At the very back is a triangular space that's clearly the stage. Along the right side is a bar, with a guy coated in tattoos doling out drinks. Taryn stops, shakes hands with a girl all vintaged out in a black dress, black platform heels, and a thin black hat with a veil. Trip would love her too.

"Come on," Sylvia says, grabbing my elbow and leading me over to the bar. "Let's get you some ginger ale or something."

I accept Sylvia's offer, and we perch against the bar, watching everyone. There are people smoking. People drinking. People done up in outfits, and people who couldn't seem to care less.

As I look around the room, Sylvia doesn't say anything to me, and neither does anyone else, but it's cooler not to talk—not to have to fill the space with our noise. I stand there, sipping my ginger ale, and order another when I finish.

After what feels like a long while, a pudgy guy in jeans and a suit jacket gets up onstage. I watch Taryn move toward him, but there are already four other people who also want to talk to him.

"There we go," Sylvia says, lifting her beer in his direction. "The ringleader of the circus, so to speak."

Taryn hovers on the edges, and then finally dives in, practically elbowing another girl off the stage. The guy looks at her at first with tolerance while she talks, and then interest. Finally he shakes her hand. She heads off the stage grinning, and I lose them in the crowd as the guy steps to the mic, welcomes everyone. There are loud cheers from the audience.

"Let's get right to it," he says. "Remember this is a judged competition, with our judges being anonymous. But trust me, they're all here, so be careful who you snub."

Chuckles from the audience, which has grown. Taryn and her friends finally appear beside us.

"Don't you want to go closer?" Taryn says.

"We're good here," Sylvia answers.

Taryn looks at her a second, and then, I guess, agrees. The emcee calls the first performer up to the stage. Her hair is dyed black and she's carrying a giant case, maybe for a cello. I lean against the bar, trying to read the looks on Taryn's and Sylvia's faces. I don't know what all of this is normally like, but for me, I can tell, it's going to be an education.

Two hours later we're back in the car. I'm up front, giving Sylvia directions to my house. Everyone is high-fiving each other and laughing.

"We are going to trounce them next week!" Taryn shouts from the backseat.

"So we're all signed up?" Sylvia wants to know.

"For the third time, yes. God. Everything's taken care of."

"And you will dominate," Veronica says.

Though I'm still thinking that that guy with the harmonica was extremely talented, and some of the other performers were also terrific, I too feel pretty good about our chances next week. Most of the groups tonight were snobby performers, hardly able to engage the audience. Our style is way more peppy and interesting. We'll definitely make an impact. Especially if we practice hard.

"You feel good?" Taryn asks, getting out to hug me when they drop me off.

"I feel good." I nod, still trying to absorb everything I saw tonight.

"You know you're going to rock, right?"

"We're going to rock."

"So Tuesday we'll just perfect a few things," she says, flitting her hand.

"We'll make it perfect all week."

She touches my face. "*You* are perfect. I'm glad you came out with us."

"Me too. And thanks for the ride."

"See you Tuesday?"

"Tuesday, Tuesday," I sing, stepping back.

Sylvia toots the horn as she pulls away, and I dance, waving at them in the yard. The whole way back into the house, I feel the happiest I've been all week.

After such an amazing Saturday night, after getting a glimpse of what life will be like in another short year when maybe I'm in college too, or at least not in high school anymore, nothing else really matters. School becomes a monotonous blur. I don't see Trip. I don't see Abe or Eli. I don't see Lish and I don't care. I pretend I don't see Oliver ignoring me in psych. I eat my lunch hunched over a book. Benji meets me before class every day, and I trade a few texts with Fabian. Tuesday night Taryn and Sylvia and I practice again, agree on the set list, and jump up and down together. It is way more fun than any Sad Jackal rehearsal—even the ones this summer with Trip. I call Jilly so that we can both squeal about the fact that she'll be home for Thanksgiving break next week. I sing, alone in my room, since Taryn and Sylvia are too busy for other practices. I duck my head down. I make it through.

And then it's Saturday again. By the time I wake up at eleven o'clock, Taryn's left me five texts. Most of them are full of exclamation points. One of them asks if I want to come over early, maybe go to the Righteous again for dinner before the show. I find Gretchen in her and Darby's room, ask if it's okay if I take the car.

"Of course, rock star," she says. "Darby's going to be mad you're not letting her do you over, though."

"Oh, no. Of course she is. I'm getting ready before I leave. I couldn't do this without her." I indicate my baggy flannel pajama bottoms, my rat's-nest hair.

"She probably has a schedule for you, then." Gretchen smirks. "You better get downstairs and see."

By quarter to seven I am in the car, blasting the stereo, singing at the top of my lungs—partly to warm up, partly because I have to get out some energy. With the sun already mostly down and everyone's headlights on, driving feels even more exotic, more grown-up. I am excited and nervous, but in a good way. Darby spent several hours blowing out my hair, treating my face with a couple of different anti-whatever creams and gels, and then meticulously applying a lot of makeup in such a way that somehow doesn't look like I've got that much on. I even like my outfit: the new sailor pants I love so much and a pretty, drapey burgundy top with some dangly gold earrings of Darby's. It probably isn't going to seem very cool compared to the fashionistas at Earhorn, but it makes me feel good, and I'm comfortable in it, which I know is what matters the most. Plus, in these pants Darby doesn't mind if I wear my boots, which helps me feel even more myself.

"Wow, you look pretty," Veronica says to me when she answers the door. She holds it open, letting me walk in. I can't help but notice she is in a robe and pajamas, with furry slippers in the shape of bananas.

"You're not coming?"

She gives her head a small shake. "Something's going on between them." She points to the floor above us. "And I want some peace while I can get it."

"Is everything okay?" I whisper back.

"I don't know. Taryn poured her first drink at four, and Sylvia won't come out of her room. Maybe it's nerves, but they're not good signs, believe me." Her voice rises so that it floats up the stairs, cheerful, "But I'm sure they'll be right down in a minute."

"Thanks." I'm not sure what to do with this news.

We hear a door open upstairs, and Taryn calls, "Hi, pumpkin! Come on up!"

I give Veronica a *Wish me luck* glance and head upstairs.

"You look pretty," Taryn says, all breathy, setting down a red plastic cup on her incredibly cluttered but very cool vintage dressing table. The kind with a round mirror.

"Thanks," I tell her, looking around. Her room isn't that big, and most of it is filled with the dressing table and a giant bed with a matching wooden headboard. There are some bookshelves anchored to the wall, crowded with books and papers and pictures and CDs and figurines, and a small table beside the bed overflowing with more books and magazines. The floor is covered with clothes and more CDs. It's worse than Darby and Gretchen's room. Worse than even Oliver's.

"Sit, sit," she says, gesturing to the bed. I find a spot near the edge where I won't crush the dresses and jackets strewn across it. Taryn drops down on the stool in front of the dressing table and leans close to the mirror to examine her face. She's nowhere near ready yet. And not just because all she's wearing is a black silk kimono.

"Are you okay?" I ask, hesitant. She doesn't seem drunk, but . . .

"Just nervous." She lets out a long breath, then straightens up and pushes her hair back away from her face, sucks in her cheeks, examines her profile. Without much apparent thought, she picks up a big powder brush and swipes it across her face, puffing more powder into the air than on her skin. "There's an important person coming tonight and I . . ." She puts the brush down, stares at herself again. "I just want it to go well."

I'm about to say I'm sure it'll be fine, so long as we get there on time, when a knock startles both of us. Sylvia's standing there, outside the partly open door. She has her guitar case in her hand.

"Are you ready?" She looks at Taryn with absolutely no expression on her face.

Taryn throws out her hands. "Duh, no."

"Hi, Charlotte," Sylvia says. Her eyes and mouth become a little more pleased. "You look very nice."

"Thanks, you do too." And she does. Her short black hair is slicked back, and her jeans and cowboy shirt somehow actually make her look more feminine than usual. I think she might even have on lipstick.

Sylvia looks at her giant man-watch. "Well, the gang is at Righteous, so I'm headed over there. We'll see you at the place, I guess. Charlotte, you can drive, right?"

"Sure." But wait. Is she really leaving? Now? I try to show her how anxious this makes me.

But she's unresponsive. "You can get her there?" she says to Taryn.

"God! Yes."

Sylvia ignores the nastiness. "Just be there no later than eight thirty, all right?"

"Why don't you take my stuff if you're so worried about it," Taryn snaps.

Sylvia looks at her a second. "I'll see you there, then. Bye, Charlotte."

"Jesus," Taryn huffs, looking back into the mirror when Sylvia's gone. When she sucks her cheeks back in, applying her blush, it's like she sucks all my previous confidence right on out of me.

Taryn's not drunk, just incredibly slow. It takes her almost forty minutes to put on powder and two streaks of thick black eyeliner over her lids, plus a smear of red lipstick. There's another ten minutes of pushing her hair back in a headband and taking it down. Finally, under my encouragement—because I am freaking out about getting there—she leaves it in the headband, with a bit of her long bangs pulled forward. After another fifteen minutes, she's in her outfit.

"I look fat, I think," she says for the fourteenth time, pausing at the top of the stairs.

At this point I want to push her down them. I'm sure my family is already at Earhorn, looking around the room at all these arty college kids, wondering where I am. And I wanted some time before we go on, just to get acclimated to the vibe. Not to mention eat some dinner, so that I can sing without passing out. But now we're barely going to make sound check, if at all.

"You look great," I say again. "And besides, I don't think we have much time."

Her eyes widen. "Shit! What time is it?"

"Almost eight."

"God god god."

Suddenly she's in motion, putting her hands on the tops of my shoulders and gently guiding me down the stairs. She keeps muttering as she flies around the corner into the kitchen and into the basement.

"Okay, thank god," she says, coming immediately back up. "Sylvie's got all the stuff. Okay, okay, let's get going, then." She's rushing to the couch, snatching up her purse, reaching for her keys in the bowl by the front door.

"Bye, Veronica," she hollers as she pushes me out the door. I don't know where Veronica went. I don't know if she even heard. But it doesn't matter. Taryn's sudden panic has me panicked even more than before. What if we don't make it at all?

"Shit shit shit," Taryn keeps muttering while I drive. She's chewing on her thumbnail too, stopping only when she has to tell me to turn.

"It's going to be fine," I say, trying to calm myself down more than her. I don't know where the bubbly, bouncy Taryn has gone, but I want to get out of the car with this version as quickly as possible.

Luckily, it's not that far to Earhorn, and though there's Saturday-night traffic to deal with on Ponce, the back streets don't have many cars. We pull into the rutted parking area just as the clock on the dashboard changes to 8:25. It's a miracle, I swear.

"Come on, come on," Taryn mutters as we strain our necks, looking for a space.

"Why don't you go on in?" I suggest. "You can let them know we're here. I'll be there in a sec."

A twinkle hints across Taryn's strained face. "How'd you get to be so smart?"

I don't answer as she jumps out of the car and runs to the entrance. I have to unbuckle and lean way across the passenger's seat to get her door shut.

There are absolutely no spaces in the lot, so I end up parking on the street, about eight cars away from any streetlights. It's dark and a little skeevy, but I make myself walk at a normal pace. I have no idea what Taryn and Sylvia are going to be like when I get in there, but I know I don't want to look panicked and frazzled. I swallow a few times, blink my eyes wide, and go inside.

Sylvia is right there by the door, watching for me. Without a word, she clamps her hand down on my arm and gives a tight fraction of a smile, leads me through the art gallery into the back room. It feels darker and more crowded than it was last week. I want to explain to her that I did the best I could, getting Taryn here, that I don't want her to be mad at me, but by the clenched look on her face I decide to keep my mouth shut.

"It's fine," she eventually says, though her face is tight. "Taryn's here, along with her *boy*friend, and we're slated to go second. Our stuff's set up, and I checked the mic. I think it sounds okay. So we're set. All right? It's going to be fine."

We have to go second? is knocking against my brain, but the first thing she said crowds everything else out.

"What do you mean, her boyfriend?"

Sylvia's eyes meet mine. "I didn't know either until just now." She jerks her head to the left of us. I look over and there, indeed, is Taryn, in her black dress, talking very seriously—and very, very closely—to some guy with a beard and a wool cap.

"She didn't tell me," Sylvia growls. "And what did she fucking think? That she'd waltz in and pull some 'Oh hi, by the way, this is *Aaron*'"—she says his name with a bitterness that makes me wince—"and la dee da I'd just go along?"

I don't know what to say to this. Things were already chaotic enough, but now my heart is truly knocking against my teeth. I have no idea what performing is going to be like with them.

Before I can react, though, I hear a loud "There you are!" as Darby flings herself around my neck. Turning, I see Gretchen, Dad, and Hannah, all holding mostly full glasses of Coke. "This place is righteous," Darby says, looking around the room in embarrassing awe. "You have to bring me here, like, every Saturday from now on."

"I'm Sylvia" I hear next as I untangle myself from Darby.

"Sorry. This is my friend Sylvia," I tell my family, trying to look like everything's fine. "She plays guitar."

"We can't wait to hear you perform," Hannah says—too loudly—leaning in like Sylvia might be deaf.

Another hand grips my shoulder, and I turn too fast, flicking the person behind me in the face with my hair.

"Oh god, sorry," I say, realizing, as I do, that it's Fabian standing there.

I grab him in a big hug without thinking, almost collapsing against him. "I'm so glad to see you," I murmur into his ear.

"I wouldn't miss it," he says. Just his presence makes me feel utterly relieved.

"I'm so sorry," I blurt, mainly for being such a crappy friend.

"Well—" His face is sweet and chastising, both. "You do owe me a real, at-length explanation about what happened."

But then the emcee guy takes the stage. *Oh god* I feel, all the way in the pit of my stomach. *Oh god oh god oh god—please not yet.*

The first group starts, and I'm like a zombie victim getting her brain sucked out. They're guys—that much I can register—playing this bizarro-but-pretty ambient music. I have never seen the instruments they're using. One of them is maybe a guitar neck turned to lie flat like a table, and the other one is—I don't even know. A box with some antennas coming out of it that the guy just moves his hands toward and back. Both are hooked into laptops. The sound coming out is so floaty and hypnotic that it almost shuts up the crazy, freaked-out feeling in my head and my stomach. Still, I must look like I'm about to collapse because Fabian reaches over and takes my hand. I cling to him for the rest of the set, not because it's sparkly, but because it's what I need.

Too soon, everyone is clapping and whistling, and the emcee guy is back on the stage saying something into the mic while the first group breaks down. Fabian is hugging me, and then Darby and my dad, and Sylvia's looking at me all serious and sympathetic and mouthing "Ready?" Somehow I am nodding and following her up to the stage.

Taryn's not far behind us. While the two of them shift their instruments from the back of the stage to the front, I stand there, wanting to be helpful but not knowing at all what to do.

"All right, Coastal!" I hear from somewhere in the audience. I turn, squinting, to try and find Benji, but the lights are almost pink in their brightness, and I can't see him. Still, I'm glad he's out there.

"Test the mic," Sylvia says, nodding toward it.

"Test?" I say. The mic gives a harsh squeal.

"Do it again." Sylvia's quiet behind me, scootching back a little. She's trying to be calm for both of us.

"Test, test."

Someone whistles—maybe over where Dad is. Or back by the bar. It could be Taryn's boyfriend.

"Okay," I hear Sylvia say behind me.

"Yeah, okay," Taryn says back.

"Okay," I say, to let them know I'm ready. Which I'm not. At all. In any way. Because I can't feel my legs, and I can't see anything but the bulbous, crisscrossed face of the mic, and I've never sung in front of an audience of judgmental strangers like this before, or with such unpredictable people. I try to take in a deep, slow breath. But then, to make everything a hundred times worse, when Taryn starts playing, it's not the notes I'm expecting. Instead she's starting with a different song: the too-high new one I've only sung twice.

Through the whole thing, it's like I'm wrapped in a blanket of awfulness: dark, shifty audience in front of me, angry, unreliable, hating-each-other bandmates behind me. I'm up there, in the lights, all alone but surrounded, my insides swirling between freezing dread and hot, angry humiliation. This is nothing like the Sad Jackal show, when I felt so awful but could sink into the songs. At least then I knew Oliver, Eli, Fabian, and Abe all had my back. Now I'm up here and everything itches like a stiff Easter dress—nothing fits, but I can't pull it up over my head and get rid of it either.

We get through it, and Taryn starts up the Heart song, which at least is a crowd-pleaser and one we planned to play tonight, only last. We end with what should have been our first song, but whatever.

When we finish there's applause, but I don't wait for it. I don't offer to help Taryn and Sylvia with their instruments, either. Instead I practically stumble off the front of the stage and move toward the bathroom, where I want to shut myself in the smallest of the three tiny stalls, press my head to my knees, and cry.

But that doesn't happen. Instead I'm blocked by Fabian, flanked by Gretchen and Darby, all three of them with concerned faces that I can't stand.

"What happened?" Darby says, as I sink into Fabian's strong-armed hug. Gretchen strokes my back.

That they know it was awful makes it harder not to cry, but I'm aware of everyone else around us—our competitors, the judges, everyone—seeing me miserable. I suck in my breath, stand up straight.

"It's fine," I say, unable to look any of them in the eye. "I just got nervous."

"Hey, you okay?" Benji says, finding us.

I dab my eyes with my fingertips. "Yeah." But it comes out all wobbly. "Thanks for coming."

Fabian gives me another hug. "It wasn't you," he says, close to my ear.

I shake my head, try to show I'm thankful.

"We can't talk about this now," I tell them. "Because I will seriously lose it."

Benji loops his arm around my shoulder. "The rest of your family here?"

I look over in Dad and Hannah's direction. "I should go back to them. But you guys really don't have to stay."

"Are you kidding?" Darby takes my hand. "Come on."

There are only six acts tonight. Four more to watch before the winners are announced. I try to shake off my cloak of embarrassment, my veil of fury at Taryn and Sylvia, and just enjoy the music. The two of them have disappeared anyway, which is good riddance, the way I feel.

Eventually Sylvia shows back up with her friends and leans in to say "Good job," though not very convincingly. I tell her the same back, but she doesn't say anything else. It's too loud for us to talk, for me to find out what she really thinks, and there's not a lot she can say. We were awful and I know it. Though really, they played fine. Played the wrong songs, but played fine anyway. It was mostly me who messed up. Me who flung away everything I know about practice and good management, all for a silly time and the approval of girls I barely know.

Jilly was right. Just because something's fun, it doesn't necessarily bring out the best in you. You need to work at it. You need what I had when I was with Sad Jackal.

•　•　•

By the time the last performers finish, I'm beyond ready for that emcee to get it all over with. I want to hear that we didn't win, so I can go home and put this entire night behind me.

There's a break first, though. Most people head to the bathrooms, the bar. Sylvia's disappeared again, though her friends still hover. Since I want to leave as soon as everything's over, this might be the best chance for us all to talk. I tell Dad I need some air and go to look for her.

She isn't hard to find. Just off the crowded patio, Sylvia's standing, arms crossed, listening to Taryn, who's making wild gestures. I'm about to step back inside—clearly this isn't a conversation for me to be in—when Taryn looks up, sees me, and heads over, eyes flashing.

"What was that?" she hisses. I've stepped out of the way of most of the smokers, but still a tall dude in black looks over his shoulder at us. "What happened? That is not what I expected from you."

Her anger slaps me worse than knowing I didn't sing well.

"I'm sorry," I say, trying to keep my voice quiet. "Everything was so intense up there. And you started this whole other thing and I was—"

"You're supposed to be able to go with the flow. You're supposed to roll with it."

"I didn't know it was going to—"

"Leave her alone," Sylvia says behind her. "You're making a scene. You intentionally sabotaged us—me—with the playlist change, so don't blame Charlotte."

"Sabotaged!" Taryn reels back. "You mean the way you've sabotaged every single relationship I've ever tried to be in?"

"Shut up right now," Sylvia growls, taking Taryn's arm and jerking her close. "You lied to me about him, when there honestly wasn't any need. You're the guilty one here and you know it. So stop taking it out on me, and definitely stop taking it out on Charlotte. It's gross."

"I know I messed up," I start, wanting them to calm down, for everyone to stop looking at us.

"Don't say anything right now, please," Sylvia says to me. "Let's all go in and try to have a little bit of dignity. I'd like to be able to show my face around here again."

Still clenching Taryn's arm, Sylvia leads the two of us back in. As we walk through the gallery, I keep my hair a curtain around my face, so that I won't have to see any smirks or snobbiness. Sylvia is practically pushing Taryn ahead of her, and Taryn's gone droopy in her grip.

In the back room, the emcee has already started his announcement.

"—for us to see all the incredible talent that comes out. Again, if you're interested in competing in an upcoming show here, please see me after, and we'll get you signed up. Now, as for our winners tonight . . ."

Fabian grabs my hand again, gives a comforting squeeze. I feel my family moving closer behind me. Benji winks. But I already know what the emcee's going to say. Or, what he isn't going to. So it's not like I'm upset when the weirdo electronic-instrument guys who went before us are announced as the winners, or when the banjo girl and accordion guy come in second. What does surprise me is Darby's scream of delight, Fabian's caught-off-guard smile, plus Benji, Dad, and Hannah pulling me into hugs, because we've just won third place.

I'm too surprised to move. Taryn bounds up to the stage first, clutching the emcee's hands in both of hers and grinning like Miss America. Sylvia stands quietly behind her, waiting to shake hands with him too. He leans forward, says a quick good-bye into the mic, and then that's it. I don't even have a chance to go up. People are already moving toward the exits or back to the bar. The DJ's set booms out of the PA. I stand there, stunned, as Taryn and Sylvia shake hands with the other performers.

"Go join them, dummy." Darby gives me a little shove. "It's your prize too."

I move to the edge of the stage, still not believing I belong here, in the circle of winners. Not believing there are three other groups we managed to beat.

"Nice job." One of the first-place guys offers his hand to me. The one who played the tabletop-looking guitar, I think.

"Thank you." I shake it. "You guys were really good."

"Eh." He shrugs. "These judges are fickle. Last time we did this, we didn't even place. So, it comes and it goes."

I only half register what he's saying, because Taryn and Sylvia are coming over, faces happy. And they're holding hands.

"Good work, kiddo." Sylvia grips my shoulder.

Taryn hands me a twenty-dollar bill, which is almost half of the fifty-dollar prize. "This belongs to you."

"But it should be three ways, equal." I try to hand it back to her.

"You put up with a lot tonight," Sylvia answers, while Taryn looks sheepishly at her. They go from holding hands to slipping their arms around each other's waists.

"I knew we could count on you." Taryn beams at me. "Our lucky charm."

Um, *what*?

"Thanks, I guess." I really cannot look at them anymore.

"We're going to celebrate," Sylvia says, nodding in the direction of their friends around the bar. "You want?"

"I think my family," I say, reaching into the air behind me.

"Let them spoil you," Taryn says. "You deserve it!"

I let them both hug me before I turn back to the people I truly care about. I have no idea what happened tonight. It's almost like

I'm sleepwalking, going back over to everyone, gathered together in the gallery, clearly all ready to go.

"We thought parfaits at home," Hannah says, reaching out to rub my arm. "That sound good?"

I look at Fabian: stable, present, fabulous Fabian. And Benji, with whom things changed but have also somehow stayed the same.

"Can you come too?" I ask them.

"Unfortunately I can't," Benji says with a sorry look.

"What, Lake House party you still gotta scope?" I tease.

He salutes. "That's what I love about you, Coastal," though he doesn't elaborate. He shakes hands with my dad and says good night to us all. I want to tell him—I don't know what—but he's already gone.

"You can come, right?" I tuck my arm under Fabian's, make pleading eyes.

He squeezes my arm with his. "Ain't nobody says, 'Oh, no thank you, I don't like parfaits.'"

I laugh. "Donkey's my *favorite*. I watched *Shrek* every day when I was little."

"See all the things you've been missing about me?"

"There's a lot," I tell him seriously as we walk out into the night, "that I have missed about you."

Chapter Eighteen

I have no idea what I want anymore. Everything is just too mixed up.

After basically sleepwalking through Sunday and the first part of Monday, I take out a piece of paper during lunch and ask myself: *when* did I really enjoy all this band stuff, and why?

All I can think of is the summer, which surprises me. Summer, when it was me, Oliver, Abe, and Trip. When we'd hang out and mess around, playing some and talking a lot. When the atmosphere of Sad Jackal was a lot more like the one in Taryn and Sylvia's basement. Maybe not with all the silly jumping around, but much less pressure. And yet more constructive. I would write something, and then read it to Trip, and he'd help me shape it into something even better. We'd show it to Oliver and they'd turn it into music. I loved watching them, and loved how Trip always helped me bring out the story in the song, teaching me how to see it too. Writing for and with him, I got braver and sharper with my lyrics. Stronger. And then there was the notebook, heavy with all our other thoughts—the things in our heads we were working out together, instead of alone. I think of lying on the floor, silent, listening to his music, learning a lot more than just the names of a bunch of bands.

The bell rings, making me jump. I've been staring into space for I don't know how long. I look down at my paper, and what I see there is a shock. I've written four words: *Our Golden Summer* and *Trip*.

Realizing that I was maybe happiest when I was working with Trip doesn't make me feel any better, though. In fact, it makes me feel worse. First of all, what am I supposed to do about it? There's no way to get that back. For one thing, Fabian and Eli are an essential part of Sad Jackal now. I wouldn't want to trade them for the old group, Golden Summer or not. On top of that, though, even if Oliver did take me back—which I doubt, because he still isn't even looking at my side of the room during psych—I have no reason to think he'd take me and Trip together.

Which doesn't matter either, because there is no me-and-Trip-together. He has Chris Monroe and his gang now. He has Lily. He's probably forgotten all about me and the notebook. He's probably burned up every page.

But I can't go back to Taryn and Sylvia, either. I don't want to be in a band with people who are so undisciplined and unpredictable. So now I guess I'm in no band at all.

I can barely do anything the rest of the afternoon.

The next day, thank god, is our last day before Thanksgiving break. There isn't much to do, since most teachers know our brains are already in vacation mode. But this just makes the time go slower. Except for 20th Cen., when Benji and I do a Mad Libs he made up from some old picture book about the first Thanksgiving. Otherwise, the day crawls.

That night, all I can think about is Oliver and the band and my own stupidity, and then—Trip. Trip's gentle hand on my shoulder. Trip's face close to mine as we work over a song; his whole face lighting up as I round a corner; his hugs that enfold me in something more than warmth. I spend hours with my headphones on in my room, lights out, listening to his playlist. It's pathetic, I know, but I want to gather as much of him around me as I can. Some of the songs he's given me are stupid, or not my type of thing, but most make my heart swell and then sink to the bottom of me, thinking of him, and missing him so completely.

I should have held on. I should have fought to keep us together. I shouldn't have let him disappear forever.

After sleeping late the next day, and lying in front of On Demand with Darby and Gretchen—a Wednesday of pajamas and maca-roni and cheese and not knowing what time it is—a horn beeps in our driveway and we open the front door. There she is, Jilly. I realize I need her so bad, my eyes start to tear up.

Gretchen, Darby, and I go out into the yard in our slip-pers and wrap her in squealing hugs, help with her bags, and bring them upstairs to my room—our room. Back down in the kitchen, Jilly is almost vibratingly hyper from sucking down too much Coke Zero on the drive. She needs a shower, she says, and has no idea what she packed besides a bunch of dirty laundry, it's good to see us—she grabs whomever's closest in a hug—and when will Dad and Hannah be home?

We sit her down on the sofa. We give her water and ask does she need anything to eat. We try to tell her, all at once, what's been going on since she left, and we ask, on top of each other, how the heck is college? Darby especially can't get enough, lean-ing over the counter, getting as close to Jilly as possible. From her questions, it's clear that Jilly's barely talked to either her or Gretchen all semester. It makes me feel glad, a little.

Still, there's so much Jilly doesn't know. So much I have to say, and so much that's been a mess without her here.

After about an hour of talking together in the kitchen, it's like someone pulls a cord and everything falls back to this normal place. Jilly heads upstairs to shower, and we put our movie back on. When Jilly comes down, fresh and fragrant and with damp hair, she plops on the floor in front of me and holds up a comb. I help her work the knots out of her long wavy hair. Hair like mine.

We stay that way, the four of us, like regular sisters, until Hannah comes home with a bag of groceries. Dad appears soon after, carrying the turkey for tomorrow. There's another round of exclamations, hugs, and questions, and then we help Hannah with dinner while Dad checks his email and Gretchen takes her phone upstairs. It is normal and it is not. It is comforting and it is not. I am happy—so happy—to focus on Jilly, but I also know she's just a temporary distraction from the whirlpool of thoughts and memories that keeps sucking me down.

After dinner, Jilly and I wash our faces side by side in the double bathroom sinks and slip, clean and quiet, into our beds. Only now do I have a chance to really talk to her.

But what do I say? Where do I start?

So I just . . . talk. It's hard to keep myself on one topic, with all the images cascading over me: Oliver turning away from me in class; Benji folding a pizza slice in half and shoving it into his mouth; Fabian hugging me in the front seat of his car; Trip cracking me up with one of his cartoons.

Jilly listens. And then, after a long pause, she says, "You need to do what makes you happiest. Don't worry where it's going right now."

My brow furrows. I wish she could see it. "It's not that. I'm just . . . unsure."

"Unsure about what, exactly?"

"Unsure what I want from all of this, from all of them. Unsure if it's about me or—" Oliver. Benji. Fabian. Trip. Lish. Taryn. Sylvia. Mom. Even Jilly.

"You can't do it for someone else." I hear her shift in the bed, can almost see her, in the dark, facing me fully. "You have to do it for you."

"Huh."

"What?"

"You sound like Mom."

She is surprised. "Do I?"

I backpedal. "Well, not exactly. But that's something she'd say."

I wait for her to get mad. To tell me how wrong I am, say it's awful for me to compare her to someone she's trying so hard not to be. But she doesn't say anything. And I don't want us to be fighting when she's only home a couple of days.

"How do I know what's really the right thing, though?" I ask, to keep things going.

"Oh, I think you know. Deep down we all really do."

I consider this, staring into the dark. "I'm afraid I might *like* Trip," I test out.

Absolute quiet comes from her side of the room. And then, finally: "Do you?"

I imagine him. His grandpa-style gold-rimmed glasses. His floppy hair. His sloped handwriting. His focus on me whenever I'm talking.

I imagine myself, the last six weeks, without him around.

"I know I'm better when I'm with him," I admit.

Jilly doesn't say anything for so long, I think she's maybe asleep. So long I regret not saying something different.

But after a while it comes out, quiet: "Well, there's a start."

The next day is Thanksgiving, so the moment we're awake, there are other, better-smelling things to focus on. We sauté shallots and chop garlic. Corn bread is baked and then crumbled for stuffing. We take pans off the stove, clean them only to dirty them again with something else. Gretchen's made a playlist for us—songs full of thanks. When Carole King bursts out of the speakers, Hannah sings along, unembarrassed. Jilly and I do harmonies up and around her, and it feels good and right in a way I didn't know I'd been missing. Even Dad joins in. We sing together all afternoon.

By four o'clock, everything is ready and we've changed from Cooking In the Kitchen Casual to Thanksgiving Dinner Outfits. It's sort of funny, transitioning into Formal Dinner Mode with each other. Why we don't eat dinner in whatever we were wearing before I don't know, because it's not like anyone's here to see. But when we sit down at the table—made bigger by the leaf we rarely use anymore and lit by tall candles in Hannah's mother's crystal candlesticks—it's actually nice.

The reliable goodness of our family joining hands like we do every year, going around the table to each say a thing we're thankful for—it feels like some of the questions inside me start to break apart and drift away. There *are* some things I know are right.

While we're cleaning up the dishes after Thanksgiving dinner, Mom calls. Right away she apologizes for not doing so before now, and it occurs to me I'd hardly noticed. She tells me about the grain salad she's making for the multifamily Thanksgiving they always have at the studio, and I wonder if she still misses regular corn-bread stuffing. But for the first time, while she talks, I can hear in her voice how content Mom is there. Holidays without her usually make me all sorry for myself, but somehow, today, I know she wouldn't be happy if she was here. She wouldn't—and neither would we. It's a strange thing to have my head around.

We're leading up to good-byes when Jilly sidles over to me and takes the phone, wanders into the living room. When she comes back into the kitchen, I can tell she's been crying a little. But I can also tell she doesn't want anybody to notice, so I toss her a towel and get her to help me with the drying.

Benji texts me on Friday, saying that he is dying of boredom and can I please rescue him. Since Jilly has plans with her high school friends, I suggest we go to the movies and out for Chinese. When Fabian texts ten minutes later, I invite him along.

Which turns out to be one of my best ideas, ever. Benji picks me up and we meet Fabian at the restaurant. We pile our plates with greasy buffet and talk so much we barely make it to the movies, all three of us jokingly irritated that we missed the first preview. When it's over we stand in the parking lot debating the pros and cons of the film, until I'm in danger of violating curfew.

Before we split up, Fabian hugs me. "I think you should call Oliver," he says.

When I start to protest, he gives me this fatherly look. I tell him I will think about it. He says he hopes I won't think too long.

Early Sunday morning I'm helping Jilly check the bathroom for all her toiletries, making sure her laundry got separated from mine when we did Laundry Marathon last night. It sweeps over me how much better things are, without me even knowing it, when my sister is here. How much I don't want her to go, don't want to go back to trying to be okay with her gone.

But it doesn't matter how much clearer things are with Jilly, because it's time for her to go, and for me to clear them up myself. We help load up her bags, and she moves around the circle of us, saying good-byes.

"You're doing so great," she says. "Just listen to yourself, and you'll be fine."

I squeeze her tighter and tighter, not knowing what to say. And then she's walking down to her car, and opening the door, and driving away.

With Jilly gone, it's best to get things back to normal, so I spend an hour turning the room back into mine—straightening the comforter on her bed, throwing the sheets in the wash, putting on my music, pulling out my binders and books to plan the week. Taking out my algebra homework, I find that reasons-I'm-in-a-band list I tried to make: the one that starts with *Our Golden Summer* and ends with *Trip*.

Immediately, I know what I have to do. I don't know why I've waited for so stupidly long. I pull on my boots, grab for a jacket, then pound down the stairs and holler to whomever is in earshot that I'm going for a walk.

As I propel myself down the street, I can't believe I've been so pigheaded and selfish, how I let all *this* get in the way. Oliver and I have lasted through so much. Like the time we got busted for trying to walk off campus during lunch as freshmen and had to serve detention together for a week. The month in seventh grade when he was in love with Zoe Blackstone—how silently devastated he was when she started wearing Will Stanford's hockey jersey, and how I spent one entire afternoon filling up his locker with *Her loss!* notes. How grateful he was every day that I took notes for him while his arm was in that cast in tenth grade, so much so that, for a while, I confused it for a crush. Our fifth-grade science fair project, and the poetry project last semester in Mrs. Stenis's class. How he's always needed me, and I've always needed to be the one he counts on.

I think of the tiny things that make us what we are: the way he sees I'm irritated even when I'm doing my best to hide it, how I can make him laugh when he least expects it. How he understands that I get freaked out and will blow things out of proportion, but then how I will always calm down and come back, even if I'm convinced I never will. How he's so cool and great and mysterious when he sings—and how he admitted that I'm better. Years and years of the two of us ending up, somehow, together. A team.

He said I didn't have to be around. But all this time—he didn't have to be either.

The closer I get to his house, the more anxious I feel, wondering if he's back from his grandparents'. Seeing all the cars in the driveway washes me in relief, and I practically jump up the stairs to his porch. I'm impatient, waiting for someone to answer my knock, afraid he'll see me and won't answer.

And then he's there, holding the door open. He's wearing sweatpants and a hoodie—something I hardly ever see him in anymore. He's got on a baseball cap and his glasses, which he never wears. He looks like the boy I met in fifth grade, only a lot taller. He looks like my friend.

We blink at each other a minute.

"Apparently," he says finally, "I can't write songs for shit."

I hold up my notebook—the empty, fresh one I grabbed with my jacket. "Well"—I smile big—"apparently I can."

We don't talk about what happened. We don't bother comparing Thanksgivings or families or what's been going on since our fight. Instead we go down into the rec room to get some ideas going. When freewriting yields very little, I tell him the story of Taryn and Sylvia and Aaron. I don't mention the band thing, or anything about Earhorn, only the story of two lesbians and a grungy hipster boy. This gets him to talk about Whitney: to admit, at least sideways, that it was weird when she started hanging out with some senior right after the Halloween dance. I tell him about Lish dropping me again. He brings up that week in ninth grade when she fake flirted with Abe, just to get revenge on him for pointing out how she talks with food in her mouth.

We laugh. We remember. We write and write. After almost two hours we've come up with a couple songs that, with some revision, could become something.

"I knew we'd make it back," he says, giving me a high five.

His words make my eyes go wide.

I stand and reach for my jacket. "I gotta go."

He gets up too. "What, homework?"

I can see he wants to tell me this is way more vital to my future than some project for Enviro.

"No. You'll see. Keep working on those." I point to the sheets of our almost-lyrics. "And get ready for more."

"Okay." His face is confused at first, but then something in it shifts. "Spider . . ." He reaches out to give me a hug. "I'm sorry."

I feel how good it is, our being together again.

But then I can't help it: "Well, you were a jerk. But I'm sorry too."

He holds my gaze for just long enough.

"So." I snap to, pushing back my hair. "Practice tomorrow?"

"Every day until the dance."

"I'll be there," I chirp, waving and bounding up the steps.

• • •

At home, I tear through my desk until I find what I'm looking for, shoved in the back of the middle drawer: the scribbled thoughts from what feels like months ago, when Trip stopped talking to me. Some of the scrawls are so messy I can barely decipher them, and some are so maudlin you can practically smell the pathos coming off the paper. But there are other parts that surprise me with their honesty, with how clearly they say exactly what I felt. They aren't the main lines I'm looking for, though, so I smooth out each page, spreading them across the desk so that I can see, until—there they are. I'm glad I had the sense to actually record them when they were fresh.

At the top of a new page, I write, *Hansel and Gretel Crumbs.*

I hope I kept enough of them to lead me back.

Chapter Nineteen

I can't describe the happiness I feel the next day, walking out to the parking lot with Oliver, both of us excited and eager for rehearsal, not caring about anybody else around us. Though Oliver's chin is high, I can't help but sneak glances over at Trip, who's hanging out with his gang a few rows down from Oliver's car. I don't know if it was a good idea or not, what I did last night, or if he even got it, or cared, but after spending an hour reshaping all those thoughts, perfecting the last song we wrote together—I don't know. I was . . . thinking about him. A lot. And he and I don't have the accordion background of me and Oliver, so it's not like we can just snap back to the way things were. But I'm still grateful for what we had. So last night before I went to bed, I had to let him know somehow that Our Golden Summer mattered. I opened his playlist and selected one to email to him. No message, no nothing—just that "It's All Mixed Up" song he played for me over the phone forever ago.

I try not to stare as we drive past on the way to Oliver's, and when we get there, I push it totally out of my mind. I'm so happy to be back—carrying a platter of snacks down into Oliver's rec room, hearing Abe's under-his-breath "thank god" at the sight of me. Eli comes over and wraps me in a hug, lifting me off the ground. And then Fabian, when he arrives, is all Kermit the Frog, both of us twinkling at each other. None of us dwells on my little departure. Winter Formal is in less than two weeks, and there's a lot we have to do.

We stay focused and work, trying some of the new songs and going over old favorites. When I suggest to Oliver that we sing "Disappear" as a *duet*, he scrunches up his brow for a second, then agrees to give it a try. I realize I'm being my whole self here, surrounded by true friends. And it feels awesome.

Feels so awesome, for all of us, that we go until seven thirty, and Mrs. Drake offers to make us dinner. We decline, needing to get back to families and homework, since we'll be practicing again tomorrow. Eli and Fabian leave their equipment down in the rec room, and I give the new lyrics to Oliver, so he can work on melodies tonight if he has time. Fabian drives me home.

"You were better today," he says.

"Um, thanks?"

He realizes how that sounded like a backhanded compliment. "Not just better than at Earhorn, but better than I've ever seen you. I think the rest of us were too."

"We needed each other," I say.

"I think we all did," he smile-says back.

Every afternoon for the next whole week I'm at Oliver's house practicing, even on Wednesday, when Benji and I have to work on our next 20th Cen. test. I tell him to come over to Oliver's, and we sit together on the couch and work like always, except every now and again I have to stop to give critiques. Other times, of course, I have to get up and sing. And somehow it makes sense that Benji's a part of the whole experience.

The week goes by: every afternoon, practice; every night, cramming homework, ending the day—too late, usually—emailing a song to Trip. I don't know why I keep doing it, because he never writes back, but when I think about not doing it Wednesday night, it seems weird, and then the next day and the next are the same. I consider sending him the new lyrics I've written, but I'm not sure if they'd have relevance to him now, and anyway, what I really want to be doing is showing him how much I appreciate what we had when he first played these for me.

Then it's the weekend, with chores and movies with my family, and me and Fabian hitting the Masquerade Saturday night for a show. Benji comes with us, as well as Fabian's boyfriend, Drew, and I find out—now that my jealousy's had a chance to unhinge itself—that he's actually very funny. And attentive. And nice. If Fabian's not going to be into me (not *that* way, anyhow), I guess I can be glad that he has someone like Drew to be into him. Especially if he can become my friend too.

I feel a little edgy, though, wondering if Taryn might come crashing up to us, or if I'll see Sylvia lurking in some corner, full of all the things she hasn't said to me yet. They used to hang out here with us, after all. I'm not sure why they wouldn't be here tonight. The idea of bad feelings between us still makes me feel a little strange. I know I don't want to sing with them, but I feel like I still owe them something.

As the second band starts up, I pull Fabian to a quieter place in the outside stairwell to talk.

"Everything okay?" He is so nice, so concerned.

"I just want to know if there was more to it." I have to half shout it. "Between you and Taryn and Sylvia? When you quit their band?"

He pauses while a group of tattooed guys and girls thumps past us.

"It's a long story."

"So why didn't you tell me all of it?" I holler.

"Because the details aren't important. After a while . . . they weren't my thing."

"Why did you let me do it, then? When you knew they were such a mess?"

"Because you wanted to, silly. You were so cute. And I didn't know; maybe you liked messes. I mean . . ." He chuckles and leans in. "You *were* hanging out with Benji."

I twist my mouth. "You didn't even know him."

He shrugs, meaning, *I'm just sayin'.*

"I haven't talked to them since," I tell him.

He nods. "I know."

"What do they say?"

He shrugs again, annoyingly stoic and removed. "Taryn's all over the place. And, you know, for better or worse, Sylvia goes with her."

"But should I call them?"

A knowing pause from him before he answers: "*Should* you?"

So I do. On Sunday. I figure I will end up leaving a voice mail, anyway, so—

"Hello?"

"Um, Taryn?"

"Oh my god! No way! Charlotte, we were just talking about you. I swear to god, you are utterly fate. *Guess* where we were last night. Earhorn! And it was boring as all hell and all so amateur, and we were looking at each other and going, 'We really need to get back into practice.' I've found, like, fourteen songs you'd be great at, and Sylvia's working on some new ideas about maybe doing originals—though, you know, she has no real training in poetry, which I keep telling her she needs. But I wanted to write songs inspired by Sharon Olds poems. Or Elizabeth Bishop, maybe. Something, I don't know, with some teeth. But you can bring some poems too, and we'll talk about it. What are you doing Tuesday?"

I can't help being shocked. And for a moment, I'm terrified to tell her I've decided to go back to Sad Jackal. But I can't do things simply because I don't want her to get upset. I need to listen to myself.

I tell Taryn I'm not going to be able to play with her and Sylvia, and there is a long, long pause.

"Aaron said you were going to say that."

"Well, I guess, tell him thanks for understanding." And— *what*?

"I don't think so. We broke up. But thanks for noticing."

I pretend not to hear the nastiness in her voice. "Well, I'm sorry, Taryn. I really am. I learned a lot singing with you and—"

"I'll tell Sylvia you called."

And then, I guess, that part of things is over.

I don't have very long to feel weird about it, because about five seconds after I hang up with Taryn, Hannah's at my half-open door, knocking politely. She has her keys in her hand.

"You're not ready?"

"Ready?"

Brief, exasperated stepmom sigh. "Dresses? Shopping? Winter Formal next weekend? The way Darby's pacing downstairs . . ."

"Oh. Right." I guess I do remember Darby, Gretchen, and Hannah talking at dinner the other night. I just hadn't realized they meant today.

Darby appears behind her mother. "Why aren't you *ready*?!"

"I'm not going to the mall."

"Not the mall, dummy," she growls. "A boutique. Gretchen found it. Get your butt in gear."

"Wait. You have a date?"

She makes a nasty face. "Do you not hear anything I say? Having a date means you have to hang on one guy the whole night."

"Oh." I pull open a dresser drawer, look for some clean cords. "I forgot about your harem." I look at Hannah. "Is it a harem? Or are those only made up of women?"

Hannah lets out a hoot. "You two can work it out. I'm leaving here in ten minutes, because otherwise it will dawn on me how unpleasant Buckhead traffic on a Sunday afternoon is going to be."

Darby gives me a pointed look. "Hurry up."

The entire way up and across town, Darby chatters about her friends and what they're wearing to the dance, who their favorite guys in Sad Jackal are, what bets they all have about what I'm going to wear, and their general curiosity about whether this means Oliver and I have gotten back together.

"That last part is a joke," she breezes, right before I'm about to punch her. "Nobody thinks you're together. At least, they hope not. They want him themselves."

We finally find the boutique Gretchen wanted—a small, glass-front place tucked into a mini-strip of shops, one with barely any parking.

"Hello, hello!" the owner sings to us from the rear of the shop. She's attaching giant binder clips to the back of the wedding dress another woman is trying on.

Darby looks over the woman in the dress. "It's pretty," she says. But the woman doesn't seem very grateful for the compliment. She turns to face herself in the surrounding mirrors.

"Here, see?" Gretchen says, going over to the rack along the right wall—the one full of formals, instead of wedding gowns.

Hannah checks the price tag of the first dress on the rack, raises her eyebrows. "Not exactly cheap," she mutters.

"But not mall prices either," Gretchen says testily.

"Ooooh! Lookit this one!" Darby pulls out an emerald-green column dress.

"I am *not* wearing anything fitted," I growl.

"We're not just here for you," Darby snaps, my rock star position apparently eclipsed by visions of herself making some grand entrance at the dance.

"Fine, then."

I move down the row, past Darby in the sizes made for tiny ninth graders, past Gretchen in the sizes designed for average-framed girls, and onto the You Are Not a Water Buffalo But Don't Push It, Honey, end of the rack. The band's been so song-obsessed, so focused on playing things over and over until we can do them flawlessly backward, that I haven't really thought about the *formal* part of Winter Formal. I can't picture the boys in tuxes, but this isn't going to be a jeans affair for them either. I'm about to text Oliver for ideas when Hannah comes up behind me.

"What about this one, Charlotte?"

I turn around. She's holding up a cream-colored A-line, strapless dress, with a dark blue satin ribbon across the waist. A little ruffle of tulle pokes out from under the hem, but other than that, it's completely smooth.

"Oooooh," Darby sighs, looking up.

"I don't know about strapless" is my first response.

Hannah's brow creases. "Why not? You have beautiful collarbones."

It's such a random thing for her to say—and a random thing to notice—but still, it's nice to hear. "I do?"

She holds the dress up against me. "Of course you do. And you could wear your hair down, if you wanted. Or up would look good too."

I check the size. It's actually what I wear.

"Try it on." Gretchen's face is approving.

"It doesn't look like a wedding dress? I'm not going to be"—I picture stage lights glowing off me—"too pale?"

"The blue offsets that," Hannah says.

"And we can spray tan you," Darby adds.

"What a beautiful choice," the shop lady says, finally coming over to us. "Shall I start you a dressing room?"

I look at Hannah, uncertain, but she's already handing the dress to the woman.

"You can look at other things, if you want," she tells me. "But I think that one's going to be it."

And in the end, my stepmom is right. As soon as Gretchen gets the zipper up, I can feel how well the dress fits me. I don't have much of a waist, but somehow with whatever's structured inside it, this dress gives me one. My boobs have never been more than annoying most of the time, but the way the neckline curves just right at the top, they're suddenly *up*. And they're pretty. I thought the flared-out hemline would make me look wider, but really it just balances out my hips, makes me look . . . perfect.

"Such a nice hourglass," the shop lady says, smoothing her hands along my waist.

It's embarrassing, but, looking in the mirror, I see that she's kind of right.

Darby and Gretchen find dresses that make them look fantastic too. The maroon spaghetti-strap column dress Darby picks makes her look, as Hannah says sadly, like she's twenty-one already. Gretchen's dress isn't quite as glamorous as Darby's, but the shimmery pink material brings out her healthy, All-American Girl glow.

Enlivened, I guess, by her happy, pretty daughters, Hannah agrees to an unplanned stop at Lenox, to get the accessories over with. She gives us each some cash to supplement the funds we brought ourselves and tells us to meet in an hour outside of the Crate & Barrel, where she wants to do some shopping of her own. Gretchen and Darby both disappear in separate directions immediately, so I'm searching solo, not sure whether to go up the escalator or stay down on the main floor.

I wander into the first shoe store I come to and spend some uncertain time dawdling near the entrance, pretending to be interested in stiletto-heeled boots and brown leather clogs. The salesgirl is superglad to see me, and just as I'm telling her I'll let her know if I need any help, a display deeper in the store catches my eye. Or, more specifically, a single pair balanced on the clear plastic shelves. I go straight to it, surprised to be drawn to shoes at all, particularly such girly ones. But these are so perfect it's almost funny: vintage-looking heels that maybe a pinup girl would wear, with a little peep-toe front spanned by a multilooped bow. Picking them up, I know that these are shoes I could be comfortable in. The heel is more sturdy than the skinny spikes you usually see, and when I try them on, they hug my feet in a way that's supportive instead of pinching. The best part is? They're the exact dark blue of the ribbon on my dress.

I thank the shopgirl after I pay, and then I just about skip out of the store. Until I stop dead in place, seeing Lish and Bronwyn walking past.

They stop too and are—oh god—coming over to say hi.

"We're shopping for Winter Formal too!" Bronwyn squeals, indicating my bag. She hugs me, one thin arm wrapped around my neck.

"Haven't had any luck yet, though." Lish pouts a little.

"If someone wasn't so picky." Bronwyn pokes her.

"Can we see?" Lish asks, leaning forward to peek.

Why they're acting like they haven't ignored me the last few weeks, I don't know.

"I, um . . . want to keep it a surprise," I fumble. "If you don't mind."

Lish nods. "Of course, of course. We were certainly surprised—in a good way, I mean—when we heard you were back with Sad Jackal. But ooops—" She covers her mouth with her hand, makes a coy face. "Was that supposed to be a surprise too? I mean, you didn't say anything to us, so . . ."

I narrow my eyes at her. It's only slightly, but I see her see it.

"I guess I've been busy."

"Well, you can't be too busy during lunch." She pushes me gently on the arm. "You should come out with us again. I mean, you just disappeared and—"

Right. That's what happened. I disappeared. And now, suddenly, with Winter Formal a week away, I'm visible? Do you really think I'm that stupid, Lish, that I would let this happen again?

It is so, so tempting to call her out on it right now. To cut her down to the insignificant-feeling size she's reduced me to so many times. But right as I'm gathering up the words, taking in a deep breath, I look at her in her trendy mall-store outfit, her Hollywood-magazine hair—at Bronwyn, who makes sure to match Lish in every way, because god forbid she do her own thing—and I feel really sorry for them both.

"There's a lot going on," I let out. I try to make it sound like I'm disappointed, but only barely. "You know how it is. But I'll see you at the dance. Good luck with shopping."

I give them a twinkle-finger wave and stride away, head high, but not because I'm trying to prove something by looking superconfident, if they're watching. Instead it's because I honestly don't care anymore what Lish thinks or what she says. Because I know—I really know—that I have way better friends than her.

Chapter Twenty

How does a week rush by so quickly? I don't know, but it happens. Because suddenly we have gone from *Holy shit we only have two weeks to practice* to *Holy shit we only have two hours before we go on,* and I don't have much memory of anything in between. All I really know is how crazy it feels, now that it's here.

This year Winter Formal is in the Old Courthouse in Decatur. The band has to get there an hour before the doors open, for sound check and to coordinate with the DJ about when we'll go on and all that. I'm meeting the guys there, which means most of the day I get to participate in another round of Darby's Beauty

Parlor. This time she and Gretchen are doing it too, which makes it more fun. Darby gives me hot lemon tea "for my throat," and then I rest with cucumbers on my eyes for an hour while she takes a bath. Then it's my turn for an aromatherapy soak, and as I float there, I try not to think about Lily doing similar things, getting ready for Trip. Try not to think of him handsome in his suit. After that, while Gretchen's in the tub, Darby supervises my high-energy protein dinner and massages shea butter into my feet before I get dressed.

"Wow," she says, smoothing my dress down after we get it zipped up. Her face is coated in some kind of shiny peel-off mask.

I press my hands to my new waist, give the skirt a little back-and-forth twirl. We decided to keep my hair down, partly for warmth, but also because the gentle waves she makes still look great. She's swept the front part back and to the side a little, fastened with a fake-pearl clip Darby found for me at the mall, so even though it's down in the back, you can still see my face and those collarbones I apparently have. The small, dangly earrings Hannah loaned me are just the right amount of sparkle, and with the shoes, the whole thing is pretty remarkable.

I grab Darby in a huge hug. "Thank you for all of this."

"It's fun for me," she dismisses. "And you're messing up your dress. Now." She hands me the small drawstring purse she's loaning me for the night. "Lip gloss, eye smudge, mascara, lipstick, and fresh powder are all in here. Perfume, too, and a tiny deodorant, in case."

"Those fit in here?"

"Plus your phone and your money. And some cough drops."

"You are the best, seriously."

She shrugs. "First record deal, you're buying your baby step-sister some Louboutins. Just sayin'."

We hug again and head downstairs. Dad's driving me to the Courthouse, and when he looks up from the couch, the expression on his face is borderline embarrassing.

"Don't say anything," I warn him jokingly.

"Say what? You look that gorgeous to me every day."

"Yeah, right."

"It's true." His face is all innocent.

"Okay, Dad. Let's just go, all right? Before this swan turns back into a pumpkin."

We make fun of my stupid mixed metaphor, and he helps me into my coat. I take Dad's arm, and we head out.

It's a little weird to walk into Winter Formal by myself. There are no flashbulbs popping, no gaggle of girlfriends squealing over my dress, no nervous date with a corsage. Instead I climb up the marble staircase to the main room upstairs, where the stage and the dancing will be. The guys are all there, standing along the back wall, trying to pretend they aren't getting nervous while waiting for the sound man.

"Wow," Fabian says, coming over to give me a hug.

"You think?"

"Most definitely."

"You too," I tell him, admiring his green vintage jacket and crazy black-and-pink splotched tie. Eli's done vintage as well: a red jacket cut narrow to his frame, with black silk lapels and even a flower in his buttonhole.

"Sharp, man." I nod my approval.

"Not bad yourself, sister." He winks back.

"Here." I go over to Oliver, who is tugging at the knot of his tie. He's trying to make it look cool and loose, but mostly it looks like he put it on wrong. I tighten the knot all the way and then pull it down, just barely, working it a little looser as I go.

"There." I pat his lapels, and the true gratitude in his face fills me up with warm.

"Okay, you guys?" the DJ calls, ready for our sound check.

"Here we go," Abe whispers, letting out a low whistle.

"It's gonna be great," I tell him, all of them, though I have to suck in a deep breath too.

It doesn't take that long to set everything up. There are some tweaks and adjustments, and Fabian has a hard time with his monitor, but then we play through "You're Ugly, Too," to make sure everything's right, and the boys all nod at each other, nod at me. We agree it sounds good. That we're ready.

"Let's go outside, dude," Eli says, shaking out his wrists. "I could use some air."

I'm not sure how far I can walk without my shoes filling with blood, but I'm also not going to be all girly and dumb about it. It's freezing out, so we pile back into our coats and scarves, tell the sound guy we'll be back in plenty of time. We don't want to sit at the picnic tables outside the Courthouse, looking like we're waiting, but we don't want to go in anywhere, either. So we amble in the direction of school, talking about all the stuff we haven't talked about because we've been practicing so hard: video games, movies, who is stupid at school and who is not. Eli has his flask, of course, and it makes the rounds. I take a sip, part for tradition with them, part for courage. When we get down to the tracks, a limo passes us, headed toward the square.

"Must be time, then," Abe says, staring like he's trying to see inside.

"It's freezing out here anyway," Oliver says.

"You okay in those shoes?" Fabian asks.

I nod. "Just cold."

He puts his arm around my shoulders and I huddle up next to him as we turn around, head back, this time none of us saying anything. As we walk up the hill, past the Chick-fil-A, we see more and more couples hurrying toward the Courthouse, more cars in the loop with herds of kids climbing out. It's all really happening. We still won't play for a while, but it's freezing, and, as Abe says: "We have to show up and *dance*."

Inside, the lobby of the Courthouse has been transformed since we left. The entire place is lit up with white Christmas lights, and snowflake garlands stream down the rail to the stairs and up the columns, fluttering slightly. There being people in here makes a difference, too. Instead of cold and stony and a little foreboding, now the place is echoing with the sounds of couples already here and music booming from upstairs.

We wait in line to check our coats with everyone else, looking around the room, smiling *oh my god it's time* smiles at each other, watching people as they come in, and pretending not to be.

"You look awesome," someone says behind me. An arm loops around my waist.

I turn enough to see him.

"Wow. So do you."

Benji's outfit is simple: jeans, a dark blue jacket and plain white T-shirt, but it looks somehow extra-sharp on him. His hair, slicked back fifties style, adds greatly to the affect. For a brief second I picture him showing up like this at my door, being my actual date tonight, and then I remember kissing him. I wonder how different tonight would've been if we'd made a less awkward couple, if we hadn't turned out better as friends.

He can see me looking at him strange, because he pricks up one eyebrow. His eyes are sparkling, though maybe a little sad, too. We hug and he bumps fists with the other guys, and once we hand off our coats, we all head upstairs to see what things look like on the dance floor. There still aren't that many people up here—it's cooler to hang out downstairs, I guess, watching everyone make their entrances—but the decorations and the hundreds of twinkle lights make everything warm and beautiful.

"You wanna?" Benji says, holding his hand out toward the floor. Only a few brave couples are dancing, plus one big throng of freshmen, but everyone's clearly having fun. I'm not sure I want to get too sweaty before we go on, but dancing with Benji sounds better than tensing up in a bunch of nerves. I grab Fabian and Oliver, pulling them with us, when someone says to me, "Your name's Charlotte, right?"

It's the sound guy. Looking a little perturbed.

"Yeah?"

"I'm not a messenger, all right? I've got work to do here."

I take the notebook he's handing me.

"Um, thanks."

Staring down, a prickly feeling sweeps over my arms and bare shoulders. I know exactly who left this for me, and I crane my neck, trying to spot his tall blond head in the crowd.

"Can you tell me when he left?"

The sound guy gestures rudely to the dance floor. "I've had a few other things to focus on."

"Okay. I get it. Thanks."

"You okay?" Benji leans in.

"Yeah, I just . . ." I turn the notebook open to the first page. His handwriting pulls sharp, unexpected tears up from inside me. "I just need a second."

I push past the guys into the hall, to the bathroom, which fortunately isn't crowded yet with three hundred girls waving mascara wands. I do have to wait for a stall to empty up, but I don't let myself start reading until I'm safe, and alone, the door locked securely behind me.

Dear Charlotte, it starts. *What are you trying to do to me?*

Twenty minutes later I can finally come out. Girls have been banging on the door—only a few of them asking, concerned, if I'm okay—but I don't care. I had to finish reading all fifteen front-and-back pages, and then I had to make myself stop crying enough to walk out of the stall. It takes another five minutes, maybe more, to straighten my makeup halfway back to what Darby created earlier tonight. Thank god for her tiny travel makeup kit. And lots of tissues. By the time I've taken a few deep breaths, and a drink of water at the fountain outside, I find the guys—standing, again, against the back wall, watching people dance—and I hope I look at least a little bit pulled together.

"Where've you been?" Oliver looks freaked. "We have to go on in, like, ten minutes."

Next to him Fabian crinkles his brow at me, wondering am I okay.

I ignore both of them. "Have you seen Trip?"

Oliver arches up on his toes to look over my head. "Why? Is he here?"

"I think so, I mean he might be—"

But then, like that, there he is, standing in dirty jeans and a baggy sweater, his hair a mess, the rest of him blurred suddenly by a new crop of tears—tears there's no way I'm going to let fall, because I don't have time to redo my makeup a second time. Just the thought of it pisses me off all over again.

"What the hell is this?" I demand, shaking the notebook at him. "What do you mean, you couldn't help yourself? That I can't blame you for being afraid of how you felt? I completely blame you! This whole last month has been your fault, you stupid ass. What am I supposed to do, say I'm *sorry* Lily broke up with you because you couldn't shut up about me? I'm sorry you got mixed up in a bunch of stupid shit, because after our nacho date you didn't want to be just friends? I'm sorry for how jealous you got, hearing about me and Benji? How am I supposed to feel, you telling me all this now, huh? You finally coming around, showing up, pouring out your heart, when you know I have this big thing tonight, when you know I've been missing you so much and now I have to . . . to . . . get up there and . . ."

But I can't say the rest, because suddenly his arms are around me and I'm surrounded by him, and it feels so absolutely good and right to be here in the middle of him, him, him. It's a feeling I've needed for weeks now. Probably my entire life.

"I can't do it anymore." He presses his lips to the top of my head. "I don't want to be the person I was being without you. Even if you don't feel the same way—even if we're only friends— that's fine with me. I just want to be around you again. I thought about you . . . who you are to me . . . what I've been since I left—"

I step back so I can see his face. "Did you really think that splitting us up was going to make things *better*?" I'm still trying not to cry, but it's hard.

He takes my hands.

"Big dummy, I know. But once I knew how I felt, it sucked not being able to *be* with you. And you kept getting extra-fabulous, extra-hard to not be with. But after . . . Lily . . ." He says it like it's embarrassing. "Not being with you at all hurt even more."

"Um, Charlotte?" Fabian's hovering behind me.

"Oh god." I turn to him. On his face I see that it's time. And I'm so not ready.

"I'll be here," Trip says. "I know there's a lot more talking we need to do. And I'm really sorry to spring it all on you like this."

I grab him around the neck, squeezing him close. "I missed you," I say, fierce, before letting go.

"I know. It was stupid. You can tell me all the reasons why later." His face is so sincerely sorry. And sweet. And I'm just glad to be seeing it again.

But Fabian genuinely looks anxious now as he reaches for my arm to guide me toward the stage. I realize Oliver and the other guys are already up there, that the DJ's last song before us is half-way through. I take Fabian's hand and we work our way to the front of the room, pushing past people and faces and voices telling us good luck. I look for Trip, to wave to him, but he's already melted into the crowd.

"You need some more time?" Fabian's got one foot on the stage, one on the floor—half of him ready to play, the other half here for me if I need him.

Eli comes over. "She all right?"

The song around us repeats its final chorus, quieter and quieter, and people start moving closer to the stage. We're on the far edge, away from most everyone, but still it would be nice if there were some kind of curtain.

"I'm fine," I tell them both, sucking in a deep breath. "I mean, the boy I think I love more than anything just told me he's in love with me, and that this whole time he's been ignoring me and making me feel like utter crap—all because he hasn't been able to make himself happy without me, and I've been writing all these songs and doing all these things, thinking I'll never talk to him again but also knowing I won't be happy without him either, and I'm supposed to process all that in, like, ten seconds, while in the meantime I have to get up here and sing, and be there for you guys, who've stuck by me through this whole thing, but . . . yeah. I'm okay."

"Whoa." Eli looks like I might electrocute him.

"Ready?" the DJ interrupts, wanting to introduce us. Oliver appears next to him, fingers yanking through his bangs.

Fabian keeps his eyes on me. "We think so." But he doesn't sound very certain.

Oliver's beside me now. "Spider? You can sing, right?"

And everything that's happened—everything over the last six weeks of good and bad and awful and terrific—flashes around me like I'm dying. I picture where I was at the start of all this, and where I am now: who's left me, who's stayed by me, and who's grown with me through all of it.

My breath comes out a little shuddery, but strong. "I can sing."

Immediately the DJ turns and hollers into his mic, without giving us even another second. "Okay, everybody. Time now for our special musical guest . . ."

The room echoes with whistles and applause, and a visible crush of people swarms in from the back. I shake out my hands, take another deep breath, move to my spot in front of the mic. The hall swells with more noise. Oliver and I sneak glances at each other, trying not to smile under the pride we can't help but feel. When the DJ steps down and the lights brighten on us, I can't see anyone very well anymore, but I hear Benji's loud, sharp whistle, and Darby and Gretchen screaming my name. Out there somewhere in the crowd, I know Trip's eyes are on me too.

We're starting tonight with Oliver's favorite of our new songs, the one he insisted I sing first. The irony is so big, I almost laugh into my mic as Fabian's first notes of "Hansel and Gretel Crumbs" swell around me. But instead I manage to make it look like I'm the happiest person in the world to be here. And maybe I am.

Behind me Oliver comes in on his guitar, a loud, bold chord.

I take a breath.

And then I sing my heart out.

Acknowledgments

In reality, the byline of this book should read "Terra Elan McVoy and Anica Rissi." Anica, I know it's your job, but thank you for all the extra tough love, time, attention, and sparkle that you put into this manuscript. It was a mess without you.

Caroline Corder, Sumar Deen, and Natalie Spitzer, your beautiful honesty inspired these pages. And Jamie, you might not remember our discussion about what kind of solo time guys spend with girls they're not attracted to, but I do, and it helped with this book. (Bump fists.)

Scott, you were an extra trooper with this one. There's no acknowledgment I can ever write that will properly thank you for what you give to me, and my work, every day. I am glad you are so much more than my friend.

Amy McClellan, you are a million times better than a million boy (or girl) friends put together. I cherish the time we spent working out this arc, and it remains a great example of exactly why and how I love you. (Also, if we hadn't, this book would have no plot.)

Lastly, I have to recognize the purely friend guys in my life: the ones who have informed and sustained the girl I am. David Astor, John Aubry, Josh Siegel, Frank Schultz, Stewart Haddock, Tom Bell, Jamie Allen, David Lee Simmons, David Bowles, Colin Moore, Justin Colussy-Estes, Paul Stenis . . . we don't have to talk about it, but thanks.